GRADUATION DAY

GRADUATION DAY

BY JOELLE CHARBONNEAU

Houghton Mifflin Harcourt
Boston   New York

www.hmhco.com

The text of this book is set in Garamond.

Library of Congress Cataloging-in-Publication Data
Charbonneau, Joelle.
Graduation day / Joelle Charbonneau.
p. cm.—(The testing ; book 3)
Summary: "The United Commonwealth wants to eliminate the rebel alliance
fighting to destroy The Testing for good. Cia is ready to lead the charge, but
will her lethal classmates follow her into battle?" —Provided by publisher.
ISBN 978-0-547-95921-4
[1. Adventure and adventurers—Fiction. 2. Loyalty—Fiction. 3. Government,
Resistance to—Fiction. 4. Survival—Fiction. 5. Love—Fiction.] I. Title.
PZ7.C37354Gr 2014
[Fic]—dc23
2013034743

Manufactured in the United States of America
DOH 10 9 8 7 6 5 4
4500505626

To Margaret Raymo, for your guidance and vision.
I could never have done this without you.

CHAPTER 1

A KNOCK MAKES me jump. My hands shake from exhaustion, fear, and sorrow as I unlatch the lock to the door of my residence hall rooms and turn the handle. I let out a sigh of relief as I see Raffe Jeffries in the doorway. Though we share the same path of study, there is little else that is similar about us. Me from the colonies, who had to survive The Testing to be here. He from Tosu City, where students related to former graduates are welcomed into the University with open arms. We are not friends. Even after he helped save my life last night, I do not know if I can trust him. But I have no choice.

Raffe appears unconcerned, but I can read the warning in his eyes as he steps into my sitting room and closes the door behind him. "Cia, they know."

My knees weaken, and I grip the back of a chair for support. "Know what?"

That I left campus? That I know the rebellion led by the man who helped me during The Testing isn't what the rebels believe? That soon the rebels will launch an attack that will lead them to their deaths? That Damone . . . I push my thoughts away from that question.

"Professor Holt knows we both left campus." His dark eyes meet mine. "And Griffin has started looking for Damone."

Of course Griffin would be looking for his friend. When he doesn't find him, he will alert the head of our residence, Professor Holt. She will wonder why the Tosu City Government Studies student has vanished. Will Dr. Barnes and his officials believe the pressure to succeed has caused Damone to flee? Or will they launch a search for him and discover that he's dead? Panic begins to swell. I tell myself there wasn't another option. But was there?

I shake my head. Unless I want my future to contain Redirection or worse, I have to avoid thinking about what is past.

There are no rules that say we cannot leave campus. I cannot be punished for that alone. But if they know what I have seen . . .

I take a steadying breath, then ask, "Does Professor Holt know when we left or if we left together?"

My fingers trace the lightning bolt symbol on the silver and gold bracelet encircling my wrist as I think of the tracking device contained inside. The one I thought I had beaten. Only, I was wrong. I was wrong about everything. Now Michal is dead and . . .

"I don't think anyone knows how long we were gone. No one saw us leave, and I don't think anyone spotted us when we returned to campus." Raffe runs a hand through his dark hair. "But Griffin stopped me when I was going to deliver your message to Tomas. He asked if I had seen Damone. Then he wanted to know where you and I went this morning. I don't know how, but he knew we were together."

I have not told Raffe about the tracking device in his bracelet. Part of me had hoped I would not need to share my secrets. My father warned me before I came to Tosu City for The Testing to trust no one. But I have. I must again now. Because he's helped me, Raffe is in danger.

Quickly, I tell Raffe about what's hidden inside the bracelets and about the transmitter Tomas and I designed to block the signal and hide our movements from Dr. Barnes. Only, sometime last night or this morning, that transmitter fell out of my pocket. Where and when it was lost I do not know.

Raffe looks down at the symbol etched on his bracelet — a coiled spring in the center of the balanced scales of justice. "They're monitoring our movements." There is no surprise. No outrage. Only a nod of the head before he says, "We're going to have to find a better way to block the signal if we don't want them watching our every move when we do whatever you have planned next."

What I have planned . . .

This week President Collindar will stand in the United Commonwealth Government's Debate Chamber and ask the members to vote on a new proposal. One that — if approved — will shift administration of The Testing and the University from Dr. Barnes's autonomous control. One that will force him to report to the president and allow her to end the practices that have killed so many who wanted nothing more than to help their colonies and their country. But while I'd like to believe the proposal will pass and The Testing will come to an end, everything I have learned tells me it is doomed to fail. When it does, rumor says Dr. Barnes's supporters will call for a vote of confidence on the president. A vote that—if lost by the president—will signal not only the end of her role as leader, but the start of a battle that the rebels and the president have no hope of winning, since Dr. Barnes knows of their plans. Indeed, he and his supporter Symon Dean have planned the rebellion itself. Only recently have I learned its true purpose, which is to identify, occupy, and ultimately destroy any who would oppose the selection methods of The Testing. The time is fast approaching when Dr. Barnes will allow his people among the rebels to escalate their outrage and encourage open warfare, in order to crush that rebellion with violence of his own. If Dr. Barnes's plan succeeds, those who seek to end The Testing will die—and my brother will be among them.

I can't sit back and allow that to happen, but I don't know how I can help stop the events that are already spinning into motion. I thought I knew. I thought I had found a way to help. But I only made things worse. Now Dr. Barnes will be watching my movements even more closely than before. I wish there were time to think things through. My brothers always teased that it took me hours to make a decision that took others minutes, yet my father taught me that anything important deserves thoughtful study. The choices that face me now are the most important of my life.

Am I scared? Yes. As the youngest student at the University, I find it hard to believe that my actions could change the course of my country's history. That I am clever enough to outthink Dr. Barnes and his officials and save lives. But there is no other way. The odds favor my failure, but I still have to try.

"Right now the only thing I have planned is to do my homework and get some sleep." When Raffe starts to protest, I say, "You need sleep, too." The way his shoulders sag tells me he is just as tired as I. "Maybe if we're rested we'll come up with a way to help stop what's coming."

Raffe nods. "Regardless, with everything that's happened, it's probably best we stay inside the residence for the rest of the day. I'm sure Professor Holt will have someone watching you. You'll need to be careful."

A muffled series of clicks catches my attention. There it is again. One. Two. Three faint clicks of the transmission button on the Transit Communicator. The signal Zeen suggested we use to indicate one of us needs to talk. He must have found a place where it is safe for him to speak. But it is not safe for me. Not with Raffe here. I have been forced into trusting him with many things, but I will not trust him with this. Not with my brother's life.

"I'll see you later today," I say.

Raffe cocks his head to the side. His eyes narrow as the three clicks come again.

Pretending I hear nothing, I walk to the door and open it. "I have an assignment I have to get to work on."

Raffe looks around the small sitting room. My heart beats off the seconds as he waits for the clicking noise to recur. When it doesn't, he shakes his head and walks to the door. "I'll be around if you need anything."

When the door swings shut, I flip the lock and hurry to my bedroom. My fingers slide under the edge of the mattress and close around the device I brought with me from Five Lakes

Colony. It was designed to communicate across distances of less than twenty miles with a device my father kept in his office. The one Zeen must hold now while waiting for me to respond.

I click the communication button three times to indicate I have received his signal.

"Cia. I can't tell you how glad I am Michal finally told you where I am. I wanted to contact you the minute I got to Tosu City, but Michal said it would be best to wait. Are you okay?"

The sound of Zeen's voice fills me with warmth. Growing up, I could always tell Zeen anything. Of all my brothers, he was the one I went to when I needed help with a problem. I was certain he could come up with the answer for everything. I hope that is still true.

"I'm fine." For now. "But—"

"Good." I hear Zeen sigh. "That's good. Cia, I'm sorry I was so angry. I shouldn't have let you leave without saying goodbye. I was jealous because you got what I thought I wanted. I didn't know . . ."

I think about the hurt I felt when Zeen disappeared before I left for The Testing. Of all of us, he is the most passionate. The easiest to upset. The quickest to react when his emotions are stirred and hardest hit when those he loves are wounded or taken away. Which is why I understood his absence when my family said their farewells and why I can honestly say, "It's okay. Besides, if you hadn't stormed off, I would have asked permission to take this Communicator and you would have turned me down. I wouldn't have made it through the last couple of months without it."

"You should have heard me yell when I saw your note." Zeen laughs. "Mom said it was a small price to pay for how

I'd behaved, since I might never see you again. She didn't want me to come, but Dad understood why I had to. Cia, there are things happening here. Important things. I don't know if Michal told you, but these people are going to end The Testing. The leaders here have a plan that will change everything. It's dangerous."

"Zeen . . ."

But Zeen isn't listening. When I was little, Zeen used to talk to me for hours about things I didn't understand, but I didn't care. I loved listening to his voice and knowing that he understood the things he talked about. But he doesn't understand now.

"Zeen . . ."

"And it's complicated and will take too long for me to explain. I can't talk for much longer or someone will come searching for me. With everything going on, they're slow to trust. Even with Michal's endorsement. I think they would have arrested me the minute I walked into camp if it weren't for—"

"Zeen, stop!" When there is silence, I say, "Michal's dead." My throat tightens. Tears prick the backs of my eyes. Saying the words aloud makes them all too real. "I saw him die."

"Cia, that can't be true." But the hitch in Zeen's voice tells me he is shaken by my words. "I would have heard if Michal died. Symon or Ranetta would have told us." Zeen's soothing tone is the same one he used when I was small and thought there were monsters lurking under the bed. Only there is no soothing me with kind words now. I know these monsters are real.

"Symon wouldn't have told you because he's the one who killed Michal." I look at the clock beside my bed. Five minutes have passed. If Zeen is right, people will soon come searching for him. I don't want them to hear him talking into the Communicator and think he's a spy. There is so much to say. So little time to say it in. I have to decide what is important now and what can wait until we can arrange another time to speak.

"Michal brought Symon the proof the president needs to sway the Debate Chamber vote and end The Testing in a peaceful way. I was hiding nearby." I can still see the way the rebellion leader looked when he raised his gun and fired. Two shots. Then Michal fell to the ground. "I heard Symon say that he and Dr. Barnes created the rebellion to control those who want to bring an end to The Testing. The rebellion isn't real."

"The rebellion is real, Cia." Though Zeen keeps his voice quiet, I can hear the anger, outrage, and disbelief bubbling below the surface. "Don't you think I'd know if it wasn't? These people are ready to fight in order to bring change."

"I know they are. That's what Dr. Barnes and Symon want them to do."

"Cia, that can't be true. I talked to Ranetta and Symon. Symon—"

"Killed Michal. You can't trust Symon." I'm not sure about Ranetta. "Michal did, and he's dead." Once again panic simmers inside me. Zeen has to believe. "Symon's job is to make sure that the rebels fail. If the president loses the Debate Chamber vote and the rebels attack, Dr. Barnes and Symon will have Safety and Security teams waiting. They'll say it is the only way to keep the rest of the city safe. If we don't do something, the rebellion will fail. More people will die."

"Wait. If you're right . . ." Zeen takes a deep breath. When he speaks again, his voice is barely a whisper, but filled with conviction. "You have to get out of Tosu City."

"I can't. There are reasons." The bracelet on my wrist. My friends who would be left behind. Zeen, who is in the middle of the rebels Dr. Barnes intends to kill. The last is the only thing I know how to fix. "Zeen, you should go. There are lots of buildings that aren't used very often here on campus. You could hide in one of them."

"No one is supposed to leave camp without a direct order from Symon or Ranetta."

Ranetta. A woman I have never met or seen. When Michal explained the divide in the rebellion — one faction that pushed for a peaceful resolution and the other that, impatient with the delays, urged war — he said Ranetta was the leader of the latter. She must have once followed Symon's methods as all the rebels did. If she opposes them now, could she be an ally? If Zeen could talk to her . . .

No. While Zeen is smart, when his emotions are engaged he often reacts before thinking things through. He hasn't been part of the rebellion long enough to understand the dynamics and effectively gauge who can be trusted. Who knows if anyone can be? Michal thought Symon could be trusted. So did I. Besides, Zeen didn't go through The Testing. He doesn't understand what it is like or how terrible it truly is. This isn't his fight. He needs to get out.

"You could escape without them seeing you." The camp the rebels are using was an air force base before being hit by a vector tornado. The destruction was so great that the Commonwealth Government abandoned any hope of revitalizing the area. But while the land is not healthy, trees have grown. Some plants have thrived. If anyone can navigate the unrevitalized landscape and hide from those who pursue him, it will be my brother.

"Maybe. And I might have to if things go the way you say. But not yet. I'm here. I might be able to learn something useful. People expect the new guy to ask questions. I just have to figure out what kinds of answers we need. If there's a chance . . ."

I wait for Zeen to continue, but there is only silence. My heart pounds as I look at the Communicator in my hand. Zeen must have heard someone approaching. Did he stop talking in time or was he overheard? I wait for Zeen to give me a sign. Something to tell me that he is safe.

The minutes pass slowly. One. Five. Ten. The clock taunts me. My worry grows with each passing moment. Silently, I clutch the device in my hands and will my brother to be okay. My bringing Michal those recordings prompted his death. I can't lose Zeen, too. If I do, it will be one more person who died because of my actions. Part of me wants to go find Tomas. He was with me last night when I first spotted Zeen in the rebel camp. He'll want to help. But as much as I want to wrap my arms around Tomas and rely on him, I know there is little he can do. That either of us can. As University students, we have almost no control of the world around us.

But there is someone who should be able to help me. Michal might not have been certain we could trust her, but I don't see a choice. Not anymore. Zeen is in the middle of a rebellion that is ready to take up arms against Dr. Barnes and his supporters. The Testing will soon select the next round of candidates. More than a hundred students could once again be pushed into decisions that could end lives, whether their own or others'. And if my role in Damone's death is discovered, I will no longer be able to take any action at all. I will be dead. The fate of too many people is at stake for me to believe I can fix what is broken. I am not one of the country's leaders. The president is. This is her job. Not mine.

I have to convince her to help.

I pull on a pair of brown pants I acquired after arriving in Tosu City and a fitted yellow tunic adorned with silver buttons. I clean my comfortable but worn boots to make them as presentable as I can. Most days I pull my hair into a tight knot at the nape of my neck. Today, I take special care to brush it until it shines before braiding it in a style that my father lamented made me look like a young woman instead of his little girl. I hope he was right. In order for my plan to succeed, I need the president to see me as more than a University student. She has to see a woman.

Then I roll the bloody clothes I was wearing yesterday into a tight ball and shove them into my bag. There is no removing Damone's blood from these garments. While I rarely have people in my room, I do not want to risk someone seeing the clothes. I need to get rid of them.

I reach under the mattress and pull out a small handgun given to me by Raffe. The weight in my hand feels insignificant compared to the weight in my chest. Guns are used in Five Lakes. I learned to discharge a shotgun at an early age, and Daileen's father taught us to fire his handgun around the same time I learned how to multiply and divide. My father's job required us to live near where he worked, which meant living close to the unrevitalized land where meat-seeking wolves and other, mutated creatures roamed. More than once I have injured or killed an animal intent on attack. But if this gun is fired it will not be at an animal looking for food. After shoving the Transit Communicator into my bag, I slide the bag's strap onto my shoulder and walk out the door, careful to lock it behind me.

The halls of the residence are quiet. The students I pass speak to each other in tones more muted than usual. No doubt because of Damone's disappearance. As I pass students on the stairs, I am careful to keep my eyes down in case they can see the guilt in them. With every step, I find myself listening for a click from the Transit Communicator to tell me that Zeen is okay.

When I reach the first floor, I force myself to walk in slow, measured strides to the front door so no one can see the anxiety I feel about Zeen's silence. With each moment that passes I am more certain something terrible has befallen him. As I push open the door, I look behind me in case Raffe has seen me going down the stairs and has followed. No one is there, so I step outside into the afternoon sunshine. According to my watch, there are two hours until dinner is served. If I am not back in time, my mealtime absence will be noticed. But I have no choice.

I straighten my shoulders and walk around the residence to the vehicle shed, trying not to look at the place where Raffe and I pushed Damone over the edge of the ravine. Wheeling my bicycle out, I look around for anyone who might be watching, then throw my leg over the seat. My feet push the pedals. Worry about my brother propels my body forward despite my fatigue.

The wheels glide over the bridge that spans the twenty-foot-wide crack in the earth that separates the Government Studies residence from the rest of campus. It isn't until I turn down the roadway that leads to the library that I glance over my shoulder. From this distance, I can't be sure. But I think I spot Griffin standing motionless on the bridge, staring into the darkness of the ravine below. Despite my desire to find Tomas and ask him to join me on this journey, I don't. Drawing unwanted attention to Tomas is the last thing I want to do. I turn and begin to ride as fast as I can in hopes of finding help for my brother and myself.

Riding under the woven metal archway that so closely resembles the design of the band that now circles my wrist serves as a reminder that my whereabouts are being monitored. University students are not forbidden to leave campus, but if I venture too far afield, Professor Holt and Dr. Barnes will certainly question my motivation. Luckily, as an intern in the president's office, I have reason to be traveling to my destination.

Past the archway I stop my bike, pull the Transit Communicator out of my bag, and turn on the navigation display. While I have traveled these roads before, I am still not confident of choosing the most expedient path. Using a strip of fabric from my stained clothing, I tie the Transit Communicator to the handlebars. Once it is secure, I press the Call button once. Twice. A third time. No answer. I swallow my disappointment and point my wheels toward the center of the city. As I ride, I picture the faces of Zandri, Malachi, Ryme, Obidiah, and Michal. All came to Tosu City looking to help the world. All are dead. I have to help my brother avoid that same fate. I just hope I won't be too late.

CHAPTER 2

I BARELY NOTICE my surroundings as I zigzag through the city, careful to keep an eye on the Communicator's readout. As I ride, I consider what I know. The president's disapproval of Dr. Barnes is obvious. I have observed their mutual dislike first-hand. But though the president wishes to remove Dr. Barnes from power, no one knows whether she will alter or end the University selection process. The Testing is terrible in its methods, but it has gotten results. The clean water we drink and the number of colonies with revitalized land prove the leaders the University has trained are skilled.

Can the president be trusted to change the system when it is yielding such results? I don't know. But as the wind whips my hair, I realize that if I want to try to end The Testing, I am going to have to find out.

Residential streets give way to roads with larger buildings as I ride into the heart of the city. Personal skimmers hover above for those with business that demands attention on a Sunday. I turn down another street and see the distinctive gray stone turrets and clock tower of the building that houses the office of President Anneline Collindar.

I store my bicycle in the rack next to the entrance and pull open one of the large wooden doors. Two officials dressed in black jumpsuits approach. Two others hold their positions on either side of the arching door in front of us. The color of their clothing, their white armbands, and the silver weapons hanging at their sides signal their standing as Safety officials. Only Safety officials are allowed to carry weapons inside government buildings. The law was created after the Seven Stages of War when the people gathered to debate whether to form a new central government. Arguments for and against a new government body were heated. Many believed that the last president of the United States, President Dalton, and the other world leaders who held power leading up to and through the stages of war were to blame for corrupting the earth and causing so much death and destruction. Others argued that an organized government was still essential if the hope of revitalization was to be fulfilled. All citizens were allowed a voice in the debates, but some believed weapons were more persuasive than words. It was the firing of those weapons by opponents of a new government that swayed many to believe lawlessness would prevail without one. The first law passed after the vote to establish a new governmental entity banned all firearms from the Debate Chamber floor. Ten years later, the ban was expanded to all government buildings.

Today, I am in violation of the law. To obey, I would have

to surrender the gun Raffe gave me. Something I am not willing to do. I do not know how the president will react to what I must tell her. I have to be prepared for whatever might happen.

Shifting the weight of my bag on my shoulder, I walk to the broad-shouldered Safety official who stands behind a small black desk. I give my name and show him my bracelet. When he nods, I straighten my shoulders and walk through the arched doorway that leads to the president's office.

Since my internship began a few weeks ago, I have learned that while a few young, dedicated members of the president's staff can be found working on Saturdays and Sundays, rarely does the president herself walk these halls on the Commonwealth's designated days of rest. With the president scheduled to call for a debate on Monday, I expect more officials to be working. I'm not disappointed. The hallways I pass through to get to the president's first-floor office teem with activity. The air crackles with tension as officials huddle around desks, talking in hushed voices. A few look my way as I pass by, but most are too preoccupied with their own business to notice me. I walk through a large meeting space where a board displays this week's debate schedule. TESTING AND UNIVERSITY OVERSIGHT is marked in red letters under the date two days from now.

Finally I come to the large white wooden door of the president's office. The desk to the left of the door sits empty. I put my hand on the doorknob and turn it.

Locked. A knock confirms my suspicion. The office is empty.

I retrace my steps back to the main hall and climb the iron staircase to the second floor. Weeks ago, I made this climb for the first time while following behind Michal. I'd been shocked to see him here. He'd pretended not to know me as he gave me the tour of the building—one of the oldest in Tosu City. After climbing the last step, I slowly walk down the hallway toward a set of double doors flanked by two purple-clad officials. Michal said the doors lead to the president's private quarters.

Wishing he were standing beside me now, I walk up to the officials and say, "I have a message for the president."

The dark-haired official on the right frowns. "The president is not on the premises. You can leave the message on the desk outside her office downstairs. A member of her upper-level staff will receive it tomorrow."

I recognize the words for what they are. A dismissal. Though being cleared into the building says I have a right to walk these halls, no amount of confidence can hide my youthful face or small stature. Both mark me as a student who should not have any reason to send missives to the leader of the United Commonwealth.

"There must be a way to get a message to the president." I use the firm, measured tone my father employed whenever he talked to Mr. Taubs about his goat eating the new seedlings planted near his farm.

"There is," the gray-haired man to the left admits.

Before he can order me to leave, I say, "My name is Malencia Vale. I'm the president's intern. President Collindar asked me several weeks ago to speak to her about a specific subject. I would like someone to get her a message that I am here and am willing to discuss that topic now."

"The president does not take—"

The gray-haired official holds up a hand, cutting off his partner's angry words. Quietly, he says, "I will have your message sent, and I hope it is as important as you believe. If not, you'll discover there's a cost to your misjudgment. Is that a price you are willing to pay?"

Cost. I know what Dr. Barnes's price is for a failure in judgment. Does the president require the same payment? I have not worked in this office long enough to know its secrets, but I know Michal did not fully place his faith in President Collindar. I don't either, but I have only to think of Tomas and all those whose lives could be threatened to know that no matter the price, I will pay it.

A nod is all it takes for the gray-haired official to disappear through a small door to the left. When he returns he says, "I've relayed your message. You're to wait here."

For what, he doesn't say. The president? Officials who have deemed my request inappropriate? The only thing I am certain of is that my request to speak to the president has not gone unnoticed. Younger officials whom I have seen working in the cramped offices on the upper floors whisper to each other as they walk down the stairs in groups of twos and threes. While they pretend to be on some kind of errand, the looks they send in my direction speak of their true purpose. I hear one whisper that they hope I know what I am doing.

I hope I do, too. The more people who walk by, the more certain I am that news of this meeting request will spread beyond this building. Michal's job in this office was arranged through Symon's connections within the government. Symon planted Michal here to keep an eye on the president and report her plans, but I doubt Michal was the only informant assigned to that task.

Resisting the urge to pace, I keep my eyes straight ahead and hope the nerves I feel do not show on my face. After what seems like hours, a dark-haired woman in ceremonial red appears at the top of the stairs. She gives me a considering look before handing the gray-haired official a note. He reads it, nods, and walks over to me. "This way."

He leads me to the double doors of the president's private quarters. Opening the doors, he steps back and says, "You are to wait in this room. They will come for you when they are ready."

Before I can ask who "they" is, the official nudges me into a small antechamber. The doors behind me close. The dim lights and gray walls make the room feel as if it is caught in shadow. A bright white door stands directly in front of me. The silver knob is polished to a shine.

A memory stirs. Six white doors with silver handles. Five marked with black numbers. The sixth is the exit. This door resembles the ones I stood in front of during the third part of The Testing. A test designed not only to evaluate our individual academic skills, but to examine our ability to assess correctly the strengths and weaknesses of our teammates.

"Malencia Vale." A female voice emanates from a small speaker in the wall. "You may now enter."

I put my hand on the knob and take a deep breath. During The Testing I had to make a decision — to walk through the door and face the test I found inside or to leave without entering. To believe that my teammates were working toward the same goal or to think that one who should be working for the common good had betrayed. During The Testing, I left through the exit. Today, I turn the knob and go inside.

No one is there.

The large room is painted a sunny yellow. Situated on one side is a long black table. On the other is a grouping of blue-cushioned chairs in front of a crackling fire. To the right of the fireplace is a closed door.

I open my bag, turn off the Transit Communicator, and take a seat in one of the cushioned chairs as the door opens. President Collindar stalks in. Her tall stature and sleekly cut black hair command attention, as does her fitted red jacket. She nods to acknowledge my presence and turns to speak to someone standing in the doorway behind her. "I've given you all the information I have. I hope you'll be ready."

"You can trust me," a male voice says.

My breath catches as a gray-haired man comes into the room and gives me a broad smile. The same smile I saw him give this morning, just a moment before he pulled the trigger and ended Michal's life. A smile that belongs to the rebel leader—Symon Dean.

Metal glints in the light as his coat shifts. He has a gun. Most likely the same one he used to murder Michal. His eyes meet mine, and I feel the pull of them just as I did when we met before. We have met only twice, during the fourth stage of The Testing, when he gave me food and water. Aid that he supplied to give the rebels a sense of victory, to keep them from feeling they could more successfully end The Testing on their own. But I am not supposed to have those memories. Any sign of recognition will be a sign that my Testing memories have returned.

Blood roars in my ears. I swallow down the anger and fear and force my expression into one of calm interest. Seconds pass, but it feels like an eternity before Symon shifts his attention from me back to the president. "Everything will be ready, but I still think you should postpone the debate." I try not to show surprise at Symon's words as he and the president walk farther into the room. "While postponing will be viewed by many as a sign of weakness, the extra days you gain will give us a chance to rally more votes. As it stands now—"

The president raises a hand and shakes her head. "Already there are those who waver in their support. A delay could push them to change their minds. Unless you can guarantee that you will be able to find what I need—"

"You know a guarantee is not possible."

"Which means the debate goes ahead as planned. One way or another, by the end of the week I will declare victory."

"Then there is much to discuss." Symon gives a weary sigh, but I do not think I imagine the triumphant glint I see in his eyes. Suggesting the president would lose political clout by postponing her Debate Chamber proposal was his way of eliminating any thought she had of doing just that. He is smart. I hope she is even smarter.

President Collindar nods. "I will meet you downstairs as soon as I am done discussing my intern's University experience. I thought having a student refresh my memory of the curriculum would help, considering the topic of this week's debate. This shouldn't take long."

Symon casts one more look at me before nodding his head and disappearing through the door. When he is gone, President Collindar sits in a chair across from me. "I told Symon and other members of my staff that I asked you to meet with me this weekend after you finished the work you were assigned by your teachers. I thought it would be safer for you if word spread that you were here at my command instead of by your own initiative. There are events happening this week that could make it difficult for you to be seen as more than just an intern for me and my office."

"I know," I say.

One of the president's eyebrows rises, but she does not speak. She simply waits for me to continue. I take a deep breath and straighten my shoulders. How I present my information is just as important as what I say. I must keep calm. In control. This is the most important test I have faced thus far in my life. Too much is riding on the correct answer. I cannot fail.

"I know your team has been searching for tangible proof that Dr. Barnes's methods for Testing and in running the University push beyond the bounds of what is acceptable. I've been told that without this evidence, the vote to remove Dr. Barnes from control will be unsuccessful."

President Collindar leans back in her chair. Her dark hair gleams against the light blue fabric as she studies me. "Your information is accurate. Could the reason you're here now change that?"

"I hope so. Although not in the way I think you mean." I take a deep breath and explain. "The Tosu City official who escorted me from Five Lakes Colony to The Testing began working for you just before my internship started. His name was Michal Gallen." I see a flicker of awareness cross her features as the name registers. "Michal told me he was transferred to this office through the influence of a man named Symon, who was leading the movement to put a stop to Dr. Barnes and his extreme methods. I was informed that because of my age, it was too dangerous for me to be involved in the rebellion against Dr. Barnes. I had nightmares about my Testing experience. I didn't know if the flashbacks were real, but they made me determined to help in any way I could. Without Symon's knowledge, Michal gave me a task. He asked me to help find the proof needed to convince the Debate Chamber to vote Dr. Barnes from power. Yesterday, I brought Michal the evidence you've been seeking."

President Collindar leans forward.

Before she can ask for what I can no longer give, I say, "Michal took the evidence to Symon." Her smile falters as she shifts her attention to the door through which Symon withdrew. "Since Symon didn't know about my involvement, Michal was reluctant to bring me to the rebel camp. I insisted. I hid as Michal turned over the proof that would have brought an end to The Testing. And then I watched as Symon took out a gun and shot him. The evidence is gone. Michal is dead."

President Collindar studies me. Her expression is devoid of emotion. My heart thuds in my chest. I fight the urge to squirm under her gaze. I want to beg her to believe me. But I can tell she is weighing my words. Judging my motives. My honesty.

Finally she says, "You claim Michal Gallen is dead. Can you prove it?"

"No," I admit. Although maybe I could. Raffe was there. If the president were to summon him here, his account could add weight to mine. But I have not mentioned his involvement. To do so now might make President Collindar wonder what else I haven't been forthcoming about. Perhaps more important, if President Collindar does not believe me, she will certainly mention this meeting to Symon. Redirection will not be far behind. In case Raffe is truly to be trusted, I will not entwine my fate with his. However, I realize there is one fact that will lend credence to my words. "Michal will not report for work Monday or in the days to come." I ball my hands into fists as tears filled with sorrow and guilt prick my eyes and lodge in my throat. "His absence will confirm I am telling the truth, but by then it will be too late."

"Too late for what?" President Collindar asks quietly, but I can see by the tension in her jaw that she has done the equation in her head. If I am to be believed, Michal is dead by the hands of someone she's close to. Someone who has helped plan this vote and the attack on Dr. Barnes that is scheduled to come with its failure.

Still, I answer. "By the time people know for certain Michal is missing, you will have already made your proposal on the Debate Chamber floor." Commonwealth law states that once a proposal is made and the debate on it has begun, the proposal cannot be withdrawn. The debate must be allowed to continue and a vote taken. The law was created to ensure that all matters brought to the debate floor would be carefully considered. "As soon as you do that, you set in motion the events that Symon and Dr. Barnes have orchestrated. They want your vote to fail and the rebels to attack. The minute that happens, Dr. Barnes's supporters will move against them. They will remove both the threat to The Testing and you from office with this one fight."

"And look heroic doing it." President Collindar's words are barely a whisper. So faint that I question whether I have heard her correctly. Heroic is the last thing I would call Dr. Barnes's plan for eliminating those who oppose him.

But now that I think about it, I realize President Collindar has seen what I did not. Out of necessity, the rebels have been operating in secret. Their cause is unknown to Tosu citizens save for a few who may have recently been imposed upon to take up arms. And even if it were revealed, most citizens do not know someone who was chosen for The Testing. A fraction are related to those who sat in University classrooms and became the country's leaders without undergoing The Testing or experiencing Redirection. Very few would celebrate a rebellion that would likely shed innocent blood for a purpose they do not personally understand. If Dr. Barnes and Symon's plan is successful, the rebels will be killed almost immediately after the violence begins. Without the rebels to speak for their own cause, Dr. Barnes can paint their purpose as one designed to take down the United Commonwealth Government and destroy the country's revitalization mission. His supporters will claim him as a hero. History has ever rewarded the victors.

President Collindar rises and stands in front of the fireplace. "Symon is working with Jedidiah." Her voice is quiet. Controlled. Yet I hear the thin veil of tension that coats her words. "Setting up a rebellion against himself is smart. It allows him to control both those who follow and those who oppose him. Jedidiah's strength has always been in strategy."

"You believe me?" I ask. Amazement and a strange sense of peace flow through me. Not only have I passed this test, I have handed this problem to someone with the power to prevent a series of tragic events. Zeen and I can let her take care of it.

"I do believe you." The president turns back to me. "You didn't think I would. And yet, still you put yourself in danger to get this news to me. Even before we met in the Debate Chamber, I'd heard you were different from your peers. Perhaps because Jedidiah's tests are not designed to reward those who are willing to sacrifice themselves. From what I know, sacrifice during The Testing often results in a candidate's elimination."

"Elimination." A more pleasant word than "death."

"It's unusual that someone like you has gotten this far," she adds.

I think about The Testing. More than twenty of us passed the fourth test and sat for final evaluations. Dr. Barnes could have eliminated me then. Why didn't he?

President Collindar takes a seat again. "Perhaps you can answer a few questions. How many of the rebels are working with Dr. Barnes? Also, is Ranetta partnered with Symon or is she as unaware as I was?"

"I don't know." I wish I did. "I've never seen or talked to Ranetta." Something that now worries me, considering my brother is working side by side with her and the other rebels. "Symon ordered some of his team to carry Michal's body away. They didn't seem concerned by Michal's death. But I have to believe most of the rebels want to see The Testing ended." Michal would not have put his faith in the rebellion if that weren't the case. Neither would Zeen.

"I believe they do. Unfortunately, I cannot be certain which rebels are to be trusted and which would claim they are on our side in order to remove us. And since you say Michal's position in this office was orchestrated, most if not all of my staff's loyalty must also come into question. It is impossible to know which are loyal to Symon's purpose or to me."

She's right. Tension builds as the president falls silent and stares into the fire. Her lips purse — the only sign of the magnitude of the problem that faces her. It is in this moment that I understand why she was chosen to lead.

She nods. "Symon will be wondering about this meeting. I have to go downstairs. Remain here. Someone will bring work to occupy you so those who are watching will not question your continued presence. I will be back soon."

"But—"

President Collindar strides out the door and into the hallway, from where I hear her say, "Someone will be back with a project for Ms. Vale to work on. At least then her time here will not be completely wasted."

I hear the door shut and I rise from my chair. Despite the relief I feel, I cannot sit still. Pacing the length of the floor, I think about President Collindar's reaction to my words. Her quick acceptance indicates that she had concerns about the trustworthiness of the rebels already. Yet despite that, she continued to work with them. Michal once told me that though she holds the top government position, President Collindar has less power than Dr. Barnes. I think I finally understand how this can be true. The title of "leader" only brings authority if the officials and citizens you work with follow you. The term "president" is meaningless if people turn to someone else for leadership. With so many Commonwealth officials allied with

Dr. Barnes, possibly even those in this office, President Collindar has been forced to work with those she might not have full confidence in to regain the control she needs to keep the country unified. Not only do presidents have to be smart enough to understand the problems that come before them, they have to find potential solutions and a way to inspire others to follow their lead.

President Collindar took office less than five years ago, after President Wendig died. He served in the office for thirty-four years. My Five Lakes teacher called President Wendig one of the greatest leaders history has ever known. When I studied the huge advancements in clean water, power, food sources, and colonization that were made under his leadership, I had to agree. Now I have to assume that President Wendig knew about The Testing and what was expected of the students who passed through The Testing Center's doors. How many of the accomplishments he presided over were made possible because of students who were forced to sacrifice their lives? Did he actively support Dr. Barnes's program? If so, does that diminish the advancements that came under his guidance? My uncertainty about the answer disturbs me deeply.

There is a knock at the door. Moments later, a young red-clad official appears, loaded down with several large folders filled with paper. Behind her is another female official also laden with paperwork. The two place the stacks of papers on the table. The second turns and leaves as the first says, "President Collindar asked that you organize these reports on University graduates based on where they grew up. Once you do that, she requested that they be alphabetized." Her sympathetic smile says that she believes I am being punished with busywork for not providing more useful information during my meeting. Walking toward the door she adds, "A lot of us are going to be working late tonight. If you're still here when the president leaves, we'd be happy to help."

Clearly, the president's plan to make people think I wasted her time has been successful.

While I know the papers are not part of a real assignment, I choose to organize them anyway. If nothing else, having something tangible to focus on keeps me from worrying about the president's meeting with Symon. I assign areas of the table and nearby floor to the city and each of the colonies. Then I pick up the first stack of papers and get to work. Not surprisingly, since Tosu City was the only established concentration of people for the first twenty years after the United Commonwealth was founded, most University graduates have come from the city. Although, looking at the paperwork, I can see that there were fewer students at the start than there are now. Probably because more people were needed then for the physical labor involved in restoring the city.

As the first colony, Shawnee has the next largest concentration, immediately followed in number by Omaha, Amarillo, and Ames. Not surprisingly, the space I reserved for my own colony sits empty for a long time before I find the first student from eighteen years ago. Seven years after Five Lakes was created.

Dreu Owens.

Magistrate Owens's son? My father once said she had a child but that he was no longer with us. I assumed he meant that the child had died. Instead, he was selected for The Testing and survived to attend the University. According to this file, he studied Biological Engineering and was assigned an internship with a research team working on techniques designed to reverse mutations in plants and animals. Putting the paper in the section I designated for Five Lakes, I wonder what job he was assigned after he graduated and if he is still in Tosu.

The stack of unsorted papers grows smaller as I continue my work. I am starting on the last stack when President Collindar walks in holding a gray folder. Gone is the muted sense of concern I saw when she left to meet with Symon. In its place are strength and confidence.

I scramble to my feet as she says, "I apologize for the delay. Symon had a number of thoughts on this week's activities. Letting him talk gave me time to come up with a plan." She crosses the room to the table where I sit, looks directly at me, and says, "I cannot cancel the Debate Chamber vote. Not without raising Jedidiah's and Symon's suspicions. But tomorrow morning a member of my staff will be reported as missing. No one will question a postponement while my team dedicates all its resources to finding him. I believe Symon will outwardly applaud the decision, all the while sowing dissention among the rebel factions and pushing them to schedule an attack. I can convince them to hold off while we search for Michal. If I am lucky, I might be able to postpone their actions for a week. I only hope it will be long enough."

"For what?" I ask.

"I thought that would be obvious," she says. "There is no choice. We must carry out the rebels' plan to end The Testing."

For a moment I am speechless as her meaning hits home. "The rebels were going to start a war."

"That has never been the intention," she says. "The plan is for the rebels to coordinate the elimination of specific targets. The loss of life will be limited to those threats marked for termination. Of course, when violence is employed as a tool, there is always a chance of unexpected casualties. But those involved in creating this plan worked to design a blueprint that would limit losses as much as possible."

Strategic targets. Termination. Tools. Blueprint. Clean words for the bloodletting they imply.

She opens the folder she is carrying, pulls out a piece of paper, and hands it to me. On it are eleven names. The first is Dr. Jedidiah Barnes. Professor Verna Holt is also on the list, as are Professor Douglas Lee and a man named Rychard Jeffries—whom I am almost certain is Raffe's father. Just holding the sheet of paper makes my pulse race and my palms start to sweat.

President Collindar doesn't appear to notice my discomfort as she explains, "The direction of The Testing and the University is headed by a select group led by Dr. Barnes. They are members of the University, officials in key government positions, and research scientists whose work has been used by Dr. Barnes to benefit The Testing. All of the people listed have enough influence and authority to retain control of the University and Testing programs even if Jedidiah is removed from the equation. Symon helped create this document, so there is a chance it is flawed, but I believe the plan is still valid."

"You want to murder Dr. Barnes and his top administrators?"

"No."

I let out a sigh of relief as President Collindar reaches over, takes the paper from me, and slides it back into the gray folder. "I'm not going to kill Dr. Barnes and his followers." She places the folder in my hand. "You are."

CHAPTER 3

HER WORDS PUNCH through my chest and steal my breath. The fire crackles. Somewhere in the building I hear a door slam. President Collindar stands still as death, watching me.

"You can't be serious," I whisper. Though I know she is. "I can't—"

"Yes, you can." Her words are sharp. Confident. "Though the process of The Testing is kept from the public, I have heard enough rumors to understand the tests each candidate must face. For a candidate to pass, she must be intelligent, quick thinking, and able to prove she is capable of doing whatever it takes to survive."

Suddenly, I am not here. I am on the unrevitalized plains during the fourth test. Tomas whispers my name. In the dim light I can see the blood as it flows from the wound in his abdomen. Will stands in front of me. His green eyes narrow behind the gun he has now aimed at me. He straightens his shoulders and takes aim. The gun in my hand kicks. Will staggers as the bullet punches into his side. When he runs I ignore the nausea that is building inside me and fire again.

Yes. When attacked, I will do what it takes to survive. But this . . .

"I can't." My legs tremble but my voice is firm. Strong. More in control than how I feel.

President Collindar walks unhurriedly across the room and takes a seat in the chair right next to the fire. "I will postpone the vote, but that will only delay the inevitable. If you are correct about Symon's allegiance, how long do you think it will take before he incites the rebels to lead their own attack? What will happen then? Do you think Symon will allow any of the rebels or the citizens who have aided them to live? What will happen to the country if I am gone? Who do you think the Debate Chamber members will appoint to take my place?"

Dr. Barnes. If not him, someone he supports. The Testing will continue.

"Cia, I would prefer not to involve you in this, but sometimes a leader has to rely on the resources at hand. My staff has been infiltrated once that we know of. There is no doubt in my mind that where there is one spy there are more, which means the people in this building cannot be trusted. Neither can the rebels."

"The Safety officials—"

"Report to one of the names on that list. And there must be others Dr. Barnes knows will take up arms in his support. Otherwise he would not have embarked on this course of action." She turns and stares at the fire as if looking for answers in the flames, and sighs. "I would attempt to execute this plan myself, but it would be impossible for my actions to go unnoticed, and I am no longer confident of whom I can trust. You, Malencia, are the only one I can be certain of, which is why I am forced to ask you to live up to the promise you have made as a future leader and take up this task. As long as Dr. Barnes remains in control of the University, the rebels will not put aside their agenda. Emotions are running high. The rebels are insisting on change. I have talked to a number of them already."

I see a flicker of regret on the president's face, but it is gone as quickly as it came. Then all I see is her resolve. "I have been told that citizens on the outlying areas of Tosu have been armed by Ranetta's rebel faction despite my express wish for this not to happen. Symon assured me that those allegations are false and that my orders are being obeyed, but everything he's said is suspect. We must assume there are citizens aware of the rebellion and ready to take up arms in support. When the rebels do attack, those citizens could take to the streets. Dr. Barnes's forces will respond. People will be scared. Some will fight. More will die."

Michal told me that the rebels were arming citizens. The president is right to fear what could happen with weapons in the hands of so many. The fear. The desperation to survive at all cost. But that might happen no matter what.

Shaking off the images, I say, "Killing Dr. Barnes and his top administrators might gain you control of The Testing, but people will panic when they hear that many government officials have died. There has to be another way." When solving geometric proofs, often more than one path of logic can lead to the correct solution. Surely there must be a different route we can take now.

"The more we talk, the better I understand why Dr. Barnes chose you."

Despite my own proximity to the fire, the president's compliment makes me shiver.

"You are correct," she acknowledges. "The death of several Commonwealth officials will be cause for concern. But that is far more easily dealt with than the alternative. Safety officials will be deployed in larger numbers. After a week, I can say that the person responsible for the attacks was killed when officials attempted to apprehend him. Personnel schedules and power allotments will return to normal. People will believe the crisis is over because they want to believe their world is safe."

I try to imagine how I would feel if I were a Tosu City citizen who heard the president say a murderer that close to top government officials was no longer a threat. Would I believe the danger had passed and that life could return to normal?

Yes. Not because I was shown proof, but because I'd want to believe. The president's plan might work. But only if someone were to perform the step that came before.

"Murder is wrong." I'm amazed at how composed I sound, because inside my head I am screaming.

"Think of how different the world would be if someone had eliminated Chancellor Freidrich before she had Prime Minister Chae assassinated."

The assassination of peacemaker Prime Minister Chae fractured the Asian Alliance and sparked the First Stage of War.

"Leaders are often forced to make determinations they find distasteful for the good of the people they serve. Asking you to help eliminate the leaders who champion the current mission of the University is the last thing I wish to do. I do not make this request lightly. But it is the best chance we have to avoid a path that will certainly lead to a far worse fate."

President Collindar stands and crosses to me. She takes the folder from my hand, walks to the table, and picks up a pen. While she flips open the folder and writes something on one of the pages it contains, I swallow hard, close my eyes, and wish that I were back in Five Lakes. That I had never come to Tosu City or learned the secrets behind The Testing. War would still be looming but I would be unaware. The president would not have asked me to betray everything I have ever believed in order to fix what she cannot. That is not my job. Coming here and alerting her to the danger was supposed to pass the responsibility of keeping me, my brother, Tomas, and my friends safe to one who has been officially charged with leadership.

"If I thought I had a chance of successfully orchestrating this plan with my own team, I would. Perhaps I will have to attempt that as a last resort if you do not take up this task." She places the folder back into my hands. "Throughout history, leaders have used targeted means to eliminate threats that, if allowed to remain unchecked, could cause far greater damage. When the United Commonwealth was founded, our leaders vowed we would do whatever was necessary to forward the country's mission of revitalization and peace. That mission is now threatened. I'm asking you, Malencia Vale, to help keep our country and its purpose alive."

The speech stirs my blood. Since I was little, my goal has been to follow in my father's footsteps. To be selected for The Testing. To go to the University. To help my country. But this . . .

"Do not give me your answer now." She takes one step

closer and puts a hand on my shoulder. "I understand the difficult choice I have laid before you. I can hold off the rebels for at least a week. Two if I am lucky."

So little time.

"Inside that folder is the list of those who need to be removed if The Testing is to end, along with information on each of them. Also, there is a room on the fifth floor that you might find useful in completing this task. I have written the entrance code on the top page." The president squeezes my shoulder and then steps back. "I do not expect this to be easy. You may die in the trying. Even if you do not, there is a strong chance you will fail—although I would not ask this of you if I believed either to be the inevitable conclusion. If by the end of this week you have decided not to pursue this assignment, I ask that you send a message saying that the project is unsustainable."

One week to decide.

"Regardless of what you choose, I warn you to be careful. Symon has indicated that members of the rebellion exist among the University students. They could expose you without realizing what they have done." She walks toward the door. Hand on the knob, she looks at me. "Trust no one, Cia. It's not just your life but also the lives of many others that depend on that."

As she strides out I hear her say, "I think it is safe to say the young woman has now learned her lesson. I'll be in my office if anyone else needs to meet."

The door stays open as her footsteps fade. I know it is time for me to leave, but I am too stunned by what I have heard. Too overwhelmed by the task I have been asked to perform. I want to believe I imagined what just happened, but the folder in my hand belies that wish. My hands are cold when I open it and glance at the first page, which contains the code the president spoke of as well as the eleven names. No. Now there are twelve. Written at the bottom in the president's strong block handwriting is the name Symon Dean. Below the name is a series of seven numbers and the words "I am counting on you."

I close the folder and place it on top of my bag. Then I stack the piles of paper from my earlier work onto the table. At the last minute, I take the three pages that contain information on Five Lakes Colony University students. Why? I don't know. Maybe it is just because I cannot bear the thought that this information is in the hands of anyone who does not know or care about them. Or maybe I need a reminder of where I came from and who I am. My parents raised me to believe in my fellow citizens and in the United Commonwealth. To fix things. I wonder what they would say if they knew I had been told that in order to fix the country they have worked so hard for I must now deliberately take lives.

The world spins around me. Nausea stirs in my stomach and sears my throat. I shove the folder into my bag and stumble over a crease in the carpet as I hurry to the door. The president has given me a week to choose what I will do, but I don't see how I can make this choice. To allow The Testing to continue, or to do what I could not when I was Tested and kill. I am not like Will or Roman or Damone. I cannot commit murder to push myself forward. But can I end lives to ultimately save more?

I don't know.

And still, I find that instead of climbing down the stairs, I go up. I hear voices coming from offices on the third floor, but no one is in the hallway as I quickly climb the next two sets of stairs. The fifth floor is quiet. I stop in front of the door with a red-lit keypad at the end of the hall and turn toward the stairs to check if anyone is coming. I see no one. After pulling the paper out of its folder, I punch in the seven-number code, watch the light go from red to green, and slip inside. I wait for the door to close before feeling around the wall for lights. When I find them, my heart begins to hammer.

Guns both large and small.

Stack upon stack of boxed ammunition.

Knives of varying shapes and sizes.

Bulbs filled with an explosive powder that my father and his team use to loosen sections of rock in unrevitalized areas.

After a moment, I notice the room contains more than weapons. Long-range transmitters. Pocket-size pulse radios. Tracking devices. Recorders made in various shapes. Some look much like the ones I remember being used in our Testing bracelets.

And I realize that this room reminds me of the one Michal brought me to before the fourth test. During The Testing, I looked at the weapons provided and saw tools to aid in survival. Now I see them as so many of my fellow Testing candidates must have—as a means of taking lives.

I slide four of the smallest pulse radios inside my bag. Beside them I place several recorders and tracking devices as well as a small monitor that must be used to display the location of the transmitter. I look at the other shelves and consider taking one of the larger knives. But their serrated edges remind me too much of the weapon Tomas carried during The Testing. The one that killed Zandri.

Telling myself I have no need of the weapons since I do not

plan to carry out the president's directive, I walk back to the door and turn off the light. In the darkness, I listen for sounds on the other side. When I hear none, I slip out the door, wait for the light to turn back to red, and head downstairs.

One of the officials who brought the files spots me as I reach the third floor. She asks if I need help with my work, and I tell her I finished the assignment and am going home. With a wave, I continue down the next two flights, hoping she isn't one of Symon's rebels.

More officials are in the halls on the first floor than when I arrived. I keep my head down and walk to the exit. The fresh air feels cools and wonderful against my skin as I grab my bicycle and begin to ride. I try not to think about the president's request, but it is impossible to forget what she has charged me to do. Dr. Barnes. Professor Holt. Symon. Raffe's father. All people who have had a hand in killing Testing candidates either by active participation or passive acceptance. They deserve to be punished for their parts in the deaths of those who came here in hope. But do their actions mean they deserve to die? And if so, can I bring myself to kill them?

My stomach heaves as I recall the feel of Damone's blood running over my hand while life drained from his body. If the president has her way, his will be just the first blood I shed. I try to tamp down the nausea, but after three blocks, I jump off my bike and run toward a group of bushes huddled near the side of a sandy-colored brick building. My bike clatters to the walkway behind me as I empty my stomach onto the ground. I wipe my mouth and try to stand up straight. But my stomach tightens again and I hunch over. My legs feel like jelly. Sweat breaks out, and I start to shake as the images of those who have died run through my mind. Ryme's empty eyes. Roman's bloody body. Michal's face as it drained of color just before he crumpled to the ground.

Slowly, the shaking subsides and I straighten. I take careful steps. The weakness I felt seems to have passed, but when I pick up my bike, I choose to walk with it down the city street instead of riding. I fumble with the fastenings on my bag and dig out a bottle of water. The water cleanses my mouth and throat of the taste of bile, but it cannot wash away the cause. I wheel my bike north while taking sips of water, not paying attention to where I am headed. When I come to a small fountain in the middle of a grassy area surrounded by a small square of shops, I set my bike on the ground and take a seat on the stone lip of the fountain.

It is cool, but the early evening light has encouraged many to come out of doors. Children play a game of tag. Several couples sit on benches along the walkways that surround the park. Everything seems so normal. No one here feels the tension of the power struggle that is about to threaten their world.

I pull the Transit Communicator out of my bag, hit the Call button, and close my eyes as I wait for Zeen to respond. But no matter how much I want to hear his voice, the Communicator remains silent and I have no idea what I should do now. I went to the president so she could save him and everyone else from Dr. Barnes, Symon, and the destruction the false rebellion will cause. She was supposed to take charge and solve this problem. Instead, she has turned it back on me and I am not sure I am capable of walking the path she has pointed me toward.

Swallowing hard, I open my eyes and stare at the clean, clear water gurgling next to me. The fountain is not simply decorative but is used by citizens to fill their drinking bottles, and I find myself thinking of the people who survived the Seven Stages of War. The fear they must have felt when the South American coalition attacked. When President Dalton responded by ending the stance of isolationism he'd adopted in hopes that avoiding conflict would bring peace. It didn't. Nor did the violence that came after. Cities around the world were leveled. Millions killed. Finally, leaders decided to lay down their weapons before they destroyed not only their enemies but themselves. The Fourth Stage of War ended and peace treaties were signed.

Despite the devastation, there must have been a sense of hope. A feeling that the worst was over. But the earth did not sign a treaty. The biological and chemical warfare employed during the first Four Stages could not be wiped away with the stroke of a pen. Peace would not be so easy. Earthquakes. Chemical-laden rainstorms. Floods. Tornadoes. Hurricanes. By the time the Seventh Stage of War ended, the weather and landscape had been unimaginably changed.

It's amazing that humans survived. How easy it would have been to look at the horror around them and give up. Food was scarce. Uncontaminated water was almost impossible to find. But they didn't surrender. They salvaged what they could from their homes and set out to find other survivors. They came here. They revitalized this city. Brick by brick, tree by tree, they began to restore what their leaders had destroyed.

There must have been terrible choices to be made. People who refused to endorse a centralized government created trouble. They hoarded resources. Caused fights on the Debate

Chamber floor and turned the focus away from the good of everyone to themselves. City officials encouraged them to leave Tosu. Eventually, they did.

When my Five Lakes classmates and I were studying this part of history, our teacher told us that the dissenters disappeared from the city. I assumed she meant that they set out to find a new place where they could live as they chose. Now I wonder. Would those intent on bringing down the newly created government have been able to leave so easily? Especially when their dissent was causing the governing body so much trouble? There were food riots. Solar panels were destroyed or stolen. Vigilantes patrolled the streets, fighting with and sometimes killing those the government had assigned to ensure their safety. With a shortage of resources and a flurry of lawlessness, there must have been concern that the new government was flawed. That it was not in control. That, maybe, not following the new rules for resource distribution and revitalization would make things better.

How difficult those days must have been. With new food resources available and plants and trees thriving in the revitalized soil, it seems impossible to imagine that anyone could have believed trying to survive on their own would be better than working together and following the same rules. But quite a few did. Yet somehow the government regained control. In order to do so, did they eliminate those who were intent on wreaking havoc?

Maybe.

If so, were they wrong?

I look at the sparkling, uncorrupted water and then at the children laughing as they play. Would these things be here now if the dissenters had destroyed what was just being created? Does this end justify a means paved with blood?

I don't know.

At one time I would have been certain. This situation would have appeared black and white. I wish it did now. I told President Collindar that I could not eliminate those whose names are written on the paper in my bag. I want to believe that this is the truth, but the pressure I feel growing in my chest as I look around at a city that was forged in struggle and in hope makes me wonder whether there might be another truth. That like the Seven Stages of War and the time that followed, peace will come accompanied by sacrifice and death.

I glance at the watch on the strap of my bag. The sun will soon be setting. I need to return to campus. I know I should get on my bike and return, but I find myself pulling the gray folder out of my bag again and opening it. There are the twelve names, the code to the fifth-floor room, and the note President Collindar wrote to me. Under that page are several more sheets of gray recycled paper. Eleven of them, to be exact. One for each of the original eleven names on the president's list. At the top of each page is a name followed by the person's residence, family information, and role in The Testing.

Not surprisingly, the first page of this group centers on Dr. Jedidiah Barnes. The location of his home means little to me, since I am not from Tosu City. Although I do remember other students mentioning that his personal dwelling is on one of the streets that surround the University campus. I read the name of his wife and picture the woman I met last summer, after The Testing was over. His two children are sixteen and twelve—approaching the age when they can apply to the University. With their father as head of the program, they no doubt would be selected. But will they want to be a part of the trials that follow? Dr. Barnes has been in charge of The Testing for fifteen years. During that time, 1,132 students have sat for The Testing. Of those, 128 were passed through to the University. Over one thousand students who wished to help the world are gone. Because of him.

As the light fades, I read through the other pages, committing as much as possible to memory. Professor Holt — an advocate for adding another section to The Testing to push the ability of students to think critically while under emotional strain. Professor Markum — head of Medical studies, who created the newest version of the memory-erasure serum and is working on a neurological implant to help officials better monitor the way each prospective student deals with the strain of The Testing process. Professor Lee — who, according to this information, not only helped create the scoring system for each group of students during the first round of The Testing but is advocating for a larger pool of candidates to ensure that none of the best and brightest escape notice.

Page after page of leaders. All working to make The Testing harder. More invasive. Deadlier.

White-hot anger builds inside me as I start over and reread the descriptions by the fading light. These people were entrusted with the lives of the next generation of leaders. They have betrayed not only that trust but also the faith of the entire country.

Emotions cloud my vision, making it hard to read through the last few pages. Rage. Sorrow. Fear. Despair. They chip away my resolve to refuse the president's request and pull at the beliefs I have been taught to hold dear. When I finally finish my second read, I slide the papers back into the folder, fill my water bottle at the fountain, and climb onto my bike. Using the Transit Communicator to guide me, I head back to the University, taking the same path I used to get to the president's office. The route isn't the most direct, but getting back quickly isn't my purpose. While I would prefer to destroy the papers the president gave me, there is a chance I will have need of the information they contain. Hiding them so I cannot be caught with them is my best option.

I spot a neighborhood where the roads and sidewalks are cracked and broken and the grass less green, and turn to enter it. The roofs of the houses sag in the middle. Boards across windows and doors signal a lack of materials to make repairs. Stairs are missing steps. Swirls of faded paint decorate the houses' exteriors. The front yards are mostly dirt with a few patches of scraggly yellowish grass. If it weren't for the hopeful budding of the healthy trees on the street, I would think this area had yet to be revitalized and that people did not yet live here. But they do. A rag doll sitting near the rotted front steps of a squat brown house with a porch that is carefully swept of debris and a metal shovel that is free of rust sitting outside another dwelling tell me that people are here.

Since coming to Tosu, I've realized that despite the best intentions of the government, it is almost impossible for a city this size to treat all citizens the same. Streets that government officials call home are repaired more frequently than those of people who do not hold influential jobs. But the run-down appearance of some areas notwithstanding, I have never seen another so poorly tended as this one. While that disturbs me, in a way I am glad. It's clear that the government rarely if ever notices this street, so it could be a perfect place to hide the papers I don't want anyone to find.

In the last rays of daylight, I study the dilapidated, graffiti-laden houses on either side of the roadway, ignoring those that show signs of habitation. A small one-story structure with boarded-up windows and a sagging roof catches my eye. The houses across from it show subtle signs of occupancy, but this one and the two on either side look as though nothing but rodents and small animals have gone near the front door in months.

Careful to keep to the grass so I don't leave footprints in the dirt, I cross to the back of the house. The door in the rear hangs precariously from its hinges. I can see at least one spot where an animal has constructed a nest in the eve of the roof.

I lean my bicycle against the back of the house and walk to the door. The hinges let out a shrill protest as I shift it open. I go still and wait to see if anyone appears. When no one does, I walk inside into a small kitchen. Doors of cabinets are missing. In the center of the room, the remains of a collapsed table lie sprawled on the floor, surrounded by three wooden chairs. Leaves and twigs are scattered on the ground. Still, I search the rest of the structure to make sure this place is not in use.

The living room floor is coated in a thick layer of dust. The lone sofa in the room is so worn that springs poke through its cushions. I search the bathroom and two bedrooms. When I see no obvious signs of habitation, I pull my pocketknife out of my bag, then open the bedroom closet. Kneeling, I use the knife to prod around the floorboards. Several are loose. I pry up three, stand up to pull the folder out of my bag, remove the list of names, and tuck the rest of the papers into the spot I dug out. I replace the floorboards and pile the clothes stained with Damone's blood on top of them. Then I close the closet door and hurry out.

I save the coordinates of this location on the Transit Communicator, then climb onto my bicycle and ride. When I reach the end of the street, I look back at the house where the papers lie hidden, knowing that if I return to retrieve them it will be because I have chosen to take up President Collindar's charge.

And not just me. Because this task is not one that I can complete on my own. My father told me to trust no one. I have broken that edict more than once — often to my detriment. And if the president is right and there is no other way to end The Testing and the destruction to the country that might come, I may have to break it again.

CHAPTER 4

THE SKY IS dark as I cross under the arch that marks the entrance to the campus. Solar lights illuminate the roadways and the buildings that I pass. I see fewer students than usual. Many spend their Saturday evenings in their rooms, catching up on sleep or blowing off steam, but normally there are more than the handful of students I see going to and from the library or sitting on the benches outside the residences. The inactivity makes my heart race as I pedal across the bridge toward the vehicle shed. I store my bike and hurry around to the entrance of the residence.

"Cia."

I jump at the sound of my name and squint into the shadows, looking for the source. For a moment I see nothing. Then a figure moves away from the trunk of the weeping willow tree into the faint moonlight.

Enzo. Of all the University students, Enzo is the one I think I most understand and the one I am more inclined to believe has my best interests at heart. He is not like the others, whose families have ties to the Commonwealth Government. He could not rely on his parents' connections in order to get accepted to the University. Enzo worked for it. He, like me, wanted to come to the University to help better our country. That similarity and the lack of connection to those who currently lead the University are the reasons I cross the grass instead of going inside. If Enzo has been waiting outside the residence for me, the reason must be important.

As I walk toward him, Enzo looks around to make sure we are alone. When I reach his side he says, "Professor Holt is looking for you."

I swallow hard. "Do you know why?" Does she want to know what I was doing in the city today? Does she suspect what the president has asked of me? Or is this about what happened last night?

"Professor Holt has been interviewing everyone in the residence to see if anyone has information as to Damone's whereabouts."

"Maybe he went to visit his family," I say, hoping Enzo doesn't hear the strain in my voice. Many Tosu City students use their free hours on the weekends to spend time at home. The action isn't encouraged by University staff, but neither is it condemned. Their being able to visit those they love is just one more aspect that separates those of us from the colonies from the students born in Tosu City. Even Enzo has taken time away from his studies to make the trek to the south side of the city to see his family.

"I told her that I spotted Damone this morning from my window. He had a bag over his shoulder as he came out of the vehicle building with his bicycle. Professor Holt is checking to see if Damone went home." Enzo looks toward the bridge as if searching for answers. After several long moments, he quietly says, "I couldn't sleep last night."

Five words. Enough to make my pulse pound.

My heart ticks off the seconds as I wait for what comes next. Ten. Twenty. Finally he says, "My bedroom window next to my desk faces the back of the residence. Normally I don't bother to look outside. But I did. I saw Damone." His head turns toward me. "And you."

"I . . ." I what? I wasn't there? I was, and Enzo and I wouldn't be having this conversation if he had any doubt that it was me he saw in the moonlight. "What did you see?" My voice sounds harsh. Panicked. I'm both. If Enzo has lied about what he said to Professor Holt, I will have two choices: run or be Redirected. Maybe that is why he is telling me now. To give me a chance to flee.

"I saw Damone and you fighting. I was going to come help, but by then my help wasn't necessary. Damone is dead, and I'm not sorry. He shouldn't have attacked you. He shouldn't have even been here in the first place. It's people like him that made my father agree to help change things. He and my brothers—" Enzo looks back to the horizon. Taking a deep breath, he says, "Look, I'm not telling you this to make you afraid. I just want you to know that I could see you and Raffe. If I could, someone else might have. Professor Holt is talking to everyone inside the residence. You need to be prepared."

"Why are you telling me this?" I ask. "You could go to Professor Holt, tell her what you saw, and collect your reward."

"I'm not Damone." Enzo's voice trembles. "He and Griffin

want to be important. I want to make a difference. I promised my family I would. They're counting on me. Selling you out to Professor Holt wouldn't make them proud or help them. They are fighting against what she stands for. I am too." Enzo takes several steps toward the residence and turns back to face me. "I don't know why you were out of the residence last night or why you let Raffe help you. He's one of them. I think you and I are on the same side. So be careful. Okay?"

For a moment we just look at each other. Enzo watching me for signs of agreement. Me waiting for . . . I don't know. Something that tells me he really is on my side. That he is not repelled to know I am responsible for taking a life. That he can be trusted to aid me if I see no other way to end The Testing than to follow the president's command.

Whatever he sees on my face must be enough of an answer because without another word, he turns and leaves me standing under the willow, struggling to think through what he has told me. Is it safe for me to stay, or should I pack my bag and run now while I still can?

Part of me wants to flee. If I could talk to Zeen, I know he would tell me to run. But he still isn't answering. I want to believe that he hasn't been able to find a place isolated enough to contact me. To think otherwise would shatter me. My brother is smart and resourceful. I just have to be patient. But I cannot wait to hear from him before formulating a plan. If I were to run, Tomas would go with me. The two of us are resourceful. We would have a greater chance of survival than most. Our survival of The Testing proves that. Running would mean I wouldn't have to face the choice I have been given.

For a moment I look at the bridge. I imagine what it would

be like to leave behind this place and everything I know. Then I turn and walk to the residence. Because there is too much at stake. I might not be able to stop what is to come, but I cannot leave without trying, or without learning what has become of my brother.

The sight of two officials in ceremonial purple greets me as I walk through the entryway of the residence. Enzo is nowhere to be seen. The minute the officials see me, the one on the left takes a step forward and says, "Malencia Vale?"

I try to keep the concern I feel off my face as I nod.

"Professor Holt asked that you report to her in the main common room once you arrived. She'll be glad to know you are safe."

While I am not sure Professor Holt will feel delight upon seeing me, I thank the official for his message. I then head in the direction of the common room, hoping I did not make the wrong decision when I chose to stay instead of run.

I walk down the hall to the large room that we use for residence gatherings, studying, and relaxing in between classes. Professor Holt is seated near the large stone fireplace. Her squared shoulders, her short cap of red hair, and the crimson color of her clothing give her an undeniable air of authority. Across the room, several upper-year students are standing in small groups. It only takes one of them noticing my approach for Professor Holt to turn toward me. Her almond-shaped eyes narrow behind her thickly framed glasses before she turns back to the students gathered nearby. A look from Professor Holt sends them hurrying out the door, leaving the two of us alone.

Forcing a smile, I say, "You asked to see me, Professor Holt?"

I stand motionless while Professor Holt studies me. My heart hammers as I think of Enzo's words, the lie he swore he told, and the gray paper in my bag. In my mind I picture Professor Holt's name written in firm black letters beneath that of Dr. Barnes. Would she understand the purpose of the list if for some reason she asked to see the contents of my bag? And what would she say if she saw the gun and the transmitters?

"Please, take a seat." Professor Holt waves me into the faded armchair across from her.

I sit, wishing I could have found a plausible reason to stand, since I had the advantage of height and the ability to run. Sitting with my bag on my lap, I am very aware of being at the mercy of Professor Holt and the University if the answers I give are not correct.

Professor Holt leans back in her chair and asks, "Have you been experiencing any problems in your classes or with your internship?"

The subject matter catches me off-guard. I blink twice and consider her seemingly innocuous words. After being assigned to the Government studies program, my fellow students and I were given class schedules. I was assigned nine classes—the most of any first-year student. Failure to keep up with the course load is monitored closely. Some students who struggled have already been Redirected out of the University. According to my guide, Ian, I have been watched more carefully than my peers for signs of difficulty. There was something about me that Dr. Barnes and Professor Holt found troubling long before my untracked disappearance from campus this morning. Something that goes back to The Testing. Even with my returned memories, I have not been able to puzzle out what that something is. And not now, with Professor Holt staring at me, waiting for an answer.

My admitting my workload is difficult could give her an opening to doubt my abilities as a student, but saying I am managing my schedule with ease is a lie. One she will certainly call me on. Without understanding her agenda, I carefully say, "It's a challenge to keep up with all of the work, but I'm deter-mined to succeed."

"I'm sure you are." Professor Holt's smile fades. "Damone Pyburn was determined as well, but he appears to have van-ished from campus. He has not been seen since last night. When your friends could not find you, I was concerned you might have disappeared as well."

Her eyes flick to the bracelet on my wrist. A sure sign that my whereabouts were never in doubt. I wonder if Damone's bracelet is currently able to be tracked and if Professor Holt knows he is at the bottom of the chasm that surrounds this building. Or does the tear in the earth go too deep for her and Dr. Barnes to trace with a short-range transmitter?

Giving her an embarrassed smile, I say, "I apologize if I caused anyone to worry. I had some questions about a project I'm working on and decided to go to the president's office to get some answers."

If Professor Holt looks for the lie in my words she won't find one.

Nodding, she says, "I appreciate your dedication to your studies, as I'm sure the president does. And, of course, you left before I requested that students remain in the residence so that I could discuss Damone's unusual disappearance with all of you individually. So, you had no way of knowing that you went against my explicit instructions."

"I would never have left had I known I was instructed to stay on campus."

Her lips purse. "Well, now that you're back, perhaps you can tell me whether you had cause to speak with or spend time with Damone Pyburn before he went missing."

I consider my words carefully as I say, "Despite our being on the same team during Induction, I don't know Damone very well. He made it clear that he wasn't interested in being friends with colony students, so we rarely if ever spoke."

"And yet you saved his life — twice."

Only to end it later.

I stifle the urge to shift in my seat and say, "It was the right thing to do for my team."

"And you always do the right thing."

"No," I answer honestly. "Growing up, I was taught that it's impossible to know what the right thing always is. The best you can do is to try to do what you think is right for yourself and the people around you."

Professor Holt stares at me for a minute as if trying to read hidden meanings in my words. Finally she says, "I have been told that you were absent from the residence *twice* today."

Blood pounds in my ears. Cautiously, I nod. "I went into the city."

"The first time was with Raffe Jeffries. Yes, I spoke with him earlier. He gave me an account of your outing. Perhaps you'd like to give me yours."

What to say? I do not know the explanation Raffe gave Professor Holt for our leaving campus. If my answer does not match the one he gave, Professor Holt will question everything I have said thus far. And I have used my internship to cover my journey to the city this afternoon. I can't use the same excuse for Raffe and me going out this morning.

Hoping Raffe didn't tell an elaborate story, I say, "Raffe knows I haven't had much of a chance to explore Tosu City. We ran into each other before breakfast and he volunteered to show me around."

Professor Holt tilts her head to the side. "What time did you and Mr. Jefferies meet?"

Breakfast starts at seven-thirty. "Around seven, I think." Most students don't get up on the weekends until after the allotted time for breakfast has already begun, so the time I quoted gives less of a chance for her to question why other students didn't see us. I can only hope the logic Raffe used to give his answer was the same I employed to create mine.

"Are you certain that time is accurate?"

I'm certain it is not, but I cannot change my answer now. Instead I force a laugh and say, "It might have been just before or just after. I wasn't watching the time all that closely."

"Mr. Jefferies said the two of you planned to meet this morning, but you implied it was a spontaneous trip."

I feel color fill my cheeks and I clutch my bag as my mind races, trying to decide how best to explain the discrepancy. Out of the corner of my eye, I see someone hovering in the doorway of the common room. Turning, I lock eyes with him. His long dark hair frames his pale face and deep green eyes.

"Do you need something, Mr. O'Donovan?" Professor Holt asks. Her tone is clipped, indicating her displeasure at being interrupted.

Will doesn't seem to be bothered by Professor Holt's annoyance. Flashing a crooked smile, he shoves his hands into his pockets and leans against the doorjamb. "No. I was just checking to make sure Cia was okay. I ran into Tomas Endress earlier, and he was worried that he hadn't seen her all day. Don't worry, Cia." Will's smile grows wider. "I didn't tell him that you spent most of the day with another guy."

He winks.

Frowning, I look down at my hands as though embarrassed by Will's words. In reality, I feel relief as Professor Holt dismisses Will with a reminder that all students are to remain inside the residence until after breakfast tomorrow.

When she turns her attention back to me, I quietly say, "Tomas and I aren't as close as we used to be, but I don't want to upset him if I don't have to. We're both from Five Lakes and . . ." I shrug and take a deep breath. "I thought it would be better if he heard that my visit to the city with Raffe was spur of the moment instead of something we planned."

My nerves jump as Professor Holt stares at me, her eyes unblinking behind her glasses. "It is always difficult to decide whether emotional attachment is due to shared experiences or to something deeper. If you aren't careful, those kinds of attachments can cause distractions you don't need. That's only one of the many reasons I'm pleased Dr. Barnes continued the practice of eliminating Testing memories in successful candidates. The last thing we need is students who have formed personal attachments as a mechanism for dealing with stress."

At Professor Holt's mention of The Testing, I find myself recalling the information I read earlier today and her placement on the list of people marked for death. While I don't like

Professor Holt, the idea of deliberately ending her life makes my heart cringe. "Professor Holt, can I ask a question?"

She blinks behind her glasses. "Of course."

I choose each word with caution as I say, "Do you think The Testing is the best way to select future leaders?"

"Why do you ask?"

"I heard people at the president's office discussing The Testing. Since I don't remember my experience, I thought I'd ask your opinion. Do you think putting candidates through The Testing is necessary?"

"We need strong leaders more than ever before. One wrong choice could cause everything we have rebuilt to collapse." Dark eyes filled with conviction meet mine. "The Testing is not only necessary—in my opinion, the process is not nearly hard enough."

The confidence in her stride as she walks out the door leaves no doubt. If Professor Holt has her way, even more Testing candidates will die.

CHAPTER 5

THE RESIDENCE HALL is quiet as I go to the dining area to get something to eat. I fill a plate and balance it as I walk up the two flights of stairs. Unlike most nights, no one is wandering the halls, which makes me wonder about Will's arrival during my interview with Professor Holt. Why was he out of his rooms? Was he looking for me? His appearance helped me come up with a plausible answer to her question. Was that on purpose or just a coincidence?

I have not come up with answers to these questions about Will as I turn the key in my lock and enter my rooms. Pushing aside all thoughts of Will and whatever agenda he might have, I unfasten my bag and look at the things I took from the room on the fifth floor. Why I selected these items is still a mystery to me. Perhaps instinct had me grabbing anything that would give me comfort. Fixing, creating, and modifying technology has always been what I have done best. Since being assigned to Government Studies, I have felt removed from that part of me, just as geography and our different fields of study have made me feel cut off from Tomas. Suddenly, I realize that the pulse radios in my possession mean neither is an obstacle.

After the Seven Stages of War, scientists utilized the higher concentration of electromagnetic radiation in the air to restore communication with these devices. Pulse radios were designed to record chunks of information and, using pulselike signals, send them to receiving devices that are set to a corresponding frequency. Because any device set to the same frequency as the sending radio can receive the recorded message, pulse radio signals are not a secure form of communication. But if we pick frequencies unused by the Commonwealth and alternate them often, Tomas and I will have a better form of communication than has been available to us thus far. For that, I am willing to take the risk.

The other items from the fifth-floor room I have less of a sense of purpose about. I turn a small recorder over in my hands. It resembles the one I remember finding in my Testing bracelet. Perhaps it will be useful, but at the moment I'm not sure how. Setting this recorder aside, I look at the tracking devices. While I am unsure how to use them to my advantage, there's always a chance they could be valuable.

I glance at the clock. It's after nine, but still the Transit Communicator is silent. Forcing myself to eat, I contemplate how best to modify the frequency of the pulse radio to something not typically used by Commonwealth officials. The knot of worry in my chest dissolves as I focus on a problem I can solve.

Using the screwdriver part of my pocketknife, I remove the back cover of the pulse radios and examine the transmitters and receivers. The receiving frequency is easiest to modify. Just a couple turns of a screw and it will shift downward. The transmitting frequency is more challenging, since these pulse radios do not contain oscillators but rather use surface acoustic wave filters. To alter the frequency, I will need to swap the SAW resonator and several other parts.

I look through the items in my desk drawer, hoping to find what I need. But while I come up with a few pieces I can use, others are missing. The lab rooms downstairs will have those. I hope.

After placing the cover back on the radio, I put everything back in my bag and head for the door. Downstairs, the corridors are empty. The officials in purple are gone. Everything is as still as a tomb. I turn to the right and head down the hallway in the opposite direction of the common room toward the four labs we are allowed to use for our studies.

Labs 1 and 4 are occupied, telling me that not everyone has chosen to hide in their rooms. Treading as lightly as possible, I walk into Lab 2, put my bag on the metal counter, and walk to a set of small drawers to search for the items I need to create my SAW filter and additional components. Bits of copper. A small ceramic square. Small screws. I work quickly. My confidence grows as I solder metal, connect the wires, and put that radio aside to begin work on the next one. The second is easier, since I have completed this manipulation once. When I am finished, I speak my name into the first pulse radio's recorder and press Send. Moments later I hear my voice address me from the other radio. It worked. The two are now functioning at a different frequency.

I start to work on the other two radios but then stop to

consider my options. By making all the radios the same frequency, I can allow four people to send messages to each other. While this sounds like a reasonable idea, I'm not sure it is the best plan. Whatever communication I have with Tomas I want kept private. He is the only one I am sure is on my side. The way to keep what we say between us is to set the other radios to a separate frequency and modify mine with an oscillator so it can change between the two.

The work calms me. My mind empties of everything except equations to determine frequency. Creating the oscillator circuit. Adding the pieces necessary to allow mine to swing between the other pulse radios. The higher frequency I keep for Tomas. The lower works with the other radios. Who I might give them to or why is still to be determined. When I am done, I pack the radios in my bag and go back to my room proud of the job I have done. As I curl up on my bed with the Transit Communicator clutched in my hands, I can only hope Zeen is safe.

I awake with a start. The sun is streaming through my bedroom window. The Communicator lies on the bed beside me — silent. There is no way to know if Zeen tried to contact me last night and I failed to hear his call. I push the button on the side twice and wait for my brother to respond. When he doesn't, I scramble off the bed and check the time. It is after eight.

I take the Communicator into the bathroom with me as I wash the sleep from my face, and study myself in the reflector. With the tip of my finger, I trace the five scars on my left arm. While almost all the students from The Testing were healed of injuries and began their University studies unmarked, these could not be removed. The poison that infected me was too powerful to be healed with the available medicines. Now that my Testing memories have returned, I know how I received these scars and I am glad they remain. Professor Holt might believe that removing The Testing memories allows us to come into our studies with a better ability to focus, but while that might be true, she is wrong about the importance of knowing the choices we have made and what we have done.

I killed.

Not because I wanted to. But because I had no choice. Not if I wanted to live. Not if I wanted to help the others I cared about to survive.

I came to Tosu City unmarked. I thought I understood what leadership meant and what I would face if I was selected for The Testing. These five raised scars remind me how far I have come and how much I have changed. Because it is not just the outside that has been marked. Where my beliefs were once black and white, I now see shades of gray. My father must have seen those shades, too. He suspected what The Testing entailed. He could have made the choice to help me flee. He and the other leaders of our colony could have found a way to eliminate the Tosu City official before he had a chance to inform the four of us that we were chosen.

Looking back, I see so many things my father could have done had he wanted to keep me from The Testing. And still he let me come. Because no matter what he believed about the process of The Testing, he believed in this country and the strength of the leaders who run it. He made a choice to believe in this system despite its flaws. I think of the piece of paper that sits inside the bag I now slide onto my shoulder, the task I have been given, and my belief that The Testing must end before it is allowed to kill again. I will have to decide whether to pretend I am still the girl from Five Lakes who climbed into the skimmer on her way to Tosu City or to take the best of that girl and allow it to be forged into something new.

A faint clicking sound stops me as I start down the stairs. Zeen. Relief fills me. And when the sound comes again, I hurry back to my rooms, unlock the door, and pull the Communicator out of my bag.

I click the button twice in response and say, "Are you okay?"

"I'm fine. What about you? I was worried when you didn't answer last night. If everyone around here weren't so jumpy, I would have come to check on you."

"I can take care of myself," I say. That I survived The Testing and everything the University has thrown at me should be testament to that. Still, it is nice to have my brother thinking about me and expressing a desire to protect, even though there is little he can do to keep me safe.

"Well, if you want to take care of yourself, you have to get out of there. Now," Zeen hisses. "The girl I talked to last night says there are rebels on campus who Symon has been using to collect information. They're also part of a plan to attack Dr. Barnes and other University officials from inside."

"Michal told me there were rebels among the University students," I reply. He was worried they were armed. He feared that if fighting broke out, they might start open warfare here on campus and that students might be caught in the crossfire. From what Zeen says, Michal was right.

"This morning Symon and Renatta spoke to everyone at camp. With the vote coming tomorrow and the attack scheduled to begin on Friday, we're now under instructions to re-move anything or anyone we believe could interfere with the rebellion's success. If the rebel students are under the same or-ders, it won't take much to convince them to come after you."

"That doesn't make any sense. I'm a colony student. They should know I'm on the side of shutting down The Testing. Removing me isn't logical."

"Logic isn't what's leading this rebellion, Cia. Emotion is. They want to end The Testing, but after investing their time and energy, what they want even more is to make Dr. Barnes and all those who were part of The Testing pay. They don't care if they die as long as those they believe to be responsible for The Testing are dead, too. If they see you as a threat to victory, they'll have no problem sacrificing you in order to secure the greater cause. Get out of there while you can. There's nothing you can do to stop what's coming."

Yes. Yes, there is.

"Zeen—"

"Quiet."

I obey the harsh whisper and wait. Metal bites into my fin-gers as I clutch the Communicator and wait for Zeen to speak again.

"Look, I mean what I said. Get Tomas and get out of there. He can help you stay safe until I get word to you about what is happening here."

"I'm not going to leave unless you do." If it would keep my brother safe, I would run.

"You have to get out of the city, Cia. This isn't something you should be dealing with. Let me know when you're out of harm's way, and I'll try to join you after this is all over. Don't worry if you don't hear from me. It might be hard for me to get somewhere private enough to speak, but I'll contact you as soon as I am able."

"No. I'm not going to leave knowing you're still in danger."

"Don't worry about me," he says with a hint of the self-assured tone I have always associated with my brother. "I can take care of myself. I have to go."

"Zeen . . ." I whisper. As much as I want to speak his name again, I don't dare.

Tears of frustration fill my eyes as I shove the device back into my bag and again head for the door. People will be starting to wonder why I am so late for breakfast. If Zeen is right, some of them might be rebels waiting for a chance to strike at any target, even me.

Two officials, one in red, the other in purple, stand at the base of the stairs as I reach the first floor and head down the hall to get breakfast. Only a handful of students are seated at the breakfast tables when I walk into the dining hall. During most meals it is noisy here, but now the room is quiet. Those who speak use hushed tones. Some watch me as I weave between the tables to the one where my final-year guide, Ian, sits along with Raffe. Most students keep their eyes on their plates. Enzo does not. As I walk by him I see concern and what looks to be a warning in his eyes.

Something has happened.

I try to catch Raffe's eye as I slide into the seat across from him, but he does not look up from his plate of grilled egg bread and fruit. Ian passes me a platter of food, and I place a slice of bread and a piece of ham on my plate. The food tastes wonderful, but it is clear no one is enjoying the meal. One by one, the remaining students finish their breakfast, push back their chairs, and leave. "What's going on?" I quietly ask Ian, who has remained in his seat.

"University officials have confirmed that Damone didn't go home."

"Do they think he ran away?" I ask.

Ian shakes his head. "Professor Holt seems to think he might still be on campus. The officials spotted blood behind our residence, and they're concerned Damone might be injured and unable to find help. So she's ordered a search of every building on campus, including this one. No students are allowed back in their rooms until the search is complete. We've been asked to confine ourselves to the common room or the labs or to wait outside until the officials are done."

I think of the clothes I left in the abandoned house and the items that currently sit in my bag. If I had left any of them in my rooms, officials would be looking for me now. They would suspect what I know. Would they consider those objects a sign of treason? If so, I would be dead. Still, I am worried about what else they might find. Is there something in my rooms that would lead officials to question me or remove me from campus? I don't think so, but it is impossible to be sure.

Anxiety bubbles inside my chest, making it hard to breathe. Trying to sound unconcerned, I say, "Enzo told me he saw Damone leave campus on his bike. If that's true, why is she searching the residence?"

Did Professor Holt not believe Enzo's story? Or is the transmitter in Damone's bracelet sending out a faint signal that shows he is somewhere nearby? Either way, I suspect this search isn't just a method of looking for Damone. Professor

Holt knows about the rebel students. This might be her way of causing anxiety and maybe stirring them to action so she can have them removed.

"She says she's making sure all avenues to find Damone are explored, but I get the feeling she's looking for something."

"Like what?"

"I don't know." But his eyes say something different. "At least one student has disappeared every year that I've been attending the University. This is the first search like this I've seen. Professor Holt must have a reason." Ian's tone warns me that more is going on here than is being said. Perhaps Professor Holt's search has indeed spurred the student rebels to act on their own. "Also, until further notice, students are not allowed to leave campus for any reason. She has asked Dr. Barnes to post officials at the University gates to serve as a reminder to students who might otherwise forget."

Extra Safety officials. A ban on leaving campus. Both will make aiding President Collindar more difficult if not impossible. I should feel relief that I now have a valid excuse for not being able to fulfill the president's assignment. But I don't. I feel cornered and helpless.

"When will we be allowed to resume our internships?" I ask. "There are things I've been asked to do."

Ian pushes his plate away and turns toward me. "Whatever assignments you've been given can wait until this whole thing passes. I get the feeling things are going to be different soon. Just go to class, do your homework, and sit tight. Okay?"

His eyes hold mine. Just for a fraction of a second, but it is enough for me to know that there is a deeper meaning to his words. He is confirming what I have believed since I was first assigned to Government Studies and Ian offered me assistance. Ian is one of the rebels. Which means he must have weapons somewhere nearby. Is he concerned Professor Holt will find them? If so, he is good at hiding his apprehension. I wonder whether that would be the case if he knew the rebellion he follows is being undermined.

When Michal was transferred to the president's office, he told me a friend would be near to watch over me. I believe Ian is that friend. If so, telling him what happened to Michal and warning him about Symon's true purpose in creating the rebellion could make Ian an ally. But there is an equally good chance that his dedication to the rebel cause will make him discount what I say. Worse, he could report my words back to Symon or act as Zeen suggested and eliminate the threat he might think I pose to the rebel plan. The president told me that whom I put my faith in will affect not only my life but the lives of those around me. Knowing that, I find it impossible to decide. Do I take the chance of gaining another ally—one who might be able to help convince other rebels to ignore Symon's directives—or wait to learn more?

For the first time, I find myself wishing that Ian had gone through The Testing with me. Knowing the choices he made during his Testing would help me now.

The thought shocks me. The Testing is wrong. Wishing that I knew what decisions Ian made during his Testing is wrong. And yet, despite the horrific nature of the tests, I think of what The Testing taught me about myself and about my fellow candidates. I understand that when pushed, I can shove back. That I am stronger and more resourceful than I ever thought possible. That my willingness to assume everyone believes in the values with which this country was founded and I was raised is flawed.

I think of Professor Holt and her statement that The Testing should be made even more strenuous. Of Dr. Barnes and his belief that The Testing's purpose succeeds when the pressure of the tests causes a girl to take her own life. Of Symon, who has chosen to lead those who want change — boys like Ian and my brother — to kill even as he facilitates their own deaths.

Ian stands. "Are you done, Cia?"

I look down at the mostly full plate in front of me. But when I say, "Yes, I've had enough," I know I am referring to so much more.

CHAPTER 6

THE SUN IS bright. The vibrant green grass looks cool and inviting as I stride across it to an unoccupied area not far from the bridge. I want to be close to the only exit from this area in case I have forgotten something in my room and safety officials come for me. I doubt I would be able to flee, but I won't let them take me without a fight.

The two officials on the other side of the ravine watch me as I look for a spot where I can settle. Some students who have chosen to treat being banned from their rooms as a holiday from work play a game of catch not far from the weeping willow tree. Others sit in groups, quietly talking. A few, like me, have gone off on their own, reading from books they must have brought with them to the morning mealtime.

For a moment, I stare off in the distance toward the Biological Engineering residence where Tomas is. I want nothing more than to go to him. To find out if his residence is also being searched. To tell him what I have learned and what I have been asked to do. To share the burden of the decision that deep in my heart I have made. Will he approve? Will he stand beside me and help me complete this test as he has done so many times before, or will this crackdown of University officials convince him once and for all it is time to run?

I don't know.

But I know I cannot succeed in bringing down The Testing alone. For that I require help. I need people who are not only capable of doing what I ask, but whom I know I can trust.

"Where did you go yesterday afternoon?" The soft-spoken words make me turn, and I see Raffe standing next to a small sapling. "You were supposed to stay inside."

Had I done so, I would not be planning what I am now. One choice has led to so many others.

"Too much had happened for me to stay in my room. So I took a ride to clear my head." I'm getting good at telling shades of the truth.

"And now you have a plan."

Instead of answering the implied question, I say, "While I was riding yesterday, I ended up going down a street that looked as if it hadn't been repaired in some time. Are there a lot of streets like that near the University?"

"A few. Although not as many as there are on the other side of the city. There are more government officials in this area, so there are fewer areas that have not been kept in good repair. My father doesn't even notice those streets exist."

His father.

"But you've seen them."

Raffe shrugs. "I made a point of visiting some of those neighborhoods last year. I was hoping I'd find some answers."

I wait for him to tell me what answers he sought and what he found. When he doesn't, I say, "The street I rode down is ten minutes from campus. A lot of the houses had graffiti on them."

He cocks his head to the side. "I think I know the street you mean."

"Do people live there? The houses look empty, but I thought I saw signs that some of the buildings are still in use."

"There are always people who don't want to adhere to the rules of the world they find themselves in. Since those streets are outside the notice of most government officials, they make good places to hide."

That's what I thought, too.

"Why do you ask?"

As much as I want to confide in Raffe, I am not sure I can. Despite everything that has happened in the last few days, I still don't know if I am confident enough in what he believes to tell him about the president's assignment. Without understanding his motivation in helping me, I cannot tell him more.

"I was just curious," I say. "It's different from the way we do things back home. Especially the different-color paints and drawings on some of the houses."

"There are always kids looking for places to get away from their parents. Some of them liked to mark the houses they used to let other kids know the space was claimed. Officials put a stop to that when my brother was in school. Once that happened, the government lost interest in those sections of town. But mere curiosity isn't the real reason you're interested, is it?" When I don't respond, he nods. "You still don't trust me."

Nearly everything inside me says that I should. But my

father's warning before I left Five Lakes haunts me—as does the outcome when I failed to heed his advice during The Testing. Though I want to trust, I can't. Not yet. In this case, once trust is given it cannot be taken back. I have to be sure. "You still haven't told me why I should."

"When you trust me with your secrets, I'll trust you with mine." With that, Raffe heads off across the grass and around the back of the residence. The next time I notice him, he's standing next to Griffin. Both are laughing. Both are looking at me.

The room-by-room search continues for the next several hours. Some students complain. Others stretch out on the grass and go to sleep. Careful to make sure no one is nearby, I pull out a paper and pencil to organize my thoughts. First I write my name, followed by Tomas's. Beneath our names I write others.

IAN
RAFFE
STACIA
ENZO
BRICK

All have knowledge or skills that could be useful in the days to come. Ian with his connection to the rebels. Raffe because of his knowledge of Tosu leaders. Stacia for her ability to put aside emotion and coolly analyze a situation. Enzo with his awareness of the tensions among the citizens, his clear dislike of the current system, and his father and brothers, who must be working with the rebels. And Brick, who might have skills to support this kind of action, since his parents went through The Testing. They both graduated from the University and now work at a former military facility, developing techniques to improve colony security against wild and mutated animals and other possible attacks.

All good reasons to ask these individuals for their assistance. But there is one more factor that has to be taken into consideration. Who will be able to kill? More, who will I be willing to ask to take lives?

Closing my eyes, I take deep breaths and think about these people one by one.

Tomas. Just focusing on him makes me feel more grounded. I love and trust him without reservation. He might not like the decision I have made to end The Testing using the president's method, but my heart wants to believe he will stand at my side. At the very least, he will not reveal my plans to anyone who might act against me.

Stacia is my friend. She is also assigned to the Medical field of study. The field that is headed by one of the people on the president's list. Stacia is focused, strong-willed, and more than capable of handling whatever comes her way. The Testing and her Medical Induction prove Stacia will do whatever it takes to be successful. Can she be trusted? Under normal circumstances, I'm certain I would say no. But if she can be convinced that the president's assignment will aid her own advancement, she can be counted on to help. And I am certain she would approve of the president's determination that the ends justify the means.

I draw stars next to both names and move on to the others. Raffe has already shown he can turn deadly, and the unemotional way in which he disposed of Damone tells me he is not squeamish about doing what needs to be done. But I do not know what secrets he holds or what he would do to protect them.

Brick has also shown his ability to wield a weapon. If I close my eyes, I can see his bullets tearing into the mutated humans that he thought threatened me. The Testing taught me Brick is willing to place faith in my observations when it comes to passing a test, but he's the son of two University graduates who believe in The Testing. Brick's parents wanted him to come to the University, so Brick obeyed their wishes and studied in order to be selected. I am not sure he would be willing to ignore what he was taught by his parents on my word alone. In fact, I am almost certain Brick would not see reporting my actions as a betrayal, but as the act of a good citizen. I draw a line through his name.

I shiver as a breeze rustles through the nearby tree, and I rub the scars on my arm. Out of the corner of my eye, I see the flash of a smile and the intense gaze of green eyes.

Will.

Someone I have not added to my list, but one who can kill. From experience, I know Will to be cunning and resourceful, and capable of a ruthless determination. He made the choice to kill other candidates who did nothing more than stand in his way for a spot at the University. Will he be willing to eliminate the people who gave him what he fought so hard for? I think about the Will I first met. The one who joked with his twin. Who, under the most pressure-filled circumstances, found ways to make the people around him laugh. It was when his brother failed to pass the first test that Will began to change. He felt alone. He was desperate to prove that he could survive without his brother. That the sacrifice of that lifelong anchor was not for nothing.

Does that make his betrayal less heartbreaking? No. But now that I have my memories back, I remember something else. A conversation we had after the tests were over. Despite the callousness of his actions, he took the time to learn the name of a girl he'd killed. Perhaps he never thought her death would matter to him as more than a method of achieving his goal. But it did. I can't forgive him for his actions, but there was something about the way he talked of her that makes me wonder if Will wouldn't make a different choice during The Testing now.

I shake my head and mentally draw a line through Will's name as Professor Holt steps out of the residence entryway and calls to us. When we gather near, she thanks us for our patience and tells us that we are free to go back to our rooms or to any of the University buildings. However, until the investigation into Damone's disappearance is complete, no student is allowed to leave campus.

Relief fills me. If they had found something incriminating in my rooms or in the rooms of the rebel students, I doubt they would allow us to just go about our business. Foreboding returns as I realize there is an equal chance Professor Holt and her team did find something and that they are just using that information to focus their attention on the student or students who are now under suspicion. Most of my fellow students seem unconcerned as they follow Professor Holt back inside the building. Worry that my movements might be watched even more closely makes me consider doing the same. But sitting inside will not help my brother. So instead I head for the bridge, to find Tomas.

The officials who were guarding the bridge are gone as I pass onto the main part of campus. The Biological Engineering residence is to the northwest. When I get close, I see students milling around the building. They too must have had their rooms searched. Shielding my eyes from the sun, I look for Tomas and finally spot him. He is listening to a girl who is trying to hold his attention. But I can tell the minute he sees me. His shoulders sag with relief, and his smile transforms from one of kindness to one filled with love.

As much as I want to cross the space between us, I turn and head toward the northeast, hoping that Tomas will understand and meet me in the place where we have met in the past. I take a less direct path to better determine whether anyone is following me now that the search of the residence has been completed. Fewer people are wandering around the campus, which makes me feel more conspicuous than usual. Especially since I am alone and those whom I do pass are walking in groups of three and four. I wave as if not caring who sees me and hurry along the walkways until I reach my destination.

I enter the small brick building that was once used to house genetically altered roosters. Once scientists had successfully boosted the roosters' immune systems and filtered out the mutations caused by wartime chemicals, the roosters were distributed to new farms and this building was cleaned in preparation for a new use. And now, because of the building's small size, only students seeking privacy have been interested in using the space.

Sunlight from a small window in the back provides the only illumination in the dim, musty room. It is enough light for me to decide to remain standing instead of taking a seat on the dusty floor. I check to make sure the transmitter I left here to block the tracking signals in our bracelets is still in place and then pace as I wait for Tomas to walk through the door. When he does, I drop my bag and run to him.

Wrapping my arms around his body, I lean my head against his chest, grateful to have him near. Tomas and I have known each other our whole lives. We have grown, worked, and survived The Testing together. Perhaps it shouldn't surprise me still that we are joined now by love as well as friendship. I'm not sure what I would have done without Tomas beside me during the weeks after we left Five Lakes Colony. His faith in my abilities kept me strong. His strength and love helped me survive.

When his lips find mine, I throw myself into the kiss, knowing that when it ends I will have to tell him everything that has happened since we last saw each other. It has been less than two days but it feels like longer. For a moment, I allow myself the luxury of forgetting. I press myself against Tomas, feeling the warmth of his body seep into mine. His mouth becomes more insistent, and I meet it with a passion I didn't know I possessed. We are both alive. We are together. With what is to come, I am not sure how long that will last.

The kisses grow in intensity until finally we step away from each other. My heart pounds. My breathing is shallow and quick. I long to kiss him again, but there will be time for that later. I hope. For now, too much has to be said.

As quickly as I can, I explain the events that transpired since I insisted he leave the rebel camp and return to the University without me. Raffe finding The Testing recordings. Michal's giving them to Symon. Symon's betrayal. Michal's death. Tomas starts to ask questions but I keep talking. If I don't, the emotions I've kept at bay over Michal's death and the things I have now vowed to do will overwhelm me. I speak about contacting Zeen. The search for Damone. Enzo reporting Damone's departure to Professor Holt. My trip to the city to find the president. The search of our residence.

"I'm glad your brother is safe, and he's also right. You need to keep your head down and stay out of this from now on. Especially now that they appear to be searching for trouble here on campus." Tomas takes my hand and squeezes it. "You've done all you can. The president can take it from here."

I shake my head. "President Collindar can't cancel the vote without losing the authority she still has left. She thinks she can postpone it for a week—which gives her time to implement a second plan to eliminate Dr. Barnes."

"What plan is that?"

I lace my fingers through his, take a deep breath, and say, "Me."

Tomas goes still. "I don't understand. What does she think you can do that her own staff can't?"

"She thinks I can kill Dr. Barnes and his top administrators."

"That's crazy. She can't be serious."

"It's the same plan Ranetta's rebel faction was supposed to

execute," I explain. "And it makes a terrible kind of sense. If Dr. Barnes and the other leaders are eliminated—"

"I'm not referring to the plan. I can understand why she'd believe that tactic is her only choice. What I don't get is why she's asking you to do it."

"Symon was able to get Michal assigned to her office as a spy. There could be others who report back . . ." I pull my hand away and wrap my arms around myself. "I think she's right. Asking me could be the only real chance of her plan succeeding."

"Except that you aren't a killer. Even when we were betrayed during The Testing, you refused to kill deliberately." I start to protest but Tomas cuts me off. "If you really wanted to eliminate Will during the fourth test, you would have."

But I did try. I can still feel the kick of the gun. My desperation as Tomas lay bleeding on the ground—a victim of Will's desire to win at all costs. I wanted Will to pay for his betrayal. I failed then. This time I cannot.

"I know you want to end The Testing, Cia. I do too, but this is too much for the president to ask of you. This shouldn't be your job."

But it is.

Straightening my shoulders, I say, "I have been given an assignment by the president of the United Commonwealth, and I'm going to accept." Fear wells up inside me, but alongside it is a determination as strong as steel. "I don't want to hurt anyone, Tomas, but to end The Testing and save my brother and Daileen and everyone else, I will do this."

"Are you sure?" I hear the unhappiness in his voice. Not long ago, he asked me to leave the University with him. When

I refused, he chose to stay with me. But I know that's still what he really wants. To flee. To go home. To pretend none of what we have seen and what we know is real. As much as I have planned to have him at my side during the weeks ahead, I love him. Because of that, I have to let him go.

"I am." Two words from which there is no going back. I will do what I must. But Tomas doesn't have to. "You don't have to do this. You can leave."

Pressure builds in my chest. Tears pool behind my eyes. I feel one fall as I steel myself against the pain. "I might not succeed," I say. "If I don't, one of us should go back to Five Lakes and tell Magistrate Owens what's happening here. Our families and friends need to be prepared for whatever comes. They need you."

I wait for him to respond. Another tear falls.

"Tomas?" I reach out to him, but he steps away from my touch.

"Promise me that if we fail and war breaks out, we run," he says.

"You can't—"

"Yes, I can." He steps closer, and in the dimness I see his face. So handsome. So dear. "I won't leave you to do this alone."

"But—"

His mouth touches mine, silencing my protest. I wrap my arms around him and sink into the kiss. After this I will find a way to convince him to go. But I want this one memory to hold close. This moment.

His arms wrap tight around me. In their circle I am safe, but I feel a fire start to burn. My hands touch his cheeks, his neck, his arms, memorizing the feel of him. My breath comes faster. I allow myself one last kiss, then step out of the warmth of Tomas's arms.

Taking a steadying breath, I say, "I want you to tell me that you'll leave."

"I'll leave only when you do. Until then, we're in this together."

He kisses me again. His fingers lace through mine. We stand in the shadows, facing the unknown like we did on the plains during the fourth test. "Together," I agree.

Maybe if I pushed harder, he would promise to return home. But I don't. Because this is his fight, too. Because I know, if I am going to succeed, I need him at my side. Because my heart cannot bear to push him away.

"How many names are on the president's list?"

"Twelve." I run down the list of names I memorized earlier.

"The president can't believe you can handle all of that by yourself."

"She might, but I know I need help," I say. "I was hoping you'd stand with me, and I think Stacia might. But we'll need more. People who believe as we do and can handle the decisions we are going to have to make. People we can trust."

"Trust takes time. That's something we don't have."

Tomas is right. Trust does take time. So does understanding a person's strengths and weaknesses. The task I have accepted should seem impossible, yet, in a matter of weeks, Dr. Barnes was able to determine not only who was smart enough to lead our country but how we would comport ourselves when faced with extreme pressure and life-threatening situations.

Everyone here at the University was chosen to lead. But what I will need to know is that those on my team believe as

I do that The Testing must be ended. That those who have worked for the rebellion, thinking they were bringing change, must be saved. That we need new leaders who will change the system that brought us here in order to secure the futures of those younger than us who dream of someday being selected. And if the people I decide to ask to participate in this terrible task are willing to fight for those things, there is still one question that must be answered.

Can they be trusted?

To learn the answer Tomas and I have only one choice. We will need to stage our own Testing.

Tomas listens as I tell him my idea as well as everything I learned about the people on the list and their visions for the future of The Testing. When I am done, he doesn't make another plea for us to leave. Instead he says, "A week doesn't give us much time to assemble a team and carry out a plan."

"I'll talk to Stacia tomorrow after class," I say.

"Are you sure we can trust her? I know she's your friend, but . . ."

I'm certain he is remembering the encounter we had with her during the fourth test. I remember it too. She was with two candidates from her colony—a blond girl named Tracelyn and a boy named Vic. We spent only a few hours with them, during which Stacia was standoffish. When she did speak, she casually expressed the belief that Testing officials would be justified in passing candidates who chose to kill. When the fourth test ended, Stacia and Vic had crossed the finish line. Tracelyn had not. And the smile Stacia wore on the days leading to our interviews and selection made me think she had something to do with Tracelyn's failure to pass that test.

"No," I admit. "But I think I understand what motivates her." Which might be more important. "I can't say the same about the others I'm considering."

"I wish there were more students from Five Lakes." Tomas says. "At least we'd understand where they came from and what they were taught to believe."

Knowing Tomas is thinking of Zandri, I give his hand a squeeze and think about how much I wish she were with us too.

"I think there might be others from Five Lakes here in Tosu City." Quickly, I tell Tomas about Dreu Owens and the information I found about him. "If he's still in Tosu City, he might be willing to help us."

"Maybe." Tomas smiles for the first time since I told him about the president's directive. "I know a number of Biological Engineering graduates, like your father, are sent to the colonies, but a lot of them are assigned to work in Tosu City. One of the people I work with in my internship might know where to find Dreu. If not, the head of my residence should have an idea where he is. It would be good to have someone on our team who knows how things work in Tosu City."

True. Which is why Raffe and Enzo are both on my Testing list. The idea of Raffe as a team member doesn't make Tomas happy, but instead of arguing he says, "If you can find a way to test Raffe that shows he isn't like Will, I'll be okay working with him."

In my mind I see a flash of Tomas's face going pale as Will's bullet hits home. Red blooming on Tomas's shirt. Him clutching his torso as he falls to the ground. Whatever test I create for Raffe to prove he is capable of being on our team will have to be definitive in order to gain Tomas's agreement.

I check the time. Dinner will be served soon. With Professor Holt and rebel students scrutinizing all that is happening around them, I dare not be late. We will meet after classes tomorrow. By then I hope Tomas will have learned something about Dreu Owens and I will not only have secured Stacia's agreement but will have come up with ways to test Raffe, Ian, and Enzo.

"If you need to contact me before then, use this." I pull out the pulse radio that uses the frequency I chose for just the two of us.

Tomas takes the radio from me and smiles. "I like knowing I can get in touch with you whenever I want. You're probably going to hear from me so often that you'll be sorry you gave it to me."

"I doubt it," I say, taking his hand in mine. "I know being a part of this isn't something you want."

"No. And it isn't what you want, either." He reaches out and runs his fingers across my cheek. "We're going to get through this, Cia. I promise you. One way or another."

One way or another.

We agree to test the radios later. After one last kiss, I turn and walk out the door to head back to my residence. Tomas will wait ten minutes and then go to his. We will meet again tomorrow. By then our own version of The Testing will have begun.

CHAPTER 7

I LEAVE THE dining hall as soon as I finish eating. Between Griffin's glares, Raffe's forced smiles, and Ian's concerned glances, I had little interest in the meal. Most of the other students didn't have the same problem, especially when it was announced that the ban on leaving campus would be extended one more day. Not having to attend internships made some of the students cheer. I couldn't help but notice that Ian wasn't among them. No one seemed concerned about the search of their rooms that had occurred just hours before. But I was.

When I return to my rooms, I brace myself as I slide the key in the door. During dinner, I heard a few annoyed whispers about items that were taken from students' rooms. An old straight razor Sam's grandfather taught him how to shave with. A journal one girl had kept since she first started at the University. An old map of Tosu City from the days when it was called Wichita. Nothing that seemed important. Not a single object that could help Professor Holt discover Damone's whereabouts.

But I did notice people casting glances at those who confessed to discovering items missing from their rooms.

Despite the search that took place, my rooms look almost exactly as I left them. I search to see if anything is missing. The vase of dried flowers and my clothes are here. The books for my classwork are accounted for. The homework I need to turn in tomorrow has not been disturbed. One by one I pull out the desk drawers and check their contents. Pencils and page clips. Straightedges and old assignments I have not yet recycled. Bits of wire, pieces of metal, small copper plates, some screws and other hardware—the things I used to make the transmitters I designed to interfere with the signal of the tracking device in my bracelet. Not that these things are unique to that purpose, but there is a chance someone who knows about the tracking device could look at them and divine my reason for having them. If so, there is nothing I can do about it now.

Almost everything seems as I remember seeing it when I left this morning. The only changes I have spotted are a desk chair out of place and the wardrobe pushed several inches away from the wall. I slide the chair back to its place under the desk and walk to the wardrobe. The large wooden case is heavy and hard to shift on the carpeted floor. I'm amazed the officials went to the trouble of moving it, since I can't imagine what they could hope to find in the space between it and the wall. I slide one hand behind the wardrobe to see if there is any way to get a better grip on the wood and feel something cool and metallic. I pull my hand back and peer behind the wardrobe to see what it is that I touched. The object is small, round, and silver. The same listening device I discovered in my Testing identification bracelet.

I think of the conversations I had before I went to meet with the president. Was this device placed here during the search by Professor Holt and her officials today, or has it been here longer? I searched this room when it was first assigned to me and have repeated the procedure at least twice a week to make sure no one has found a way to watch my actions when I think I am alone. But the last search I conducted was days ago. Before my conversation with Raffe. Before speaking to Zeen. If this device was put in place before I spoke to either of them, then someone knows that I am responsible for Damone's disappearance and that I'm aware of the rebels and their purpose. They will also know that my brother is now among them and is working from the inside to put a stop to their mission.

It is only Michal's insistence that Zeen use a different name that keeps me from grabbing the Transit Communicator in an attempt to warn him. While we share my father's eyes and my mother's bone structure, that is where our resemblance ends. Zeen is tall and blond. No one will see him and think of me. If anyone has listened to my conversation with Zeen, they will never know to look for a boy named Cris. Eventually, they'll ask enough questions and put together a list of all the recruits Michal brought to the camp, but that will take time.

Now that I have found the listening device, I search the room again. Every inch of the wall. The bathroom tiles. I up-end the small sofa, round table, and chairs in the sitting room. Examine the seams of each of the cushions on the furniture to make sure none have been opened and a camera or listening device inserted. The device behind the wardrobe is the only one. I walk back to look at it. When I discovered the recorder in my Testing bracelet, my only thought was to avoid letting those who listened hear my secrets. Then the information the listeners received was only a danger if I crossed the finish line and passed the fourth test. Now whoever is listening is not just an observer, but an active participant—just as we candidates were. While I do not like knowing the recording is capturing every sound I make, I recognize the opportunity to create misdirection. Of course, while I believe Professor Holt is behind this device, I am not certain that is the case. If it was here for longer, it might have been planted by the rebel students, Griffin, or fellow classmates who are just looking for a way to get ahead. Creating misdirection will be difficult unless I determine my audience. Until I do, I will leave the device in place.

After several more tries, I shove the wardrobe back. Then trying not to feel self-conscious, I put my bag on the ground, sit next to it, and pull out the list. With Symon and Dr. Barnes waiting to spring their trap, I doubt President Collindar will be able to delay making her proposal on the Debate Chamber floor for much longer than the seven days she promised. In that time, I have to assemble a group of true rebels, formulate a plan, and execute twelve leaders of the United Commonwealth. The enormity of the task threatens to overwhelm me, but I don't have time for doubt.

Tomas has agreed to help. If I haven't misjudged her, Stacia will join the cause after our class tomorrow. While part of me considers creating a test for her, what I learned during The Testing has given me enough insight into her character.

Those two are smarter than any others I know, but no matter their resourcefulness, there are still too many targets for three of us to handle. Four if I count Zeen, although I'm uncertain how much help he can offer while entrenched in the rebel camp. Still, I write his name on the paper next to Tomas's and Stacia's. Then I consider the others.

Dr. Barnes has the resources of the entire United Commonwealth and years of trial and error to create his examinations. I have Tomas, Stacia, my instincts, and only a few days. The question of what litmus test to use on my peers is a difficult one. Clearly, I must present them with an opportunity that puts a crossroads before them. An opportunity to make a choice that shows not only whether they wish to stop The Testing but also whether they are willing to believe that violent action is necessary to obtain that goal.

Easier said than done.

I consider various scenarios, but none seems appropriate for all. And I realize that this is the problem. In contrast to the early stages of The Testing, everyone cannot now be given the same test. Each classmate has a different outlook on life and a different goal for his or her time here at the University. Yes, they all want to be leaders, but none has the same reason behind it.

Raffe is here because of his family connections. That history should tie him tightly to Dr. Barnes, but it doesn't appear to. Raffe doesn't act as though it is his birthright to be one of our country's future leaders. He's hiding secrets. As is Ian. I believe Ian wants The Testing to end. We are both colony students who have faced many of the same challenges to get to this place. That alone should be enough to put us on the same side. But I'm uncertain whether he is a member of the rebellion, and if so, how loyal he is to Symon. If he believes Symon is truly working to end The Testing, Ian will not want me interfering in the rebels plans. He will do whatever it takes to stop me.

Even if we have the same agenda, it is unclear how Ian would react if I were to tell him what I know.

Enzo is another mystery. He has his own share of secrets. After what he shared with me outside the residence, I believe his father and brothers are among Symon's or Ranetta's numbers. If they are part of Ranetta's faction, he might be able to get word to them about Symon's treachery. If Zeen and Enzo's family members both met with Ranetta, they might be able to encourage her to work independently of Symon and to remove the targets on the president's list without Dr. Barnes being alerted to the attack. However, if his family is working with Symon's group, then Enzo may not believe what I have to say. As potential members of the rebellion, Ian and Enzo could be my staunch allies or my ardent opponents.

Raffe, Ian, and Enzo. I need to test all three. But what challenge should I give each of them? And while I do not want to ask myself this, I have to wonder, if they do not pass, what the punishment for failure should be.

My eyes grow as heavy as my heart. Though I want to keep working, I know my mind will function better if I rest. Besides, who knows how much sleep I will get in the days to come.

I slide a change of clothes along with my papers into my bag, and crawl into bed with the bag tucked in beside me. Despite the bulk of it, having my things next to me is strangely comforting. I slept like this every night during The Testing and survived. With a lot of luck and the right decisions, I will survive again.

My sleep is filled with flashes of memories. The poisonous plants from the second test. Malachi as he touched the wrong part of the pulse radio, sending a nail into his eye. Annalise as she tossed her red hair and swaggered out the door. The city streets with only one path for escape. Will's green eyes staring at me from behind the barrel of his gun as he fired.

When I wake, sunlight is streaming through the window. I put my bag on the floor and slide out of bed. Today the president will announce that Michal is missing. The debate will be postponed. The countdown to the rebels' attack will end as mine begins. And the images from last night's dreams give me an idea of how to start.

I shower, pull my hair into a knot at the base of my neck, and check the time. There is an hour until my first class starts. Time enough. I place two of the half-inch round trackers I took from President Collindar's fifth-floor storeroom into my jacket pocket. The monitor I slide into my bag. Then, after a quick inventory of the mechanical parts I have stored in my bottom desk drawer, I grab my bag and head downstairs to get the other pieces I need. No one is working in the labs this morning. I search through all four of them before I find the items I require. Since I have to get to class soon, I put all the parts in my bag, grab food from the dining hall so I can work through lunch. Then I look for Ian. When I spot him at our usual table, sitting across from Raffe, I walk over and slide into the seat beside him.

Putting one hand in my pocket, I quietly ask, "Do you have time to talk? I'm leaving for class in a few minutes but there's something . . ." I drop my fork, get out of my seat, and kneel down to retrieve it. While doing so, I slip one of the small tracking devices into the side pocket of the bag at his feet. I've never seen Ian put anything in that pocket, but I'm hoping the disk will be small enough to escape his notice if he does.

Grabbing my fork, I back out from under the table and take my seat again, keeping my eyes lowered so Ian will think I'm flustered by my mistake. In a quiet voice I ask, "Is there any word on when we'll be able to leave campus?"

"Not yet. Which is good in a way. Everyone can catch up on classwork. The campus lockdown is unusual, and I can't imagine it will last very long. If it goes more than a few days, I'm sure some students will feel compelled to break the rule and leave anyway."

"What will happen if they get caught?"

Ian puts down his fork. "Every head of residence is different. I've heard Professor Markum is pretty lenient about these things. Professor Holt, however, isn't as easygoing. Unless, of course, you're one of her favorites or someone she's asked to do a job for her." The way Ian glances across the room at Griffin leaves no doubt as to whom he is referring. Although Professor Holt has asked favors of Ian in the past, like spying on me, he could be one of those she allows to break the rules without consequence. The tracker will help me learn whether he actually does cross the University boundaries. If so, I will know he is working with Professor Holt. It is not a perfect test, but it is a start. Kind of like step one in The Testing process. Once I see what his movements are today, I can decide if there needs to be a round two.

Raffe leaves the dining hall when I do and matches his stride to mine as I cross the bridge and head toward the center of campus. He glances over his shoulder then says, "The president is making her proposal to the Debate Chamber today. That has to be the reason none of the students are allowed to leave campus. Dr. Barnes and his administrators must not want us to get caught in the crossfire if the attack happens sooner than they planned."

That could be part of the rationale. Of course, Raffe doesn't know about the rebel students on campus or their orders to remove any perceived threats to the rebellion.

"So have you decided how you're going to get around the tracking devices so we can do something to stop what's about to happen? Or are you still trying to figure out if you can trust me?"

"I do." At least, I think we are fighting for the same purpose. But I believed that of Will, and Tomas almost died. "There are just some things I have to work out. Once I do, I'll share everything I know."

"Well, you'd better do it quick, Cia." Raffe frowns. "Because unless I'm mistaken, the time for thinking is running out. If we're going to try to end The Testing and change this University, we have to do it before things are locked down so tight that we no longer have a choice."

Raffe stalks off in the direction of the Science buildings. As much as I want to follow, I don't. I have only twenty minutes until class begins. I need to find Stacia. We don't have any classes together until tomorrow afternoon, and Raffe is right. I do not have time to wait.

I see her walking behind a group of older students toward the Humanities building and wave. When she doesn't notice me, I yell her name as I hurry in that direction. She cocks her head as she spots me. "What are you doing over here? Don't you have World History first thing on Monday morning?"

I nod and look at the watch on my bag. Fifteen minutes. Not a lot of time, but enough to say what I need to. "There's something I need to tell you and a favor I have to ask."

We sit on the stone bench near the walkway. I take out a book in order to look as if we are two students comparing homework.

"What's so important it couldn't wait?" Stacia asks, brushing a blond lock of hair behind her ear. "Did Tomas and you break up for real?"

She rolls her eyes and waits for me to laugh as I did when she'd say something like that a month ago. When I don't, her expression turns serious. "President Collindar has asked me to assemble a team of people to help her bring down The Testing and eliminate the people in charge of it."

Stacia blinks. "This is a joke, right?" She looks at the group of girls walking by us and then lowers her voice. "You're not joking?"

"I wish I were." I give her a quick synopsis of the tug of war happening over the Debate Chamber vote and the rebellion the president was counting on that has proved false. Only five minutes remain until the start of class when I say, "I've learned enough to know that The Testing needs to end. Unlike President Dalton in the Fourth Stage of War, President Collindar has chosen to strike against Dr. Barnes and the people who could plunge this country again into war. But I can't do what she asks without your help."

Two minutes. I'm going to have to run to make it to World History in time. Hoping I have given her enough information to at least make her consider helping, I ask, "Can you meet me here in two hours?" The Calculus building is directly across from this bench. I can make it here easily after my second class.

Stacia stands. "Sure. If for no other reason than I'm dying to hear what else you have to tell me."

"Don't say anything to anyone until we speak. There are people . . ." One minute. "Just don't say anything about this. Okay? Or we'll both be really sorry."

When Stacia nods, I race across the grass, hoping I have not just made a mistake.

Class is starting when I hurry into the room and take a seat in the back. Professor Lee's raised eyebrow is the only indication that he has noticed my tardiness. While he begins the lecture, I fish a notebook and pencil out of my bag, then leave the bag open beside me so I can see the light of the monitor telling me if Ian's position changes.

The need to watch the monitor, the worry that Stacia will not heed the warning I gave her, and the knowledge that Professor Lee is one of the people I am supposed to eliminate dominate my thoughts. Professor Lee has always seemed so interested in his students living up to their potential. It seems impossible to believe he would be an advocate for a larger pool of Testing candidates. Could he really want to eliminate the potential of so many additional candidates just to provide more competition during the selection process?

"What can you tell us, Ms. Vale, about Prime Minister Chae?"

The sound of my name makes me realize that I have not been paying attention. I'm just glad Professor Lee said my name before the topic; otherwise, I wouldn't be able to answer now. Thankfully, this is a topic that was covered not only in our school back in Five Lakes, but in Early Studies. "Prime Minister Chae was the broker for the Asian Alliance. It was his refusal to accept defeat during the Sanai Summit that pushed the talks forward. He is also credited with helping maintain peace by encouraging compromise between the leaders of the Asian Alliance, but despite the public's desire to see him lead, Prime Minister Chae refused to push himself forward to be the leader of the Alliance. Had he accepted leadership, his desire for peace could have prevented the escalation that led to the Seven Stages of War."

Professor Lee studies me. "Is that what you believe?"

I feel everyone waiting for me to speak, but I have no idea what to say.

Professor Lee smiles and glances around the room. "Is that what you all believe?"

Now everyone has been put on the spot. And, like me, no one else knows how to respond. A few heads nod but Professor Lee doesn't speak. It is clear he is waiting for someone to speak. So, I do. "That's what you taught in Early Studies."

Professor Lee's smile grows wider. "It is. We know certain facts from those years before the Seven Stages of War. We know Prime Minister Chae fought for unity and that while many believed he was out to create a power base for himself, he never tried to gain leadership of the Alliance. We also know that he traveled around Japan, China, and North and South Korea stressing the need to put aside differences and follow the new laws. After that, we know very little. Which is why you have only been taught and tested on those facts. Today, I'd like to talk about what we don't know."

The confusion on my fellow students' faces must be mirrored on my own. I'd heard about the sequence of events that led up to the Seven Stages of War before I started school. I have been tested on them in Five Lakes, during The Testing, and throughout Early Studies. The idea that there is more information that I have never been told has me leaning forward in my seat waiting for whatever Professor Lee will say next.

His smile disappears. "Prime Mister Chae's involvement in the great treaty, his call for peace, and his death are well documented. However, very little about the years when he stepped out of the limelight have been verified, which is why you have never discussed the possibilities behind those dormant years. I'd like to remedy that today."

Walking up and down past the aisles of desks, Professor Lee talks at length about the mystery that surrounds Prime Minister Chae's decision to step away from the government for ten years only to reappear when the Alliance was threatened because Mongolia seized land from China. Prime Minister Chae reemerged and once again brokered peace. A movement developed in every Asian Alliance country. People demanded that the current Alliance leader step down and that Chae take his place.

According to Professor Lee, books that survived that period suggest Chae spent the early part of those mystery years traveling throughout the Alliance countries, cultivating followers while professing to support the current leader. It has never been confirmed, but there were rumors that Chae was spotted in Mongolia not long before its president directed his troops to cross the border into China.

"Since so much of our world's history was only documented with technology that was lost during the wars, no one knows for certain whether these events are rumor or fact," Professor Lee says, pausing near my desk. "If they are true, then I think it is very possible that Chae's well-known selflessness was a cover for his true intent—to become the leader of the Asian Alliance by prompting the Mongolian president to create a threat that would thrust Chae back into the political arena. If this speculation is correct, Chae laid the groundwork so that it would appear he only took the reigns as head of the Allied governments by humbly accepting the will of the people."

Professor Lee smiles. "His plan could have succeeded had he not been assassinated. After that, you know the rest of the story."

Civil war broke out in the Asian Alliance as each country accused another of the assassination. The unrest prompted the Mid-Eastern Coalition to attack Japan. One by one, every country was pulled into the war as tensions around the world exploded. Eventually the rumors of Chancellor Freidrich's involvement were confirmed, but by then the unrest was too great to turn back. Bombs were dropped. Cities leveled. The population of the world was reduced to a fraction of what it once had been. I thought I had understood the reason why our world was destroyed. But if Professor Lee is correct, we have only been taught part of our history. That shouldn't be a surprise, considering how much was lost in the Seven Stages of War. Those who lived through the war were intent on survival, not on preserving our past.

"It is interesting to speculate on what might have happened had Prime Minister Chae not been assassinated, and even more fascinating to consider what history might look like had he chosen to retain his role in the government and not pushed for more." President Lee surveys the room and glances at the clock. Our time is up. Though after what I have learned I don't want to leave. Not if there is still more to hear. My classmates must feel the same. Not a single student has begun to pack up.

"And now for your assignment," Professor Lee says. "I would like you to consider what we know to be fact about the state of the world governments at that time and write a paper telling me what you believe would have happened had Prime Minister Chae not been assassinated. I wish to be dazzled by your keen political and historical insight. Those who impress me most will be selected to participate in a special seminar. One that will discuss what is happening outside of the United Commonwealth right now and speculate on what might happen next."

He closes the book in front of him, grins at the stunned expressions of everyone in the room, and heads out the door. Despite everything that has happened over the past couple of days, I can't help but feel a spurt of excitement at the idea of delving deeper into our past and discovering what is happening outside our country. Are there others fighting to restore the earth? Could the course of action I have decided upon affect more than just the Commonwealth?

I want to believe that Chancellor Freidrich had Prime Minister Chae assassinated not to retain power, as some believe, but because the action would keep the Alliance stable. Instead it plunged nations into a war that led to the downfall of the world. Dr. Barnes is not Prime Minister Chae. He has not been an advocate for peace. Yet his work selecting leaders has helped revitalize this country. While I think The Testing is a terrible betrayal of everything I have been taught to believe in, others might not agree. I am betting that some Testing candidates, if their memories were restored, might even see Dr. Barnes as a savior. Will Stacia be one of them?

I'm still thinking about this and the events that have made me resolve to employ some of the same principles used in The Testing as Enzo and I walk together to our next class—Advanced Calculus. I have not yet decided what test I can give him, and I wonder if the fact that he knows I killed Damone and hasn't reported me to Professor Holt is test enough.

But it isn't, because I don't know where his family's loyalty lies.

As we walk up the steps of Science Building 4, Enzo stops me and asks, "Is everything okay?"

I blink.

"I just know you're going through a lot with . . . everything that's happened."

Is he referring to my part in Damone's death or to something else?

He jams his hands into his pockets and keeps his voice low. "I just wanted you to know that if you need someone to talk to, I'm a good listener. My father always says the reason I seem smarter than the rest of my brothers is because I watch and listen to everyone else, instead of jumping in and getting my hands dirty."

"Jumping in before you know what you're getting into is a good way to get hurt," I say, wondering why he is pushing to bring himself into my confidence. What does he think I am doing, and what would he do with the information if I gave it to him? The intensity with which he waits for me to say something more makes me certain there is another agenda aside from friendship at play. Trying to sound casual, I add, "I appreciate the offer, but I'm not ready to talk."

Enzo shrugs. "Well, I just thought since I saw . . . well, you know . . . that I sort of understood and that I can be trusted."

The more he tells me I can rely on him, the less I want to.

"Thanks," I say. "It's nice to know you stand by your friends." When Enzo shifts his weight and looks uncomfortable with my gratitude, I say, "Come on. We don't want to be late for class."

It's a good thing we aren't. Our professor assigns eight pages of homework, most of which deals with equations he covered in the first few minutes. I am so busy writing notes I barely have time to glance down at the tracking monitor in my bag to verify that Ian's device is still on campus. Where Ian said he was going to be. When the professor is done answering questions about the assignment, he announces that Professor Jaed is not on campus today. My next class, United Commonwealth History and Law, is canceled along with the others Professor Jaed teaches, which gives me a two-hour window until my next lecture. Time enough to talk again to Stacia and, I hope, construct an appropriate test for Raffe.

Stacia is waiting where I last saw her. Before I can take a seat, she stands and says, "You don't have to convince me that what you said the president asked you to do is the truth. At first I thought it must be an elaborate joke, but I know you wouldn't joke about something like that. So, tell me what I can do to help."

"Just like that?" I ask. Walking here, I'd come up with all the things I could say that would convince her to be a part of this team.

"Dr. Barnes runs this University. If we were still in The Testing, I'd probably side with him—since he'd control whether or not I got here. But the president's in charge of the country. If we succeed, I'll be a hero. Heroes get more options for their future. They also have more power. I want both. So where do we go from here?"

Good question. "I have something I need to do in the Early Studies building. We can talk about it there."

From what I have heard, the building's classrooms and labs are only used in the beginning of the school year. Once students are divided into their designated areas of study, the facilities are rarely utilized until the following year. If that holds true today, Stacia and I should be able to work there on a test for Raffe while talking through the details she needs to know.

"I'm assuming Tomas is part of our little band?" Stacia asks as we head up the steps of the building. As with all of the University educational buildings, the front door is unlocked during daylight hours. The labs on the first floor are open and empty. The rest of the building is silent.

I tell her yes as I lead us into the chemistry lab—a large room with ten black tables, behind each of which stand two silver stools. Light streams in from three large windows that face the back lawn of the building. In the front of the room is a large, floor-to-ceiling gray cabinet filled with chemicals, microscopes, burners, and other tools.

I set my bag on the table least visible from the windows, open it, and take out the tracking monitor so I can watch it while I work. Ian is still on campus, only a couple of buildings away.

"What's that?"

I explain about the tracking device I placed in Ian's bag and the tests I need to create for Raffe and Enzo.

"How many people are on the list the president gave you?"

"Twelve." I run down the names on the list and the reasons the president gave for each one. Stacia seems surprised to hear that the head of her residence is on the list, but doesn't interrupt. While I speak, I pull out the other items I brought with me. Six four-inch-square pieces of steel. Wires. A switch. A thumb-size solar battery. More metal for a circuit board.

"What are you doing?"

"Building a pulse radio. Or at least something that will look like one," I say as I work to attach wires. "I want Raffe to believe there's information recorded on this that will help the president bring an end to The Testing."

"Why?"

"I'm still working out the details, but if he takes it out of my room or finds a way to steal it I'll know he can't be trusted to follow my lead." I need people who are willing to stop The Testing, but whom I can also depend on at any cost.

"And then what?" Stacia crosses her arms. "Raffe isn't stupid. If he takes the recorder and figures out that the recording isn't real, he'll know you're onto him. The minute he tells his father or one of the administrators on your list we're all in trouble."

I put down my tools and sigh. "Do you have a better idea?"

"As a matter of fact, I do." Stacia takes the box I have built in her hands and turns it over. "If Raffe fails this test, there has to be a consequence that ensures he is unable to tell anyone about it. And the only way to guarantee that is if after failing the test, Raffe is dead."

CHAPTER 8

"I can't . . ."

Stacia's cool, calculating eyes meet mine. "You're planning on killing Dr. Barnes and eleven of his supporters. You really think one more is going to matter to the president as long as you help her achieve her goal?"

"No," I whisper. I'm certain it won't. But it matters to me. Raffe saved my life. My legs begin to tremble. I place my hands on the cool worktable as a wave of dizziness crashes over me.

"Just because you like Raffe doesn't mean he's not a threat. As far as I can tell you have two choices — keep him out of this, or give him a test that will allow us to know if you're right to trust him and that will remove him from the equation if you're wrong."

Keep Raffe out of this plan? I doubt he would let that happen. He already knows about the false rebellion and the true nature of The Testing. More, he's aware of my understanding of both. He will be watching what I do. If he is not a member of my team, he will certainly interfere with or possibly work against us. Even without knowing what I am about to do, Raffe could cause this plan to fail. My brother and the rebels could die. The Testing would continue. And the rest of the country . . . It is impossible to know what the repercussions would be, but I know I can't risk them happening. Not if I can potentially stop them.

Trying not to think about what I am doing, I slide the second tracking device into the box. Then I go to the cabinets where chemicals are stored.

Locked.

Not a surprise but also not a deterrent, since the same kind of closure was on the wooden chests where my brothers used to store their personal items. When I was little, they teased me by hiding my favorite rag doll in those locked containers. Since my father believed in fair play, he taught me to pop the locks on the chests with a wire or thin piece of metal. Once my brothers learned I could open the locks, they stopped taking my doll. I haven't had reason to use that skill much since then, but I have not lost the ability. Within moments, the cabinet doors stand open. As Stacia compliments my breaking-and-entering skills, I find what I need to create something else my father taught me. Something that could serve the purpose that Stacia suggests. Potassium nitrate, charcoal powder, and sulfur powder.

Stacia nods as I put the chemicals on the table and start to measure, hoping that I recall the proper ratios. I mete out the same amounts of each chemical twice—so when I am done there are two bowls that contain seventy-five percent potassium nitrate and smaller amounts of sulfur and charcoal. I keep an eye on the clock as the two of us grind the chemicals together. The process is slow, but dividing the labor makes it go quicker.

Stacia passes the time by chatting. "I can understand why the president might want to stop it, but The Testing can't be all bad. I mean, there has to be some kind of benchmark for who gets to be in charge and who doesn't."

"Killing candidates seems like an extreme method of making that choice," I say, although I can't help but think of what I am doing now and wonder if my choices are just as extreme.

"I can't imagine they kill everyone who doesn't pass. Right?" Stacia stops and looks at me. "I mean, this country is still rebuilding. Killing off over eighty Testing candidates every year isn't logical."

"Then what do you think happened to them?" I've often wondered if the candidates who weren't killed as direct penalties for failure have survived.

"I don't know." Stacia starts her work again. "We can't remember our Testing, but who's to say it was as bad as you've been told? And even if it is, think about the penalty for leaders who fail. They're not the only ones who suffer the consequences when that happens. How else can you tell if someone can handle that?"

Stacia's calm reasoning is disturbing because I can see the logic in her words.

"There has to be another way," I reply.

"Well, there's going to have to be since we're going to end it. But you have to wonder whether the president would be asking you to do this if The Testing hadn't already told her what you're capable of. What happens once The Testing has ended and they need leaders who are willing to do whatever it takes to help this country survive? Just because someone says they are capable doesn't make it true. And just because you think something is wrong doesn't mean it isn't necessary."

"If you think The Testing is necessary, why are you working with me to end it?"

Stacia's smile is hard and so very familiar. It makes me shiver now, especially when she says, "Because I want my chance to make sure the mistakes that ruined this country never happen again. If I have to kill to make that a reality, then that's what I'll do." Stacia laughs. "Besides, *you'd* never do anything you weren't certain was absolutely right. If you believe that by ending The Testing we'll prevent a potential civil war, that's good enough for me."

My breath catches. My chest tightens as Stacia's casually spoken words settle on my shoulders like a yoke. She is here because I asked. She will kill not out of passion for the purpose we have, but because of me. My request. My beliefs. My choices. I can only hope they are the right ones.

We work in silence for the next half hour. By the time the powder is ground, our arms are tired. Stacia helps me strain the black powder, then test it by putting a small pinch of the substance on a block of wood. I put the wood on a table, touch the match to it, and step back as the substance ignites. A flame several inches high burns bright, then fades.

It doesn't take long for us to put shredded paper and the black powder into the fake pulse radio I constructed. Then I slide two wires into the holes and wrap black adhesive tape around the lid to ensure that the wires stay in place and no powder escapes the holes.

I check the switch on the radio to make sure I have built it properly. To engage the power source, someone must flip the switch and then turn a knob a hundred and eighty degrees. It is a design sometimes used to make sure power is not wasted if a switch is mistakenly turned to the On position.

Stacia takes a step back as I connect the other ends of the wires to my power source. I count to ten and then let out an exhale of relief when the device stays quiet in my hands.

"Well, that was amazing to watch. I'm glad to know I'm on your side." Her grin is wide and delighted. "So, when do you plan on giving this to Raffe? I want to make sure I'm far away in case he decides to give it a whirl."

"I don't know." Now that I'm holding it in my hands, I can visualize him turning the dial. Igniting the powder. Getting caught in the explosion.

"Take advantage of the first opportunity that presents itself. If we want to succeed, we don't have time to waste."

Knowing she's right, I carefully pour the last of the black powder into a small specimen container, seal the lid, and put it in my bag, along with a book of matches from the cabinet. Together we clean up the evidence that someone has been in this room, secure the cabinet doors, and gather our things. I remove one of the single-frequency radios from my bag and hand it to Stacia. "I'll let you know when I'm done testing the others and we can move on to the next step. For now I have to get to class."

"Why?" Stacia slides the radio next to her books and tosses her hair. "Something tells me skipping a few classes isn't really going to affect our grades from here on out."

"Maybe not, but until we start our attack, we need to stick to our normal routines."

"Well, no one will be surprised if I'm late." She smiles. "Professor Frick isn't exactly punctual himself. I'll see you in class tomorrow if I don't hear from you sooner." As she leaves, she looks down at the table where the test for Raffe sits. "And good luck."

Carefully, I pick up the device, slide it into my bag, and notice that the red message light is lit on my oscillating pulse radio. Tomas.

"I'm hoping this thing works. I've been asking some of the upper years about Dreu Owens, and I think I have news. Meet me after class at the greenhouse. With internships canceled, it should be a good place to meet. Oh, and Cia . . . I love you."

Those words give me the strength to pick up my bag and walk to the door. This test for Raffe is too much like something Dr. Barnes or his officials would have dreamed up. But Tomas suffered the consequences of my confidence in the wrong person before. This time it will not just be Tomas but the rebels and maybe the rest of the country that suffers. Stacia is right. If Raffe understands he has been tested and has failed, his reaction could have serious consequences not only for me, and those who are working with me, but for the rebels and future Testing candidates. I can't afford to be wrong about Raffe. I have to be sure, and I cannot think of another way.

The professor is ready to begin lecturing when I slip into a seat near the front of my World Languages class. Will raises an eyebrow when he catches my attention. I just smile and shrug as if my almost being late to class isn't unusual.

I take notes and try to concentrate as the professor discusses the languages of the Asian Alliance countries, but all the while I am glancing down at my bag to check the monitor. Two lights blink close together. One, not far from the building in which I sit, belongs to Ian. The other belongs to the potentially deadly device sitting at my feet.

Class ends. I turn in my homework, write down the instructions for this week's assignment, and move on to my next class: Chemistry.

Raffe sits next to me. My heart pounds as the seconds count down. Stacia said I should seize the first opportunity that presents itself. This is it.

Somehow I am able to stand without trembling when class ends. My voice is dispassionate when I ask Raffe if he has a minute to talk.

"Are you okay?" he asks after the other students head out of the room. "You look upset."

"Are you going back to the residence now?"

"I was planning on it. Do you want to walk back with me?"

"I can't." I wait for the last student to leave before saying, "I have to meet somebody, but I don't want to take something with me while I do. It's too important." I open my bag and remove the metal box I created.

"What is it?" He turns the device over in his hands.

"It's a recording Tomas found. One that might be helpful in ending everything—if I can get it to the president." I take a deep breath. "I'm hoping the restriction against leaving campus will be lifted by tomorrow and I can get it to her then, but I don't want to have it on me now in case something goes wrong at this meeting. I'd give it back to Tomas, but—"

"I have it covered," Raffe assures me. "But it sounds like wherever you're going might be dangerous. Are you sure you should be going alone? Maybe you should let me—"

"I'll be fine. This is something I have to do by myself. But I need you to promise me that you won't play the message. The recording device sounds faulty. I'm worried the pulse signal might not hold up for more than one additional play." A tempting opportunity for someone who is looking to aid Symon and Dr. Barnes. Tracking down the recordings of The Testing should have proved that Raffe and I have the same goals. But there is a chance that he learned through his father about Symon and the false rebellion and knew those recordings would eventually be destroyed. If he plays this recording, I will know where his loyalties lie. And if he gives it to someone else to play, they will pay the price. Either way, I will have the answer I seek.

A flicker of annoyance crosses Raffe's face. Almost as quickly as it appears, it is gone. "Are you at least going to tell me what's on it? Or is that information only for you and your boyfriend?"

"I'll tell you everything later tonight. Everything," I stress, meeting his angry eyes. "I promise."

I see the anger fade. "Okay," he says, "then I promise too. Take care of yourself and don't forget what you just said. I'm holding you to it."

I watch him tuck the device I created into his bag, and I wonder if this is the last time we will see each other. The explosive I built is much like the ones my father and brothers used in their work when they needed to break apart rock. The amount of powder I used should severely injure or kill. If Raffe decides to listen and potentially eliminate the message he believes is there, he'll flip the switch, turn the dial, and draw a spark from the wires that should ignite the powder I created.

Raffe and I walk out of the building together. As he heads

toward the residence with the device, I picture the paper and powder igniting and then the blast. I want to run after him and take the device back, but I remember Stacia's words. That which is wrong is sometimes necessary. As I turn and walk in the other direction, I wonder if The Testing officials tell themselves that too.

The sun is bright. The warmer weather combined with the brisk walk makes me sweat. Surrounding me are signs that spring has come to Tosu City. Greener grass. Buds transforming into leaves and flowers preparing to bloom. All signs of hope.

I cling to that hope as I check the tracking monitor. Both devices are close by. One looks as if it is near the Government Studies residence — Raffe. The other is somewhere southeast of my position. I would guess that Ian is at the library. Regardless, I know he is still on campus. Taking that as a good omen, I pick up my pace as I head for the stadium and the greenhouse that sits at its center.

Long ago, the structure was used for sports events, but after the Seven Stages of War, scientists needed a controlled environment in which to plant and cultivate their new specimens. Since this building had no logical purpose in the new culture of revitalization, the country's top botanists enclosed the open space in the center of the structure with glass to create an enormous greenhouse and modified the surrounding rooms within the outer ring to function as genetics labs. Depending on the day, this area can be filled with activity as students, biologists, and various officials go about their work. Without internships compelling students to work, the building appears to be deserted.

I check the pulse radio recorder to see if Tomas has left a message as to where exactly he wants me to find him, but the light is not illuminated. While the stadium seems to be a good place to meet, it is huge. Just inside the front entrance seems like the most logical place, so I head in that direction.

As I walk, I turn on the Transit Communicator in case Zeen has news. When he doesn't answer my call, I look around to see if anyone is nearby and looking my way. No one. I have toured this building, but I have had little need to use it—although Tomas has. After being assigned to Biological Engineering, he was forced to go through a potentially deadly Induction test here. Of all the designated fields of study, Biological Engineering most often works in this building, which is why it makes sense that Tomas wants to meet here.

The stadium entrance is open. I walk through the doors into the dimly lit corridor and look up and down the two hallways that lead away from here. No Tomas.

I've taken a couple steps down one hall to look for signs of a common waiting area when I hear footsteps behind me.

"Cia," a male voice whispers.

I turn and squint down the shadowed corridor. Since this building is so large, the halls and most of the rooms are not illuminated unless they are in use. Most of the power collected by the enormous solar panels affixed to the roof is directed into maintaining the controlled climate in the greenhouse.

A figure steps into view.

"Tomas?" I ask, but I know it is not. The shoulders are too broad. The hair just a fraction too long.

My instincts scream for me to turn and run.

And I do.

CHAPTER 9

I HEAR A voice curse. Someone must have known about our meeting and followed me in. To do what? I don't know, but I am pretty sure I don't want to find out.

Blood pounds in my ears as I run. Away from whoever is now running behind me. Away from the entrance. Away from what I am almost certain means an end to a plan I have barely embarked upon.

The footsteps behind me sound like they are getting closer. I dart around the large steel beam supports and follow the hallway as it curves to the left. I'm fast. The person behind me is faster. And chances are whoever it is knows this building far better than I do. I am at a disadvantage, but if my pursuer thinks I will give in easily, he or she is mistaken.

My bag bounces against my side as I run. The jostling throws me off balance, and I shift the strap over my head to better secure the bag at my side. I glance at the closed doors that I pass. Any one of them could give me a place to hide, but if the door I choose is locked, my pursuer will catch up.

I see a set of stairs to the right and race to them. My muscles burn as I climb. When I reach the first landing and head for the second flight of stairs, I brave a look. Dark hair. White jacket. Angry expression. Dark eyes that are focused on me.

There is something vaguely familiar about him. If I had time to stop and think, I might be able to place him, but at the moment I've learned what I need to know. The boy behind me doesn't have a weapon and he's halfway up the staircase to the landing. The first gives me the advantage I've been missing. The second tells me that if I want to capitalize on his lack of defense, I have to move even more quickly.

My breath comes hard and fast as I climb step after step while unfastening the closure to my bag. My fingers find the wooden butt of my gun as I hear the boy reach the landing below and begin to climb the next flight of stairs.

Good. Let him come. The higher he climbs the better.

When I reach the top, I don't allow myself time to think. I just pull the gun out of my bag, turn, and fire.

The boy jumps to the left and then stumbles and goes tumbling down the stairs. He groans as he hits the platform with a thud. The sound gives me a hum of satisfaction as I race down the corridor to the left. Behind me I hear the boy swear and start his climb again. Even though I missed, the pain and frustration in his voice tell me he isn't as fast as he was. Which is all I can really hope for. Hitting a moving target while I am also in motion requires far more skill than I have. The only way

I'm going to hit anything is by chance. But my pursuer doesn't know that. And now that he is aware of my weapon, he will be forced to move more cautiously.

I glance behind and see he has reached the top of the stairs. I fire again. This time the bullet hits the ground somewhere in front of him. He drops to the floor. I keep running. Around the curved corridor. Down the hall. I turn and fire once more to ensure he stays off balance, then bolt for the stairs that lead back down to the first floor. If I am lucky, I will find an unlocked exit and make my escape. If not, I will learn how accurate my shooting skills really are.

I fight to breathe. My muscles burn from exertion. Sweat streaks down my back as I fly down the stairs.

One flight.

Two.

I dash down the hall toward the doors I first came through, glance back to see if the boy has gained on me, and hear the rustle of fabric a second before I collide with someone.

Hands grab my arms and I fight to get free as a voice yells, "Cia?"

Tomas.

"Cia, what are you doing? What's going on?"

Somewhere above, footfalls sound.

"Someone's upstairs. We have to get out of here."

"A couple of students might be working on a project. I thought the place would be empty, but we can always —"

"No. Someone was waiting for me to arrive and he's chasing me now. We have to run."

The sound of shoes pounding the metal stairs makes Tomas

look up. From my position I see a leg step off the landing. Tomas's eyes widen as he spots the person's face.

"Kerrick." For a moment Tomas goes still. Then he shakes
his head as Kerrick barrels down the stairs. Tomas looks around
the room and takes a step to the left. "But if Kerrick is here,
then —"

A gunshot punches the air to my right and a figure steps out
of one of the rooms. I don't think. I set myself, aim, and fire.
The answering scream tells me I have managed to hit something. I don't wait to see who I shot, I just grab Tomas's arm
and yell for him to move. I don't understand what's happening,
but I do know that if Tomas hadn't moved, he would be dead.

We reach the end of the hall. Gunshots rip through the air.
Tomas flinches with each shot, but whoever is shooting must
be as skilled at hitting a moving target as I am, because the
bullets don't come close to our position. Of course, that could
change at any moment.

I spot an exit to the right, but Tomas grabs my hand and
pulls me down the hall to the left. "Come on."

He leads me through a wide, arching doorway that runs into
the center of the stadium. My throat burns with each breath.
I climb the steps that lead to the entrance to the greenhouse.
Tomas punches a code into a panel. The door slides open and
he pulls me through.

The smell of growing plants and rich soil hits me first, followed by the air thick with moisture.

"This way."

I have been in this room only once before, during my first
University tour, and then only for a few minutes. Nothing here

is familiar, and I am running out of ammunition. I can only hope that whatever Tomas has planned will get us out of this situation.

Tomas pulls me through several rows of oak saplings and through a grove of reed-thin elms near an area that is surrounded by a small, red wire fence. "There's a control booth over this way that runs the irrigation, power, and climate for the greenhouse. Go there."

He begins pulling the knee-high red fence out of the earth. "Kerrick and Marin can't be allowed to leave here. Not unless we want them coming after us again or reporting us to someone who can do something worse. Go."

Understanding what he's trying to do, I run to the twenty-foot-square patch of the greenhouse and help yank the fence out of the ground, removing the barrier that warns people about the plants contained inside. Plants my father has spent his lifetime eradicating. Mancinella Flowers. Pink Ivy. Poppy Doll Eyes. Red Jessamine. Flowers and plants that if touched or tasted can shut down nervous systems and cause cardiac arrest, blindness, vomiting, and dozens of other awful side effects. For some, ingestion is necessary to trigger the poison, but the Mancinella Flower and Pink Ivy only require the simplest touch for infection to occur. And Poppy Doll Eye berries can cause severe hallucinations, the walls of veins to thin, and hearts to stop beating. Terrible plants. Mutations caused by the chemicals unleashed upon the world. Those grown here are used for study so that scientists can figure out how to eradicate their effects. Today, Tomas and I need their deadly qualities to keep us alive.

Careful not to touch the toxic plants, Tomas and I shift the fence to an area that contains edible vegetation.

"Now what?" I ask.

"Now we have to get them to come in this direction and hope they don't notice what they're stumbling into. Kerrick is in Biological Engineering, but he deals more with animal studies than plants. I just wish we had a way to burn some of the plants. There are burners in some of the labs, but we don't have time to waste getting them. Maybe —"

"I have an idea," I say, opening my bag and grabbing the matches I took from the chemistry lab and the specimen container where I stored the excess black powder.

"What's that?"

"Something that can set the plants on fire."

I keep one eye on the entrance in the distance as I place the paper with the black substance near the patch of plants Tomas thinks has the best chance of making this plan work. Poppy Doll Eyes. When burned, this plant gives off fumes that will overload the nervous system. Something people from Pierre Colony learned when a spark from a researcher's campfire landed on dry grass near a large patch of the plants with the white bulbs that look like tiny eyes. The fire combined with high winds caused everyone living on the outskirts of the colony to suffer muscle spasms, blindness, or, in many cases, death.

With the amount of powder I have used, a flame should flare high and wide enough to make the white bulbs hanging nearby catch on fire. The only tricks will be to get our two attackers to come in this direction and to create a fuse long enough to allow me to get to the exit eighty feet behind this point before the smoke caused by the burning plants can reach me or Tomas.

"Here." Tomas hands me a thin ten-inch strip of paper. Not as long or as reliable a fuse as I would like, but the shouts I hear and the figure bursting through the greenhouse door tell me I am out of time.

I lay the fuse on the paper and push a coating of powder onto the end. I fumble for the matches and pull one from the book.

"Get their attention," I whisper as I poise the match against the strike pad.

Tomas looks at the black powder and the match, then back at me. Nodding, he stands. He takes several steps toward the greenhouse door. He pretends to stumble over an evergreen shrub and swears. That's all it takes.

Kerrick's head swings in our direction. "They're over there."

Tomas looks back over his shoulder and makes for the exit behind us. Kerrick and Marin trample plants and weave around young trees as they race for our position. Tomas yells, "Cia. Come on."

"My foot is caught," I yell back. "Go. I'll catch up."

Kerrick and the other person come closer. For the first time I get a glimpse of Marin. She's someone I have seen around campus. I think I've even noticed her talking to Tomas. Her most distinctive features are her smile and contagious laughter. She isn't laughing now as she closes the distance between us.

A gunshot rings out. I hear the bullet hit the ground far behind me. Aimed at Tomas. Another shot. Kerrick and the girl move closer. Everything inside me screams at me to flee, but I hold my position as I pretend to struggle to free myself from the phantom vine that holds me hostage. I need their attention directed at me, not on the nearby plants. They come closer. Just a few more seconds.

Five.

Another shot.

Four.

Kerrick spots me and yells.

Three.

The girl sees me and smiles.

Two.

I press the match hard against the strike pad and pull.

One.

The match flares. A gunshot makes me jump. The bullet slams into the ground to my right as I touch the flame to the paper fuse. The second I see the flame traveling up the paper, I scramble to my feet and run.

Another shot. I stumble and pitch forward as pain sears my calf. I swallow the scream that wants to erupt from inside me and tamp down my body's protest as I climb to my feet. Marin calls out to Kerrick. Tomas yells for me to hurry. I glance behind me and realize too much time has passed. The fuse should have ignited the powder. The plan didn't work, and Kerrick and the girl are coming.

I will myself forward.

"Come on, Cia."

One step. Two. Faster.

"What's that?" I hear Kerrick yell.

The smell of sulfur reaches me. I hear another gunshot and someone starts to cough. I don't look back. I just keep moving one boot in front of the other, clenching my teeth against the pain that would otherwise bring me to my knees. Tomas already has the exit door open. His eyes are bright with fear as he holds out his hand, beckoning to me. Someone is still running behind me. I stumble through the door and Tomas slams it shut. His fingers fly over the control panel. The light above the door shifts from green to red, and now it can only be opened from this side.

A smart move, although one glance through the door's glass pane tells me it wasn't necessary. Kerrick is on the ground twenty feet from the exit. His body jerks as if connected to a stream of electricity. I can see the agony on his face as the toxins he breathed in take over his body. Shut down his systems. End his life.

CHAPTER 10

I FORCE MYSELF to watch Kerrick die. No matter the reason, I helped caused this. I do not know anything about Kerrick save his name, his field of study, and the fact that he wanted to harm me.

Tears swell behind my eyes and sear my throat as I try to hold them back. But there is no denying them. The death of the boy, the pain burning my calf, and the knowledge that more people will die before this week is done are impossible to suppress.

Tomas's arms pull me close. He tries to make me look away, but I can't. My eyes stay focused on the scene behind the glass as feelings storm through me. Sorrow. Despair. Fear. Kerrick's still body swims in and out of focus as tears continue to flow. I feel Tomas's hands touch my injured leg. Fingers probe my wound. The screams I have been holding back claw out of my throat.

"I'm sorry, Cia," Tomas says. His voice soothes even as his

hands continue to touch the wound and cause pain. "We need to clean and bandage this. It looks like the bullet only grazed your calf, but it's bleeding pretty bad. There's a first aid room just down the hall. I think there should be something in there that I can give you for the pain."

"It's not that bad," I lie. "We should get out of here while we can. I don't know where the girl went, but she could be nearby."

Tomas looks toward the greenhouse and shakes his head. "She's not going to be coming after us. Marin's in there."

Despite the angry protest of my leg, I push to my knees. I follow the direction of Tomas's gaze, squint through the haze of smoke that still lingers, and see Marin sprawled among a group of small shrubs. Marin. A name that until minutes ago I'd never heard and now will never forget.

"Do you know how to turn on the irrigation system?" I ask, concentrating on the smoke instead of Marin's lifeless face. The plants inside are too green and healthy and the air too humid for everything to catch fire. Only the plants that were directly under the flare from the black powder burned, and while I doubt that they still burn, turning on the irrigation system will ensure that the fire goes out. It should also help dissipate the poisonous fumes that linger in the air.

"Stay here."

"No." I struggle to my feet. "I'll come with you." Despite the pain that moving causes, I don't want to be alone.

Tomas slides an arm around my shoulder and helps me walk down the hall to the control booth. I ease into a wooden chair and watch as Tomas works the controls.

It takes him three tries to remember the sequence of buttons but eventually water sprays from pipes that hang from the greenhouse ceiling. After several minutes, Tomas turns off the water, hits a button marked Fan, and says, "Stay here. I'll be right back."

"Where are you going?" I ask.

"The fence needs to be put back where it was, and I need to move the bodies where they won't be discovered. Between the water and the fan, it should be safe to reenter the greenhouse."

"I'll help," I say, starting to rise again.

"No." Tomas puts his hand on my shoulder and pushes me back into the chair. "Stay here. Please. This is something I need to do by myself."

Unshed tears shimmer in his eyes. I want nothing more than to hold him and help ease his pain. But I don't. I know Tomas is trying to stay strong in front of me. So I just squeeze his hand and watch him leave.

Several minutes pass before Tomas appears behind the observation glass window. I watch him replace the fence so that it once again signals danger. Then he reaches down and picks up Marin's lifeless body. His jaw tightens as his cheek brushes against Marin's shoulder. Then with the body cradled in his arms, he disappears from view. When he returns, Tomas tries to lift Kerrick, but the weight is too much. He grips Kerrick's ankles and drags the body away. I find myself wishing I had asked him to remove their bracelets as we did for those who fell during The Testing. To remember. As if we could ever forget.

I reach into my bag and check the tracking monitor. Both devices are located near each other, not far to the south of where I am now. I am glad to see two lights on the screen. It means Raffe's is still active. He has not yet failed his test. It is something to be grateful for.

Tomas's face is flushed but free of tears when he returns with medical supplies.

"Are you okay?" I ask, even though I know he's not. How could he be after what has happened?

"Let's worry about getting you patched up. Then we'll talk." He kneels on the ground and rolls up my pants leg. I flinch when I see the bloody tear in my flesh. I focus on Tomas's face as he wipes the wound with a wet cloth. I bite my lip and taste blood but I do not call out.

Tomas's hands shake as he spreads a healing ointment on my leg. As the medication begins to leech the pain from my flesh, he grabs the bandages and says, "Kerrick likes to help first- and second-year students with genetics homework. He has a way of explaining things that makes the most complicated theory accessible. He's easy to talk to, and he never forgets a single detail. His memory is incredible."

Likes. Has. Is. All present-tense. Despite carrying his dead body, Tomas has not accepted that Kerrick is gone.

"You talked to Kerrick about Dreu Owens."

"You said Dreu had been given a job in Genetic studies. I was hoping that because Kerrick's internship involves genetics, he might have heard of him."

"Had he?"

"Kerrick says Dreu was assigned to the lab where he interned during his first year. He was working with a team to identify mutated genes in raccoons and rabbits. They were hoping once those genes are identified they can find a way to isolate the mutation and eventually eliminate it."

"Where's Dreu Owens now?" I ask.

"Kerrick wasn't sure." Tomas frowns. "He suggested I go through the files he used for his research project. The files he said are kept in one of the offices in this building."

"Did you talk about anything else?" Anything that would cause this kind of attack?

"He was curious why I was looking for Dreu now instead of when I first came to the University. When I said you overheard someone at the president's office mention Dreu and the fact that he, too, was from Five Lakes, Kerrick said I might want to wait to go through the records and look for Dreu. Otherwise teachers might assume I have too much free time and come up with more work for me to do. I thought he was just joking the way he always does."

Instead, Kerrick was issuing a warning to Tomas. To stay away from Dreu Owens. Tomas didn't, and now Kerrick and Marin are dead.

"They must have been members of the rebellion." It's the only explanation I can come up with. "Zeen said the rebels had been given orders to remove anyone who might interfere with the success of their mission. Either Dreu has something to do with the rebellion or just mentioning his name was enough to cause worry that you could disrupt their plans."

The sound of a door slamming makes us jump. Someone is in the building.

"You need to get out of here." Tomas helps me to my feet.

"What about you?"

"I'll go, too, but first I want to look around the offices and see if the files Kerrick talked about really exist. I doubt it, but if Dreu is important to the rebellion, it would be good to know why. Kerrick and Marin lost their lives. I'd rather it wasn't for nothing." Tomas looks out into the hall. "This way."

He leads me to the unlocked westernmost entrance he arrived through and tells me to wait as he steps out and looks around. A moment later, he leads me out into the cool, crisp air.

"How's the leg?" he asks.

"Fine."

"Good." Tomas runs a hand over my cheek but then frowns. "I don't think we can wait much longer to put the president's plan into action. If Kerrick was ready to attack on the chance I might interfere with the rebellion, there's no telling what the other rebel students might do. This place could end up as a battleground any moment. If we're going to finish this, we have to act now."

Anger simmers below Tomas's logic. One of his hands is clenched in a fist at his side. He who once wished to flee has found in Kerrick's and Marin's deaths the need to fight.

"Stacia is in. If everything goes according to plan, by tomorrow morning the others will be, too." I entwine my fingers through his. "Then we make this right."

I stand on tiptoe and place a kiss on Tomas's jaw. Then, as much as I hate leaving him, I turn and walk toward the south. When I glance back to look for him, he's gone. My leg aches as I hurry down the walkway. The pain reminds me that the bullet that ripped open my pants also left them stained with blood. I can't go back to the residence looking like this.

I duck into one of the Science buildings at the edge of campus, locate the bathroom on the first floor, and change into the pair of gray pants I have in my bag. I wash the blood from my hands and then run my fingers through my hair in an effort to erase all evidence of my time at the stadium. In the past several days, three students have died on account of my actions. At any moment another might be injured or killed because of something I created. Somehow, remarkably, my image in the reflector looks unchanged. How wrong that seems and yet how lucky it's true. Because there is still so much more to do before this ends. Maybe once it is over people will understand what I have become. Maybe I'll understand as well.

Since classes have ended, I am not the only one hurrying to get back to the residence. That allows me to move quickly without worry that I will attract attention. Despite the dread that churns inside me, when I reach the Government Studies building I put a smile on my face and walk through the residence's front door. The sound of laughter trickles down the hall. After everything that has happened, I long for the relative safety of my quarters upstairs. Instead, I head down the hall and glance into the main gathering room. Raffe isn't there, so I head for the stairs.

When I reach the second-floor landing, I make a decision. Instead of going up to the third floor, I turn and walk toward the door marked with a coiled spring. Raffe's symbol. For the first time I wonder which kind of spring Raffe's symbol is meant to be: a tension coil that stretches and shifts to work with the machine it's a part of or a compression coil that will not allow itself to be pushed down. Is Raffe the type who truly wishes to resist the current methods of selecting our leaders, or is he working with his father and Symon to prevent change? I raise my fist and pound on the door. The time has come to find out.

When the door opens, in spite of the monitor's assurance, I let out a sigh of relief to see Raffe alive and whole.

As soon as I step over the threshold, Raffe closes the door and throws the lock. "I was starting to worry. Did you find what you were looking for?"

"Not exactly." I look around for signs of listening devices or cameras. The room is almost the same size as mine and contains the same table, chairs, and sofa, but Raffe has transformed the space. A blue and white quilt hangs over the top of the couch. A handwoven rug with a circular blue design lies in the middle of the floor. And hanging on the walls are paintings. Some framed, others affixed at the corners with adhesive strips. Abstract swirling colors. Beautiful renderings of flowers and trees. And in the center is the largest canvas. Deep brown wood frames the portrait of a girl with light blue eyes, dark blond hair, and a chin the same shape as the chin on the boy who stands in front of me. She isn't what I would call beautiful, but there is something striking about her face, and the look in her eyes is haunting.

"I don't normally let people in here." Raffe stands next to the painting. Now that his face is beside the girl's, the resemblance is even more pronounced. "I don't think we have a lot of art lovers under this roof."

I look at the slashes of vibrant colors next to muted earth tones and find myself wishing Zandri were here to explain why these paintings make me want to catch my breath. She'd understand the emotions on these canvases because she had this kind of talent. The talent to make someone feel without saying a word.

"They're wonderful."

"Thank you."

The pride in his voice makes me turn. "You made these?"

"Only a couple of them. The rest belong to my sister." He glances at the girl in the frame and I wonder—is she the sister he referred to long ago? If so, she is part of the reason he sought to ally himself with me. Raffe promised he would trust me with his secrets if I trusted him with mine. This painting and his having passed my test tell me the time for sharing those secrets has come.

"Do you have a piece of paper I can borrow?" I ask.

Raffe looks confused, but disappears into his bedroom and returns with a paper and pencil. Taking a seat at the table, I write a note and hand it to him. He reads it, shakes his head, and together we begin to search for signs that we are being recorded. Because Raffe has more possessions than I, our search takes longer than mine did, but when the two of us are done, we haven't found anything. Whoever is listening to me has not found reason to be suspicious of Raffe.

Quickly, I tell him about what happened at the stadium. The ambush. The dead students Tomas disposed of. And finally, I tell him about my trip to see the president, what she asked of me, and what I now ask of him.

"I knew Kerrick," he says, taking a seat across the table from me.

"I'm sorry."

"You and Tomas did what you had to do to stay alive. Now we're going to do what is necessary to end this. Right?"

"Before you agree to help," I say, reaching into my bag, "you need to see this." I slide the president's list of names across the table and watch Raffe as he reads. When his hand tightens on the paper, I know he has reached his father's name. If I saw my father's name there, I would rip up the paper. Yell. Cry. Plead. And if that didn't work, I'd find a way to warn him. I would do anything to keep him safe. Raffe just stares at the paper in his hand.

The silence stretches until he quietly says, "Some of these names don't belong here."

"Your father—"

"No. These names—" He grabs a pencil and puts stars next to five names on the list. "I've heard my father rant enough about them to know they don't get along well with Dr. Barnes. I've even heard my father ask Dr. Barnes why he keeps them around instead of insisting on their transfers. Unless I'm mistaken, they don't believe in The Testing any more than you do. The president or maybe Symon has reasons for wanting them dead, though I can't tell you what they are. But my father . . ." Raffe's anger-filled eyes meet mine. "My father belongs on this list. He's a part of what needs to end. We both know my father's aware of what happens to Testing candidates who don't pass. There's a penalty worse than simple failure for Tosu City students who fail even the entrance exam and my father not only knows this, he believes it is right."

I blink. "I assumed Tosu students were allowed to go home after they were told they didn't pass." Otherwise, why would their parents let them risk failing the exam? Or does the chance to be one of the country's leaders mean that much to those who live here in Tosu City?

Raffe stands and walks toward the portrait. "They don't go home, but everyone in Tosu City believes the unsuccessful applicants are assigned to jobs outside the city. I believed that. It's what we've all been told, so why would I think any different? There are even people who swear they've heard from family members who were assigned jobs in the colonies. Important jobs working with new solar power technology or on innovative communication systems. I've heard friends of my parents brag about their child who has succeeded despite failing to pass the University entrance exam. Some have even mentioned it to Dr. Barnes in order to point out that he made a mistake grading the tests."

"I don't understand. If people have heard from their family members who have been assigned to colony jobs, then maybe the students really were sent there." I want that to be true.

Raffe shakes his head. "You asked why I insisted on helping you. It's because I learned that those letters aren't real. That nothing I grew up believing is as it seemed." He reaches out and touches the girl's portrait. "My sister Emilie created most of these paintings, including this one. I asked her to make a portrait of herself for me to have after her application to take the University entrance exam was approved."

He runs a finger over her long hair and lets his arm drop to his side. "Emilie never wanted to go to the University. She wanted to be an artist and work with one of the revitalization teams to make the city beautiful. But my father insisted she apply. The only way he would allow my mother to get Emilie art supplies was if her grades were the top in her class and she submitted an application. Emilie was smart, but she struggled with her homework, especially science. So I helped. When I didn't understand something, I asked my teachers. Then Emilie and I would figure it out together."

"She got accepted to take the entrance exam."

"She did." The words are filled with regret and pain. Raffe shoves his hands into his pockets and turns to face me. "My father was thrilled, and all the extra studying had me so far ahead that I was guaranteed a spot in my University class. Before Emilie began attending prep classes for the Early Studies exam, Dr. Barnes himself came to our house to inform me and my father that my teachers had recommended I apply to the University and take the Early Studies entrance exam a year early. I was ready to go, but Dr. Barnes believed I would do better if I had the extra year to develop my other talents. I was so proud knowing I was going to be able to attend the University like I'd always dreamed. Never once did I consider what could happen if I didn't pass the entrance exams and get assigned to a field of study. It's probably not surprising that I was too excited to sleep when I went to bed that night. So I went downstairs to get a drink and heard my father's voice. Dr. Barnes and he were talking about some possible changes to the current education program in the city that would better prepare future University students so that a higher percentage would pass the Early Studies entrance exam."

Raffe gives me a bitter smile. "Had I gone upstairs at that moment, I wouldn't be talking to you now. I'd be pissed you're so damn smart, and I'd be studying day and night to make sure my grades were better than yours."

"I would've liked to see you try," I say with a grin. The passionate way he talks reminds me of my brothers. Proud. Stubborn and strong in their convictions. Not always the easiest to work with, but people who would die before betraying what they believe. That thought comforts even as the strain in Raffe's voice makes me ache with sympathy and dread.

"When this is over, I promise to give you a run for your money." He walks over and sits back down in the chair across from me. The humor in his eyes fades as he says, "Things would have been easier had I gone back to my room, but I liked how important I felt listening to that kind of conversation. I was so busy imagining how it would feel when I was able to make decisions that changed the course of people's lives that I almost missed what Dr. Barnes said next. He asked my father if he was sure he was willing to risk Emilie sitting for the entrance exams. If not, Dr. Barnes would allow her to back out of her acceptance. He assured my father that the list of accepted students had not yet been made public. Emilie could be removed without anyone being the wiser."

"I'm surprised Dr. Barnes offered to let your sister step away from her application acceptance," I say. "It's considered treason for a colony candidate to refuse to appear for The Testing."

Raffe shrugs. "Dr. Barnes and my father have worked together for years. My father considers Dr. Barnes one of his closest friends. So I wasn't as surprised as I might have been, especially since I understood the concern. Emilie's smart, but she takes a long time to think through answers. She doesn't perform well on timed exams. Especially when they are math- or science-based. Her teachers mentioned that issue in her evaluations, which is why Dr. Barnes presented my father with an opportunity to withdraw her name. I assumed Dr. Barnes wanted to give my father the option of having his daughter remain in Tosu City, because failure on the exams would ordinarily mean a job assignment in the colonies. But when my father refused the offer, Dr. Barnes said something that made me wonder if there wasn't something more."

"What did he say?"

"That once the list was public there would be no going back. If Emilie failed her exam, she would face the same consequences as the others and become a resource for the Commonwealth. No exceptions could be made, not even for the daughter of a good friend." Raffe's gaze drifts to the portrait. "My father said he didn't care. If Emilie wasn't strong enough to take her place at the University, then her Redirection would mean she'd still make a valuable contribution to her country. Nothing else mattered."

Redirection. "Maybe your father just meant that your sister would have a purpose in one of the colonies."

"You didn't hear the tones of their voices, Cia." Raffe closes his eyes as if hearing it all again. "Whatever Dr. Barnes was talking about had nothing to do with a remote colony job. If it had, he would never have asked my father to withdraw Emilie's name. That night I lay in bed, thinking about the words Dr. Barnes had used. He said Emilie would become a resource. Something to be used. Since my father refused to change his mind, I did all I could to help Emilie pass the exam. I made her study late into the night and practice taking timed tests. But no matter how hard we studied, it wasn't enough. I should have told her what I'd heard and made her run, but I didn't. I thought my help was all she needed. She didn't pass." Tears color his words and pull at my heart. "When my father told me the news, he said she had been assigned to a job in Five Lakes Colony."

"Five Lakes?"

"I know." His eyes meet mine. "There's no one named Emilie Jeffries working with first- and second-year students at the school in Five Lakes Colony."

"No."

Raffe rises and walks the length of the room. "For the last two years, I've been looking for her and the other students who didn't pass the entrance exams. That's how I found the street you saw today. The people who stay there want to live separately from the government, but are too afraid of what lies in the unrevitalized parts of the country to travel outside the Tosu boundaries. A few were students who fled before the entrance exam results were posted—certain they had failed. The others—they all have their reasons for not wanting to be a part of what the United Commonwealth stands for. I had hoped someone there would know where Emilie was. Instead one person told me he once heard that students who failed were taken to an unrevitalized area to the east. He didn't know why. I didn't want to believe him, but part of me has always wondered if it's true. My father's position in the government has made it easy for me to meet officials who've traveled to the colonies and to ask questions, and I've learned that not a single person I've inquired about has ever been seen in the colony they'd supposedly been Redirected to. They've just disappeared. Since Tosu officials aren't in frequent contact with Five Lakes Colony, I couldn't verify whether Emilie was there. When I heard about you and Tomas, I asked people what you'd told them about your colony. I learned that until the official arrived to escort you to The Testing, no one from Tosu had come to Five Lakes for years. Emilie never set foot in Five Lakes Colony. I don't know where she was sent, but I intend to find her. She deserves that much. They all do."

I think of Will's twin brother and all the other students who did not pass the first round of Testing. After The Testing was over, those of us who were accepted into the University were told that the unsuccessful candidates were directed to jobs in colonies other than the ones where they were raised. When questioned, Dr. Barnes said sending them to new locations allowed them to take their places in society as adults instead of as children who would have to convince those around them to see them as full grown and capable of meaningful contributions. The explanation was logical, but after I listened to the recording on the Transit Communicator, I knew it was false. At first, I thought all the unsuccessful early-round candidates had suffered the same fate as those who failed during the fourth exam — death. But hearing Raffe's story confirms the theory I've recently considered and just today heard Stacia echo. Those who are tested for the University are the best and the brightest. Killing all those who do not succeed in their candidacy is wasteful. And Dr. Barnes is not one to waste resources. Not when they can be used. The question is, for what and where?

Still, while I want those answers and understand his anger, I cannot believe Raffe would really want to see his father killed. But when I ask him about it, his answer is immediate. "My father has chosen his side. Now I'm choosing mine."

I study the anguish and resolve on his face. I have seen the same expression in my reflector. It is the look of a person who has come to a crossroads and chosen the more difficult path.

The sound of people in the hall tells me it is time for dinner. After the meal, I will have to find a way to test the last two potential members of our team. Perhaps Raffe can help with that and with planning the next stage. He seems to have already helped by possibly limiting the number of people we need to target. But to be certain, I need to learn more, which is why I ask Raffe if he'd be willing to meet later tonight to compare his thoughts to the information I received when I got the list.

"We can meet after dinner and go for a walk," he says with a smile. "After our disappearance into Tosu this weekend, everyone already assumes I have a crush on you. This will seal the deal."

"They don't know you very well, do they?" I ask.

Raffe's smile fades. "Not many people do."

A reminder that despite his having passed this test, neither do I.

Shaking off my concern, I return the list to my bag and slide the strap onto my shoulder. "I'll see you at dinner."

"Wait," Raffe says as I head for the door. He disappears again into his bedroom. When he returns he hands me the pulse radio test I designed. "You forgot this. I didn't listen to the message."

"I know." I take the device and carefully set it in my bag.

Raffe folds his arms over his chest and leans against the wall. "What would have happened if I had turned those switches?"

My heart skips a beat. "You knew it was a test?"

"Not right away. But after thinking about it, I realized I would only leave something that important with someone for one of two reasons. If I had no choice or if I wanted to see what they would do with the information. Once I decided this was your way of having me prove my trustworthiness, it was harder to ignore it sitting on my desk. I wanted to know what you'd designed it to do. Was it going to give me false information?"

"No." I shift my feet. "It was going to explode."

There is silence as Raffe gapes at me. I wait for anger. Instead, Raffe lets out a bark of laughter. "I'm glad I'm such a trustworthy guy. That would have really sucked."

"You're not mad?" I remember how I felt when I realized my life was on the line because of Dr. Barnes's tests.

"You did what was necessary. And now I'm especially glad I spent the afternoon doing this instead of tinkering with your toy." Raffe grabs something off a small table near the far side of the couch and hands it to me. "Here."

I take the six-inch-square piece of paper. Painted on it is a purple circle against a red backdrop. In the center of the circle, forming an X, are two yellow lightning bolts outlined in white.

"What is this?" I ask.

"Symbols are important, especially to those embarking on change. The revolutionaries who formed the United States had their stars and stripes. The European uprising against their coalition used a closed fist. I decided to create a different version of your symbol for ours." He nods at the band that circles my wrist. "In mythology, lightning represents either the loss of ignorance or punishment for those who overstep their bounds. I used two bolts since we intend to do both."

The lightning bolts look powerful against the colors of our country. Up until now, I'd looked at the symbol Testing officials gave me as an acknowledgment of my mechanical abilities. I thought it represented the ability to create solar cells and light sources. But this . . .

"It's perfect."

The loss of ignorance. The punishment of those who created The Testing. Maybe the punishment of those of us who fight against it. Despite that possibility, there are now four of us, five if Zeen is still alive and well, who will see this through to the end.

CHAPTER 11

My injured leg is starting to throb when I go upstairs to my room to drop off the books I don't need. I open the door carefully and see the tiny slip of paper that I had slid in between the door and the frame flutter to the ground. Not the most sophisticated of warning systems, but it was effective. As far as I can tell, no one has been inside since I was last here.

Closing the door behind me, I put my bag on the table. Gently, I remove the metal box containing the black powder and place it in my top desk drawer. When I have time, I will dismantle the device so there is no chance of it exploding accidentally. While I am here, I place a new change of clothes in my bag, put more healing ointment on my leg, and check my gun. Only one bullet left and I do not have any others. A problem I can remedy with a trip to the president's fifth-floor room. I will have to find a way to make that journey before my team is forced into action.

I notice that the light on my pulse radio is illuminated, and

I go into the bathroom and turn on the water so I can listen to Tomas assure me he is safe. So far no one is looking for Kerrick and Marin.

I record messages for Tomas and Stacia, letting them know Raffe passed his test. I tell them that the device I built to test him is now back in my possession and that Raffe wants to discuss the names on the list after dinner. I tell each of them to join us outside the library. If anyone is watching, they will assume we are meeting for our study group. For Tomas, I add "I love you" before pressing Send. Thinking about those I love, I try to contact Zeen to see how he is doing. I want to tell him about Dreu Owens and the tension on campus. But he doesn't answer. Hopefully, he will find time to contact me soon. Then, sliding the Communicator back in my bag and the small slip of paper back into the frame, I lock the door behind me and hurry downstairs.

During dinner it is announced that Damone has still not been found. Also, the ban on leaving campus will continue throughout the week. Most students appear unconcerned by their fellow student's disappearance and the requirement to stay on campus, but I notice that a few upper years, including Ian, exchange nervous glances.

The dining hall is still filled with students when Raffe stands up, holds out his hand, and asks if I'm ready to go. As I let him pull me out of my seat, I try to ignore people's snickers, but I cannot help the knot of anxiety that tightens in my chest when I walk by Griffin. His grim smile is not directed at me, but at Raffe—who nods to acknowledge Griffin and then winks back.

The air outside is chilly and damp. Dark clouds dim the sky. Wind whips the willow tree branches as we walk by. It feels like a storm is coming.

"I've asked Tomas and Stacia to meet us at the library," I say as we approach the bridge. "Before they meet us, I'd like you to tell me more about the people you said you believe don't belong on the list."

Raffe glances at the residence before saying, "I could be wrong, but there are a lot of names that don't make sense to me."

"Like who?"

"Professor Lee, for one. I remember my father saying that the country would fall apart if ever Professor Lee was put in charge of the University. My father believed Professor Lee always saw the best in students and wasn't decisive enough to cut away the ones who weren't strong enough to lead."

I think about Professor Lee's kindness during Early Studies and about his lecture today. The combination makes it hard to believe he's an ardent advocate of The Testing.

"What about the others?"

Raffe names Professor Markum and Professor Harring. Heads of Medical studies and Education. Both people with whom Raffe's father has clashed in recent years. Both professors petitioned the Education Department to expand the number of colony students allowed in the University. Then there's Official Parkins, head of the Resource Allocation Department, who suggested a new colony be created in the unrevitalized area southwest of the city that was once Chicago. An area that years ago was allocated to Dr. Barnes's father for The Testing.

Those five are the ones Raffe marked earlier, but there are two others that worry him. Official Frank Alkyer and Official Liza Yamatchi, whom Raffe has never heard of. "If they are important enough to keep The Testing and the current University program going, I probably would know who they are. Dr. Barnes oversees the University and The Testing. Professor Chen coordinates selection of candidates with the colony educators. Professor Holt is Dr. Barnes's second in command. My father works with all of them to make sure they have whatever is necessary to select and educate the next generation of leaders. Those four have the most power. Removing them should cripple The Testing enough for the president to stop it for good."

Four lives — five when we include Symon, whose removal is not in question — but only if I believe Raffe is being truthful about what he knows. The president gave me the list of names. She must have reasons to believe these people should be removed. But who is to say those reasons are specific to The Testing? The first directive I was given as an intern was to have faith only in the information I verified on my own. Until this moment, I had forgotten that lesson. While I am not certain Raffe's information is accurate, I do know that I cannot follow the president's orders blindly. Not questioning her list was my first mistake. I cannot afford to make another.

"So, what's the plan?" Raffe asks as we take a seat on the stone steps that lead up to the entrance of the library. "Or do I have to wait to hear it until Stacia and Tomas arrive?"

"I don't know." I thought I did, but now . . . When I chose this path, I convinced myself that the people on the list had earned their fate. "How can I plan anything without being sure who these people are?"

"Could you live with yourself if you sit back and do nothing while The Testing continues and the rebels are betrayed and killed?"

I want to say yes, but it would be a lie. "I don't know what to do."

"Yes, you do." Raffe's voice is soft but firm. "You ask yourself what your goal is. You look at the facts as you know them, and you make the call."

"What if I'm wrong?"

"Then you're wrong." Raffe's voice cracks though the swirl of confusion like a whip. "If you're looking for guarantees, you're asking the wrong person. Leaders don't get guarantees. The only thing they can do is make the most educated decision they can and hope for the best. Isn't that how you got through The Testing and our Induction?"

I shake my head. "That was different. I'm not sure I can do this." There has already been so much needless death. The weight of those lives presses on my chest, making it hard to breathe. Whom do I trust? The president? Raffe? Tomas? Myself?

But if Raffe sees my trepidation, he doesn't show it. Instead he says, "Well, if you can't, then none of us can. One person can't do it alone, and I doubt Stacia and Tomas would help if I asked. The only way this works, Cia, is with you."

"I know." I see Tomas approaching and am certain Stacia isn't far behind. Neither of them would have picked Raffe for a teammate. I doubt they would even pick each other. Raffe is right. The future is on me.

Ever since I was little, I wanted to be like my father—someone everyone turned to for answers. Until now, I'd only thought of his successes. I never considered how alone he must have felt or the courage it took to take the next step forward knowing that another wrong move could ruin us all. But though he might have wanted to, he didn't walk away. He didn't have guarantees that things would work out. He made the decision he believed was best because that was all he could do. Just as it is the only thing I can do now. I think of the symbol Raffe created for me. For us. For this purpose. I came to Tosu City because I wanted to be a leader. I thought that would come after I graduated from the University. I thought that event would signal my readiness. But I can no longer wait for Graduation Day. The time to lead is now.

"We can't reach everyone on the list," I say when Tomas and Stacia join us on the stairs. Tomas's eyes looked tired and strained. When I touch his hand, he flinches. Stacia, however, appears not only rested but eager to take the next step.

Quickly, I give them a summary of Raffe's knowledge of those on the list. "See if you can learn anything more about them. That will help us decide which people are to be given priority. Even if Enzo and Ian join us, there's no way the six of us can hit all the targets. Out of the four of us here, Raffe is the only one who knows Tosu City well enough to get to specific addresses quickly. That's going to slow us down. And once they break the ban on students leaving campus, Professor Holt and the other residence leaders will start looking for us."

"Unless," Stacia says, "we find them first."

Raffe shakes his head. "We can't remove them before we take out Dr. Barnes. Right, Cia?"

Stacia looks ready to argue but stops when I say, "Raffe is right. The minute people on the list begin to die, Dr. Barnes will know someone is coming for him and will find a way to prevent it. Removing the other targets on the list won't mean anything unless Dr. Barnes himself is taken out."

"The president wants all the targets eliminated," Stacia reminds me. "Not just the ones you pick."

"The president will understand that we have to prioritize according to what will help her best achieve her goal," I reply. As long as The Testing and the University are removed from Dr. Barnes's control, I don't think she'll have reason to complain. "Once Dr. Barnes and the top administrators of The Testing are eliminated, she'll be able to handle the others herself."

"What about Symon?" Raffe asks before Stacia can object again. "It's not going to be easy to get to him. Not in the middle of an armed rebel camp."

"I think I know a way." But I do not share it. I will trust Stacia and Raffe to help me end The Testing, I won't trust them with my brother's life.

Stacia crosses her arms and leans back. "Okay. So when do we start this plan?"

"As soon as I've decided about Ian and Enzo. Once we know the full team, we'll be ready."

We fall silent as a group of students approaches. Once they walk up the steps and enter the library, Stacia quietly asks, "Have you figured out how you're going to test Enzo? Because if you know, this might be the time to do it. He's coming this way."

Sure enough, Enzo and Will are walking toward us.

Will spots us first. He waves and yells, "Should we be offended that you scheduled a study group meeting and forgot to tell us?"

Raffe laughs as he climbs to his feet. "It just figures. I finally get Cia to go for a walk with me alone and everyone turns up. A guy can't catch a break."

"Probably because Cia is smart enough to know not to be alone with a guy like you," Will says with a grin as he reaches the library steps. "Colony guys are far more trustworthy. Don't you think, Tomas?"

"Of course." Tomas stands and gives Will a tight smile. "Although some of us are more trustworthy than others."

"Well, I don't know about you, but some of us actually need to get some studying done. We can't all be like Cia and have our homework already completed," says Will. Stacia rolls her eyes at me and turns toward Enzo. "Do you guys have time to compare answers on the physics homework? I think I might have gotten number ten wrong."

"Sure." Enzo gives her a shy smile. "I struggled with that one too."

Stacia gives us a triumphant smile as she leads Enzo and Will up the steps into the library, leaving Tomas, Raffe, and me behind.

I wait for Tomas to tell me what he found in the stadium offices. When he doesn't, I realize it is because Raffe is here.

"I told Raffe what happened at the stadium today," I say. "You can tell him what you found."

Tomas studies Raffe for several beats before saying, "There are files on every past graduate of the Biological Engineering program. They aren't very detailed, but they do list the internships that former students worked on, as well as locations and the length of every job assignment postgraduation. The last time Dreu's file was updated was five years ago when he began work on a reverse mutation research program headed up by Ranetta Janke."

Ranetta. The leader of the second rebel faction. Whatever Dreu's current involvement with her, it's no wonder Kerrick and Marin were concerned when out of the blue someone asked about him. They thought that by attacking Tomas and me, they were protecting the rebellion, which makes me feel even worse about their deaths. They died for nothing because they did not know we were all on the same side of this cause.

But learning of Dreu's connection to Ranetta also makes me feel more optimistic. If Dreu is with Ranetta in the rebel camp, Zeen may be able to track him down. The common tie to Five Lakes could help Zeen convince Dreu of the true nature of the rebellion. He could be enlisted to help Zeen in removing Symon. If that doesn't happen, then it will be up to Stacia, Raffe, Tomas, and me to finish what we will soon start.

"Has anyone noticed Kerrick is missing?" I ask Tomas.

"No, and I doubt they will until tomorrow at the earliest. Kerrick and Marin were together most of the time they weren't in class. The people in our residence won't be concerned if they don't notice him around. We just have to hope the other University members of the rebellion don't start looking for him."

The sky rumbles. Several more students approach the library and look at us as they hurry past. The rain will be here soon. "We might want to move this conversation," Raffe says. "Especially since it looks like we're drawing notice from one of your friends inside."

I look toward the library and see Will's curious face peering out.

"I want to get back to my residence anyway," Tomas says.

"I have some things I need to take care of before this project starts."

The wind whips strands of my hair free from the tie I have fastened it back with as we start toward the residences. Raffe must understand that Tomas and I need a moment alone, because he walks more slowly until we are twenty feet ahead.

Quietly, I ask, "Are you okay?"

"Sure." The lie is obvious, maybe just because I was there today and I'm not okay, either. Although, I'm not sure that I should be. That either of us should be. Focusing on the future has helped me build a wall between my thoughts and my feeling about what has happened. But at some point, I know that wall will break. When it does, who knows if I will ever be okay again.

"Remember what you told me," I say. "We're going to get through this together." My fingertips brush his.

Tomas goes still. After several long moments, the tension goes out of his shoulders. When he nods it is accompanied by the dimpled smile that never fails to tug at my heart. "Together." His fingers close over mine for a few seconds before he walks away.

I watch him as he approaches his residence, and feel Raffe come to stand beside me as Tomas disappears through the front door.

"Is he okay?"

"Today was rough," I say.

"It's going to get rougher." The sky rumbles. "Do you think he's going to be able to handle it?"

"Tomas won't let us down." No matter the cost.

Despite the threat of rain, Raffe decides we should continue on our "walk" for a while longer. In case anyone is monitoring our movements, it should look as though we got interrupted by Stacia and Tomas and now are able to spend time together as we intended. What we really are doing is looking for the best way to get off campus without being noticed.

We spend the next hour walking along the north and east sides of the University grounds as the rain-filled clouds grow closer and the sky darkens to black. To the west and south are rips in the earth caused by the Sixth Stage of War. Too wide even at their narrowest points to cross, they provide a natural barrier.

A Safety official stands under an illuminated solar lamp outside The Testing Center. It's hard to tell if there are any officials in the shadows in between that building and the next ones we pass, but we spot another not far from the stadium and three between the stadium and the Tosu Administration building on the far northeast side. The officials must assume the eight-foot-high black iron fence will keep students from leaving, because we don't see any sign of them along that side of campus until we reach the southeast corner, where four officials stand on the road under the iron archway that marks the entrance to the University.

"We'll have to go over the fence," Raffe says as the first raindrops hit. "The grove of trees that we passed not far from the Tosu Administration building will provide enough cover for us to get over without being seen."

"Yes, but we won't be able to take our bikes." It will be hard enough to reach all the people on the president's list without also having to travel on foot. I wrap my arms around myself and pick up my pace as a drop of rain lands on my forehead.

"Maybe we can lure some of the officials away from their posts."

"A distraction might get them to leave their posts long enough for us to get by, but it won't take them long to figure out they were duped. The minute they do, they'll be after us. How long do you think we'll last out in the open city streets? We're going to need a place to hide at least for a few hours until the initial search dies down."

"I'm pretty sure I found one. Remember the street I asked you about yesterday?" The drops begin to fall harder as we race up the path toward the residence. A streak of lightning illuminates the horizon as we step inside.

"Well, that was just about perfect timing," Raffe says, wiping the rain off his nose.

"Perfect for what?" I ask, tucking a damp piece of hair behind my ear.

"For having dodged the deluge." He laughs as he shakes the water from his hair like Scotty Rollison's dogs do back home. "I guess I'll think of an umbrella next time."

"If there is a next time." The sound of Will's voice makes us both turn. "Enzo and I were wondering where the two of you went. He wanted to talk to you about the History assignment you got today. He just went to grab a book from his room. He's going to meet me back in the common room."

"If you see him before I do, let him know I'm going to change into something dry," I say with a deliberate look at Raffe. "I'll be downstairs in a few minutes." I head down the hall. Behind me I hear Raffe say that he's going to change clothes, too. He's right behind me as I start climbing the steps.

A loud bang echoes in the building. My foot misses a step

as the source of the sound slams home. Not thunder. An explosion. I regain my footing and run up the stairs, not caring about the pain that streaks through my leg.

I hear shouts. Doors slam as students who were in their rooms come out to see what has happened. I hit the third-floor landing. Raffe is still right behind me. The smell of smoke and sulfur is heavy in the air. Raffe yells for everyone to go downstairs until someone checks to make sure everything is safe. That this must have been caused by the storm. A dozen girls exit their rooms and hurry down the stairs. A few cast glances at me as I disregard Raffe's suggestion and race down the hall.

Smoke rises from the crack at the bottom of my door. The small piece of paper I used to warn me of another's entrance lies on the floor. The lock is engaged, and I fumble with the key until it slides home and the knob turns. Smoke pours into the hallway. I cough as I step into the room. Through the smoke, I spot the outline of someone writhing on the floor of my bedroom as his clothing is eaten by flames.

I drop my bag onto the floor and hurry to see if I can help Griffin. Because it has to be him. He's the one who has been following me. Who hates me. Who was enlisted by Professor Holt to find a reason to remove me from this school. I yank blankets off my bed and throw them on top of the whimpering form to smother the flames and realize the body beneath the covers is too small to belong to Griffin. And the voice that screams for help . . .

I pull the blanket away and see dark hair that has been burned away at the front of the scalp. A hand blistered by the explosion reaches out to me as I look into eyes glazed with pain and whisper, "Enzo."

CHAPTER 12

CONFUSION. SORROW. ANGUISH. Tears fill my eyes as I run to the bathroom and douse a towel in water. Enzo broke into my room. He went through my things and failed the test that was intended for Raffe. After our Induction experience and the way he tried to protect me after Damone's death, I don't understand how this could be. Placing the cool, wet fabric on his angry, red-looking arms, I want to ask why, but the pain on his face and the way his body begins to shake make that question fade. All I want to do is stop the pain. To turn back time so I can dismantle my test before Enzo can find it.

"Cia." His voice is barely audible through clenched teeth. "I'm sorry. I thought . . . Stacia said . . ." He coughs, takes a shallow breath.

Stacia. Did she think I was taking too long to make a choice? Did she decide this should be Enzo's test, or is this her way of drawing attention to me so that my plan to help the president—our plan to end The Testing—will fail?

"It's going to be okay," I say, because he needs to hear the words and I want to believe them. But it isn't. Because here he is, burned. Maybe dying.

I dig through my bag for the ointment I have been using on my leg. It won't be enough to heal these kinds of wounds, but it might make them more bearable. Once I find the small tube, I have no idea where to begin. There are red blotchy patches on his face, arms, and hands. Other burns can be seen through the holes singed into his shirt and pants. There is a charred black area on his cheek that looks as if the skin has been seared beyond repair, and the tissue around his eyes has already begun to swell, making his eyes look small and incredibly vulnerable. The bomb I built did what it was designed to do. Stacia drove Enzo here, but I am to blame for this.

A pulsing, high-pitched sound makes me jump. Someone has activated the residence's emergency siren.

"Cia, help is coming." A hand digs into my shoulder and shakes me. "Cia. Do you hear me?"

I look up through my tears to see Raffe's face looking down. "I've put out the rest of the flames and have told everyone coming up the stairs to go outside, but that siren means officials are going to arrive soon. They're going to come here to your rooms and see what's happened. Do you understand what this means?"

"It means they'll help Enzo." I feel a moment's relief and then realize that I'm wrong. Raffe isn't telling me that Enzo will get medical attention. His words are a warning. University officials will be here soon. They will ask questions about what happened and why I created a device that caused this kind of injury. Enzo broke into my room, but I am the one who will pay the price if I don't leave.

"I have to go," I say.

It takes two tries to rise to my feet. Raffe moves to help me but I shake off his hands. I walk to my wardrobe, grab my extra boots and another change of clothes to add to the one already in my bag. I pull my jacket on to protect me from the rain. Then I look around rooms that still contain a haze of smoke. Books. Papers. Writing utensils. Many items have been burned, but some were untouched by the flames. They are what have defined me and my goals for most of my life. There is no way to carry more than the paper and pencils I already have stored in my bag, and even if I could, I will have no use for anything else now. Today I am being forced to leave behind the books and the knowledge they contain. From now on, I must have faith that I have learned the lessons I need to take the next step.

"What happened in here?" Ian yells from the doorway.

I have no answer to give, but I'm thankful Raffe does. Over the shrill siren he yells back, "Enzo broke into Cia's room. He must have been trying to set some kind of trap. It backfired. We figured it would be best if we got out of the way. Right, Cia?"

Ian looks to where Enzo lies shaking on the floor. Then back at me. For a moment he seems conflicted. Then he slides his hand into his coat pocket. When he removes it, a gun is wrapped in his hand.

Enzo moans on the floor. Officials must be arriving now. My time to flee is running out. I need Ian to let me go.

"I know you're one of the rebels," I say. "The one Michal told me would keep me safe."

"Michal would understand. The rebellion has to come first."

"Michal can't understand, because he's dead," I scream. I think about the listening device behind the wardrobe and lower my voice as much as I can while still allowing myself to be heard. With the emergency sirens blaring and officials on their way, I doubt anyone is listening to what is happening in here now, but I don't want to reveal more to those who are spying on me than I have to. Lightning flashes in the window. "Symon killed him when Michal gave him proof the president could use to end The Testing. I know, because I was there."

"I was, too," says Raffe, standing next to me. His hands are clenched at his sides. I know he is waiting for the right moment to strike. Ian doesn't know it, but he is now in as much danger as we are in from him.

The gun in Ian's hand shifts downward as he looks from the open door behind him back at me. "That's not possible. Symon—"

"Symon is working with Dr. Barnes," I say. "He's not trying to stop The Testing. He's working to make sure the people who want to stop it are controlled and then killed. I'm trying to make sure that doesn't happen. If you want The Testing to end you have to let me go."

Voices can be heard over the din of the sirens. Coming up the stairs or down the hall. The time I have to escape is ticking down. If I don't leave now, The Testing might never end. My brother could die and everything I have done will have been for nothing.

I see Raffe put his hand into the side pocket of his bag and nod at me. I shift my feet and prepare for flight, but before Raffe can attack, Ian yells, "Cough."

Raffe stops and looks at me.

"What?" I ask.

"Start coughing. Both of you." Ian shoves his gun back into his pocket and takes two steps toward me. "I need you to trust me or you won't make it out of here." He leans down and puts one hand around my back and the other behind my knees. Before I know what he intends, he sweeps me and my bag into his arms and hurries toward the door, yelling, "It's going to be okay, Cia. Come on, Raffe. We have to get her out of here. She can't breathe with all this smoke."

I go limp, close my eyes, and start to cough. Raffe coughs, too, as Ian carries me away from the smoke. From Enzo. From the damage I have helped cause.

"What happened up here?"

I force myself not to react at the sound of Professor Holt's voice and wait for Ian to stop moving. But he doesn't. He just yells, "Enzo set off some kind of explosive in Cia's room. I need to get her away from the smoke."

Raffe's coughing tells me he is still behind us when Ian starts down the stairs. More than once someone bumps into us as they go to help Enzo. I keep my eyes shut tight as the chatter of voices grows as loud as the shrieking sirens. Students yell above the screech of the alarm to find out if anyone knows what is happening. Ian screams for people to get out of the way. Before I know it, I feel moist air on my face.

"She's fine," Ian yells. To whom, I'm not sure. The change in his words makes me stop coughing. "She got overwhelmed by the heat and the panic downstairs. But Professor Holt asked me to tell the rest of you to come upstairs. Someone's burned really bad."

I open my eyes as two officials head into the building, leaving Raffe, Ian, and me alone outside the residence.

"We have to leave," I say as Ian sets me on the wet ground. "Now."

"I think I can buy you five minutes," Ian says. "After that, there's nothing I can do."

"You can't stay here. There's a listening device planted behind the wardrobe in my room. Whoever put it there will know I told you about Dr. Barnes and Symon." Even if they didn't hear the rest, that will be enough to put Ian in harm's way.

Ian looks back at the residence, then shakes his head. "If someone was listening, I'll just have to find a way to talk myself out of trouble. I'm not leaving. If you're right, the students who follow Symon are in danger. I can't go without letting them know." Ian puts his hand on the door. "I'll stall the officials but it won't be for long. You have to hurry."

He doesn't have to tell me twice. I run as rain again starts to pour out of the sky. Raffe reaches the vehicle shed first. He grabs my bike from the rack and wheels it out to me.

"What about yours?" I ask.

"Two of us will have a harder time leaving campus without being seen. You'll have a better chance avoiding notice if you're by yourself."

"What will you tell Professor Holt? She knows you were with me."

"I'll come up with something. Don't worry. I'll meet up with you tomorrow. I promise."

I unfasten my bag and pull a hand-held pulse radio from inside. "Make sure this stays dry. You should be able to contact me with it."

Then I put the strap of my bag over my head and climb onto my bike as the rain pounds down.

"Wait." Raffe puts a hand on my arm. "You should take off your bracelet. Otherwise they'll be able to track you. I can plant it in one of the University buildings so they'll think you're hiding here on campus."

That's a good idea. But as I look down at the bracelet on my wrist and the symbol that was meant to signify who I am now and the future I was to have, I shake my head. "I can't get rid of it yet. There's something I have to do first. Remember the building we talked about. If I can get off campus, that's where you'll find me. It's time to act."

My feet bear down on the pedals. Rain pelts my face and soaks my clothes as my bike picks up speed. Over the bridge. Onto the walkway. Away from the sirens that still cut into the night. Through the rain, I think I see running lights of skimmers approaching in the distance, so I steer my bike onto the grass, away from the street lamps and into the shadows. Although I am not sure I can truly be safe ever again.

The wet ground slows my progress, but soon I spot the fence that marks the right side of campus. There I get off my bike and wheel it toward the arching entrance to see if Safety officials are still keeping watch there. I shield my eyes from the rain and peer into the darkness. When I see no one, I pick up a rock and throw it as hard as I can onto the roadway. It cracks against the pavement and then skitters across the ground until it comes to a stop. If anyone had been standing guard, they would have come to investigate. Enzo has inadvertently caused the diversion Raffe and I had discussed.

I start to get back on my bike but remember something I

need to do. I pull out my pocketknife, a flashlight, and my pulse radio. I use the radio first. Making sure the dial is set to Tomas's frequency, I turn on the recorder. Quickly, I tell him what happened and that I am now outside the University's boundaries.

"Once they realize I'm gone they'll come looking for you. Leave your bracelet in your room. I'll be waiting three blocks directly east of the entrance gates. Please be careful. I'll see you soon."

I press Send, shove the radio back into my bag, and turn my attention to the identification bracelet. Remarkably, my fingers are steady as I detach the slick metal from my wrist and flip it over to expose the back. I hold the flashlight in my mouth so I can see what I have to do next.

Using the smallest knife tool, I wedge it into the seam of the center disc of the bracelet. It takes several tries and I cut my finger before the back pops off and I am able to remove the tracking device.

After putting the knife and the flashlight back in my bag, I refasten the bracelet to my wrist and throw the tracking device into the middle of a small group of bushes situated near the fence to my left. Then I ride three blocks and look for the group of trees and bushes that I spotted on the way to my internship. Part of me wants to ride as fast from my tracking device as I can. I don't want to get caught. But I can't leave without Tomas. I'm hopeful he will have already seen the indicator light shining. If so, he'll be here soon. If not, I intend to wait as long as I can.

The clump of bushes I'm looking for is at the end of the third block, a hundred feet from the road. I get off my bike and drag it with me into the middle of a thicket of evergreen boughs. I sit on the ground with my knees pulled tight against my chest. Thunder echoes above. Between the lack of moonlight and the misty rain, visibility is poor. Now that I have nothing to do but sit and think, tears begin to fall. And I let them, because this might be the only time I have a chance to release the feelings inside me. Bitter tears for Enzo. For Kerrick and Marin. For Damone. For Michal. And even more for me. For the girl who was raised to love and respect life and has since been forced to kill.

The tears keep coming as the sky clears. At some point, Dr. Barnes and Professor Holt will find the tracking device near the campus entrance. They will know I am no longer on campus. Will they believe I have done what Tomas has suggested and gone home? Will they send someone to Five Lakes? Will they believe my family when they say they have not seen me? If not, what will become of them and everyone else in my colony? Because the people I know there will not stand by and allow my family to suffer at the hands of whichever officials arrive. They believe in peace, but I have no doubt they will fight if necessary. They will fight and keep fighting.

I can do no less.

I take a deep breath, wipe the tears off my face, and try to think. Part of me wants to head for the rebel camp and find my brother. He was the one I always turned to when I needed help solving a problem. Even if he didn't have the answer, he always made me feel more confident and in control by discussing the dilemma with me. But I can't go to him now. If the students who attacked in the stadium are any indication of the lengths to which the rebels will go to ensure nothing threatens their cause, going to the air force base will only lead to trouble for Zeen. Even if I could find him, my brother would insist on my leaving Tosu City, which is something I can't do. Besides, he is in the perfect place to remove Symon when we are ready. Until then, I will have to rely on myself to think things through.

I doubt Dr. Barnes and Symon will allow me to roam free for long. Once they begin to search in earnest, President Collindar will be unable to intervene on my behalf. Not without making them aware of her interests. Starting tomorrow morning, word will reach the president and her team, and I will be cut off from any assistance on that front. This means if I need anything from the fifth-floor room, I have to get it before sunrise. And now I know what I will need.

If only Tomas would arrive.

According to the watch on my bag, it has been two hours since Tomas, Raffe, and I parted ways. So much change in so little time. The minutes crawl by as I peer through the branches toward the roadway that leads to the University gate. If I'm to reach the president's office before a search for me is launched, I have to go now or risk being spotted and captured.

Still, I wait. I need to know that Tomas is safe.

Ten more minutes pass. I picture Tomas being caught. Questioned. Injured. Worse. Part of me wants to ride back onto campus to find him. But I stay put and squint into the shadows.

There.

I see the outline of a figure riding a bicycle. I know it's him. Turning the frequency knob on my pulse radio to the one that Raffe uses, I shove the radio into my bag and then crawl through the mud out from my hiding place. I pull my bike free from the branches and wheel it toward the roadway. Tomas looks over his shoulder, toward the University entrance. Looking for someone chasing him or for me?

The second he spots me he stops his bicycle, climbs off, and whispers my name in the dark. When I reach him I throw my arms around his waist and squeeze tight, so grateful that he is safe and here with me now.

"I was worried you'd leave when it took me so long to get here." Tomas presses his lips against my forehead. "There are lots of skimmers and Safety officials on campus, especially near the residences. I had to double back a lot in order to avoid them. Are you okay?"

"We have to get out of here." Reluctantly, I step out of his arms.

"If you've changed your mind, we could still leave. Five Lakes—"

"I'm not going back to Five Lakes."

Tomas takes a deep breath and nods. "I didn't think you would, but I'd hoped . . ." He looks past me, down the roadway. Despite his desire to see The Testing ended, he wants more than anything to go home. To forget. I understand that longing, but there is no forgetting what we have seen and done. The only way to live with our actions is to end the very thing that caused them. Or die trying.

He sets his shoulders and asks, "Where do we go from here?"

I climb onto my bike and say, "First to the president's office. There are weapons there that we'll need. Then we're going to hide in a place where no one will find us and plan our attack. If the others get off campus, they'll meet us there."

I can tell Tomas wants to question me further, but there isn't time. I push off and begin to pedal down the darkened road-way, scanning the area for any movement near the buildings that we pass. The structures in the area immediately outside the University are used by professors and their families, although a few are designated for use by colony officials and scientists who have come to Tosu City. Since it is approaching nine o'clock, past the time the law allows the use of electricity in nongovern-ment and University buildings, the houses are dark. Here and there I see a flicker of light coming from a window, telling me some families are using candlelight.

The clouds dissipate and the moon appears. It is only a sliver, but even that meager, hazy light helps us move faster than we otherwise could. It is hard to spot the places where the road has fallen into disrepair. But we continue to head south-bound, toward the heart of the city.

Everything about this journey, us riding bicycles, Tomas's breathing, and the nervous clench of my muscles, reminds me of the fourth phase of The Testing, when Tomas and I had only our wits and each other to help us survive. Perhaps it is because I remember how we beat the odds that I do not feel the same fear now that I did then. And strange as it seems, for the first time since I was selected for The Testing, my actions are my own. Yes, Dr. Barnes and his officials will be searching for me. Yes, President Collindar expects me to do a job that almost everyone in my colony would find unthinkable. But my flight from the University means I no longer am accountable to either of them. For the first time in a long time, my life is in my own hands. Though I can't know if that life will last much longer than the next couple of days, I at least know that this time belongs to me.

CHAPTER 13

THE TRANSIT COMMUNICATOR and the lights from the windows of the government buildings in the center of the city guide our travel. The residential neighborhoods we ride through are quiet. We hear nothing to give any indication of pursuit. Still, I find myself casting glances over my shoulder and pushing my legs. We need to get to the president's office and leave again before the search for us extends past the University grounds.

Because government officials are known to toil late into the night, I have little doubt there will be people working on the president's projects when I arrive. If I am lucky, they will not question my presence. They will, however, wonder about Tomas, which is why I lead him to the building where Michal once felt it was safe to talk.

"You won't be allowed to come into the building with me. You can stay here," I say, testing the door. When it opens, I heave a sigh of relief.

While individual offices and rooms are often locked, the

doors to most buildings are kept unfastened because of what happened during the Fifth through Seventh Stages of War, when chemical-laden rain fell from the sky. People caught in those downpours sought shelter, but those who were not near their homes or vehicles succumbed to the toxins in the deadly rains because they had nowhere to take cover.

I wait for Tomas to protest. He only warns me to be careful and hurry back.

Using one of the windowless rooms inside the building, I change into fresh clothes from my bag and untangle my hair with my fingers. I walk back toward the front door and into Tomas's arms. I hug him tight before striding out. While the streets we rode coming here were empty, here in the heart of the city I spot several skimmers as they travel to or from government buildings, as well as two people in the distance traveling on foot. I store my bicycle in the holding rack and walk into the building with my shoulders straight and my head high. As if I belong here.

One of the two Safety officials inside the foyer looks up from his log and gets to his feet to verify my clearance. His movements are annoyingly unhurried as I pull up the sleeve of my jacket and display the bracelet on my wrist.

He checks his clipboard and nods. I force myself to keep a moderate pace as I head for the stairs and start climbing. Still, I am out of breath when I reach the fifth floor and punch the code into the keypad next to the door. Once again I find myself in the storage room, taking stock of the inventory. But this time, instead of avoiding the weapons, I reach for them.

I open a box of bullets and reload the gun Raffe gave me. I then slide several boxes of ammunition, three additional handguns, and several long, deadly-looking knives into my bag. This isn't The Testing, when I could only choose three items to keep me alive. Now I can take whatever I can fit in my bag. I turn and walk toward bins containing canisters of explosive powders and chemicals. Seeing the explosives makes me think of Enzo. I can't help wondering if he is still alive and whether the medical team will be able to keep him that way and repair the damage he has suffered. I hope Raffe will have the answers to those questions when next we speak. Until then, I cannot let the memory of Enzo or the guilt I feel stop me from doing what must be done.

Stepping closer, I inspect the explosives and other containers on the shelves.

My insides curl as I carefully add three canisters to my cache. Finally I turn and look at the technological devices. My fingers itch to take them all, since these are the tools I understand best. But my bag is almost full. So I take three tracking devices that are tuned to the same frequency as the monitor in my bag. I am not sure if Raffe will be able to meet Tomas and me or if I will come into contact with Zeen. But if I see them and we are all forced to separate during the hours and days ahead, these devices will give me a way to find them. After one last look around, I lift the strap of my bag onto my shoulder and walk out of the room, hoping I have not left behind anything I need.

Aside from the sound of my boots against the gray tile, everything is quiet as I head for the stairs. On the third-floor landing, I pause when the murmur of voices reaches me. I'm tempted to walk down the hall to see if anyone there knows whether the president really did postpone her Debate Chamber proposal and if the search for Michal continues. But as much as that information would help me understand what is happening with the president, I cannot afford the time or the risk of being seen by too many people. I continue down the stairs.

I am crossing the lobby when I see the front doors open. Several officials in ceremonial purple and red walk in. The two Safety officials near the front desk stand as one last person enters.

President Collindar.

There is nowhere to hide.

Stepping to the side, I tilt my head down in what I hope looks like a respectful gesture. My hair fans out on either side of my face, giving me some cover, but when the president looks my way, I see her eyebrows rise. I hold my breath. Has she heard about Enzo? Will she decide that my being on the run makes me more of a liability than an ally?

"Official Dresden." Though the president is addressing one of the Safety officials, she takes a step toward me. "Can I see the list of all personnel who have checked in tonight?"

The official takes the clipboard off the desk and hands it to her. She looks down at the list and then back at me. "It's nice to see that so many of our staff are dedicated enough to overcome the concern Official Gallen's disappearance has caused. The increased number of Safety officials that I have just ordered to participate in the evening patrols should also ease fears. Don't you think?"

When the Safety official agrees, President Collindar hands the clipboard back to him. "I'm hopeful this upheaval will be smoothed over and things will return to normal. We need everyone from the Debate Chamber to focus clearly on our proposal." With an almost imperceptible nod in my direction, the president turns and heads down the hall. "Fredrik, what can we do to convince Nigel's department to vote with us? I've heard they are wavering and might be willing to come to our side if given proper incentive." Her officials trail after her, debating ideas, and I head for the door.

As I step out of the building, a black skimmer passes by. The white seal on the door marks it as a Safety and Security vehicle. One of the extra patrols President Collindar just warned me about. The fact that she chose to give me such a warning speaks volumes. Some of the Safety officials who roam the streets are doing so to reassure the Tosu population. But there must be others who are searching for me.

I duck back into the entryway alcove and stay there until the skimmer has disappeared down the street. Then I head for my bicycle. Coasting, I approach the roadway that leads to the building where Tomas is waiting and only turn when I see no one is around.

I click on my flashlight when I walk into the building, shine it down the hallway, and whisper Tomas's name. He doesn't appear. My heart stills. I whisper again. Panic resonates in my voice. Finally I see someone step out of a doorway on the right, far down the corridor. Tomas.

"Sorry," he says, walking through the shadows toward me. "I decided to see if there was anything on this floor we could use. Did you find what you needed?"

"I saw the president. She warned me additional Safety officials have been added to the evening patrols. We have to be careful when we go to the next location. Once we get there, we should be safe."

"Where are we going?" Tomas's hand finds mine in the dark.

"Someplace no patrols would go."

Tomas exits first. He waits several moments before motioning for me to follow. Then we climb onto our bikes and ride. Twice we stop and crouch behind bushes or duck around the edges of buildings to wait for a skimmer to pass us by.

The buildings we pass grow smaller. Tomas asks if I am sure we are going the correct way. I know he is concerned that we have veered to the north. The same direction as the University. I check the Transit Communicator and assure him that we are on course.

When my front wheel hits several holes in the pavement, I know I have found the street I have been searching for. In the dim moonlight, I study the dilapidated, graffiti-laden houses on either side of the roadway to find the one I entered two days ago.

"That one," I say, pointing to the small one-story structure. After taking a closer look, I pick up my bike and walk carefully across the grass to the back of the house. Tomas does the same.

Tomas leans his bicycle against the wall and then walks to the door and eases it open a crack. Just enough for us to squeeze ourselves and our bicycles through.

We search the house as I did the first time I was here. Aside from several puddles of water in the bedrooms where the ceiling leaks, the place looks the same. Tomas turns the faucet on in the bathroom to check if it works. The water that runs into the sink is tinged with orange. I find the pile of clothing in the same place I left it, and when I pry up the floorboards I see the folder I hid there.

My muscles tremble as I place my bag and the folder in the corner of the room. Tomas pulls a blanket out of his bag and spreads it in the middle of the dust-coated floor. Since the windows are boarded up, we leave the flashlight on as we sit down. I lean my head on Tomas's shoulder and snuggle close. There is so much we need to talk about, decisions to be made—but now that I am relatively safe, fatigue makes it hard to speak. Tomas doesn't seem to want to talk either. Instead, he just holds me. I don't know how long we sit like this. Ten minutes? Twenty? All the while I keep my eyes closed and imagine us back in Five Lakes, in a time and place that made sense. But as much as I try to hold on to the idea of us sitting near the fountain in the Five Lakes square, surrounded by all things familiar, the images of Michal's bloodless face, Kerrick's and Marin's corpses, and Enzo's burned body will not stay out of my mind.

When I shiver, Tomas holds me tighter and asks, "Are you okay?"

I shrug and burrow closer, but Tomas won't allow me to hide. His hand lifts my chin so that I am forced to look at him. In his eyes I see the same sadness I feel. But, I also see love. His lips brush mine. Once. Twice. The gentleness of his touch makes me want to cry.

Tomas leans back and looks at me again. His fingers brush my cheek, wiping away a tear I wasn't aware had fallen. When his lips find mine again, they are still gentle, but instead of kindness, the kiss shimmers with desire. I snake a hand around the back of his neck and pull him closer, deepening the kiss.

There is nothing more I want than to feel this way forever. I allow myself two more kisses before easing away from his touch. If it were just about this moment, I would allow myself to get lost in Tomas's embrace. If it were just about us, I would forget what tomorrow could bring. But I want a future that can happen only if we are successful in what we intend to do.

My breathing comes fast and my pulse pounds as I look up at Tomas, worried he'll be upset that I pulled away. But his face is filled with tenderness as he asks again, "Are you okay?" The same question, but this time he's asking about us.

I swallow hard and nod. "Are you?"

My breath catches when he doesn't answer right away. Tomas webs his fingers through mine, holds my hand tight, and says, "It's only been eight months since we left Five Lakes, but it seems longer. So much has happened. Some of it we understand, and much we don't. But there are two things I am certain of. I love you and you love me. We'll figure out what that means for us after all this is over. Until then, I'm grateful we're here together. Okay?"

I lean up to kiss him. Then I grab the flashlight, walk over to my bag, remove the weapons, and dig out the pulse radio. The message light is on. The first voice I hear when I press Play is Raffe. He sounds raspy and is speaking so softly I have to strain to understand him.

"Professor Holt called a meeting for everyone in the residence. The medical team thinks Enzo will recover."

One of the knots inside me eases.

"We've been given an order to report any sighting of you to the Safety officials or to Professor Holt. Any student who aids in your capture will be rewarded with the presidential internship and a special independent study with Dr. Barnes."

Tomas takes my hand and I squeeze his tight. All students, including my friends, have now been given two reasons to betray me. If Stacia's intent in testing Enzo was to help instead of hinder, I doubt she is still willing to aid in my plan. Not with an easier path to success in front of her. Frowning, I rewind and replay the last part of Raffe's message. "Stay safe. Let me know if I should meet up with Stacia. I'll do what I can to join you tomorrow."

The recording ends but the light doesn't go dark, which means there is at least one more message.

"Raffe didn't ask you to tell him where we're hiding." Tomas frowns. "Did you already tell him how to find this house?"

I shake my head. "I told him about the street, but not which house we'd be in. He didn't ask to confirm the location in case the signal was intercepted." I changed the frequency to one I believe is not typically used, though there is always a chance another pulse radio within reception range could pick up the signal. But there is one person who I know has a pulse radio tuned to the same signal. I push Play again and hear her voice.

"I got Raffe's message. Enzo must have decided to find the recording. Sorry about that, but I guess it's better to know now if he can be trusted. Right?" Stacia's tone is matter-of-fact. "Raffe, if you get this I'll meet you first thing tomorrow morning so you can tell me where to find Cia. See you all soon."

The light goes dark as the message ends. Stacia wants to know where to find me. In order to join in the fight or to report me to Professor Holt and receive her reward for that betrayal?

"Now what do we do?" I ask. "I don't know if we should work with Stacia, and I can't leave a message for Raffe without her getting one, too." Will Raffe believe she is supposed to come here with him tomorrow? "I don't know how to tell him to make sure to leave her behind and not let her know where he's going."

"You can't." Tomas looks at the radio on my hand. "Stacia knows too much to be left behind. She knows who is on our side and who our targets are. If we cut her out of the plan now, she will probably tell Professor Holt and Dr. Barnes everything she knows. By leaving her behind, we'll decide her loyalties for her. And let's face it, we need her."

"But—"

"There's no way we can do this alone. We need all the help we can get, and Stacia's proven she's willing to do whatever it takes. Including turn on us if that's the only way to be rewarded for her actions. It's better to have her with us where we can see what she's doing than wonder what she's up to."

Tomas has a point. I selected Will to be in my Induction group for the same reason, but then I knew we had the same agenda. Stacia wants to be rewarded for her actions. Who she plans on seeking that reward from—Dr. Barnes or the president—is still in question. But at the moment we have no choice in the decision we must make.

Pressing Record, I say, "Both of you be careful. I hope to see you tomorrow. And Raffe, if you have trouble, ask our other friend for help. He might know how to get away without being seen."

"Ian?" Tomas asks.

I nod. "I don't think he'll leave the rebels, but he helped me get away tonight. I think he'd do the same for Raffe and Stacia."

"That still leaves the problem of how Raffe will find us. All the windows are boarded up, so we can't see when they arrive. You said there are people living on this street. Some might not react well if strangers come too close to their dwellings. How are Stacia and Raffe supposed to know which house we're staying at without knocking on doors and alerting the people who live here to our presence?"

Good question. With the people on this street trying to live in the shadows, I'm sure they will not want the attention we could bring on them. To keep a low profile, they might ignore us, but it would be best not to test that hypothesis.

As I consider the problem, I put the radio back in my bag and catch sight of the painting Raffe gave me. Of the symbol he created that gives an identity to what we have planned. Seeing the crisscrossing slashes of yellow gives me an idea. Digging through my bag, I find the black charcoal pencils I carry and say, "I'll be right back."

"What are you going to do?"

"This house is covered with graffiti," I say, handing him the flashlight. "I'm just going to add a little more."

Tomas helps shift the door wide enough so I can slip out. The night is quiet. Clutching the pencils, I walk slowly to the end of the structure. I peer around the edge. The street is empty. Nothing moves. But that could change at any moment, so I have to do this fast.

I carefully make my way to the front of the house, pick a spot on the stoop that is bare, and begin to draw. My artistic abilities are lacking. The lines I create aren't filled with the same raw power as Raffe's. But when I am done, the design in the center of the slightly egg-shaped circle is unmistakable.

Two crossed lightning bolts.

A symbol of power. Of the elimination of ignorance. And of a rebellion that must overcome insurmountable odds in order to succeed. A symbol that combines my past with my future. And the time has come for that future to begin.

CHAPTER 14

When I go inside, I try to hail Zeen on the Transit Communicator. Never have I wanted to hear my brother's voice more. When he doesn't answer, Tomas convinces me that we should sleep. Lying on the blanket with the Communicator near my head and our hands linked, I listen as Tomas's breathing evens out and try to clear my mind so that sleep can find me too. But there are too many worries.

Eventually sleep comes. As always, in my dreams I see the faces of those who died during The Testing. I see those who have fallen since, too, as well as the faces of students back home who I know might suffer the same fate if I fail. In the middle of them all is Enzo. His burned hand reaches out to me as Stacia appears behind him. I jerk awake with the image of Stacia's unreadable smile etched firmly in my mind. It is only the sight of Tomas next to me that allows me to lie back and relax enough to sleep again.

When next I wake, small beams of sunlight peek through

the windows. They bathe the room in a pale glow. For a moment I smile. Then I realize Tomas is not on the blanket beside me. I sit up. Both our bags sit next to the ratty sofa. Seeing them makes me feel better as I get up and go in search. I find him standing next to a freshly cleaned counter in the kitchen, cutting up apples he must have taken out of my bag or brought from his own residence. When he sees me, a smile lights his face.

I take the apple slices he offers and realize the counter is not the only thing Tomas has cleared. The broken table has been removed and the floor has been swept.

"I couldn't sleep, so I decided to tidy up a bit and check out the place, since we might be here for a while."

We both know most likely we will not be here long at all, but it is nice to pretend if just for a moment that we can relax. That this is our house. That we are eating breakfast at the start of a typical day.

"I ran the water in this sink for about five minutes. That seems to have flushed out the worst of the rust buildup. I was worried the noise would wake you. I'm guessing you didn't sleep very well."

I put a hand to my hair and smooth it down. "I look that bad?"

"No." Tomas tucks a strand of wayward hair behind my ear. "But I had trouble sleeping. I figured you might have, too. Yesterday was hard."

I take Tomas's hand. "Today will be harder."

His fingers tighten on mine. "I know."

We sit on the blanket in the living room with the list of names, the apple slices sitting on a chipped but clean plate between us. I treat my leg wound with more ointment. I'm glad when I see it is not as swollen as yesterday, and rewrap it with a fresh bandage. Then, in between bites of apple, I explain what Raffe told me about the people on the list.

Tomas takes a pencil and crosses out the names that I have indicated, leaving the other five. "These are the ones we have to find."

"I think that Raffe's father and Professor Chen have information we need."

"What kind of information?"

I explain about Raffe's sister's disappearance and his search for her and the other students who were Redirected from the University program. "I think The Testing candidates from the first two rounds of tests were Redirected to the same place as Raffe's sister. If we get these officials to tell us what they know, we might be able to find them."

As much as I want to end The Testing, I am equally determined to find those who have not lived up to Dr. Barnes's standards. My eyes glance at the bracelet on my wrist. I no longer have a use for it, but I have yet to take it off. I may have need of it again, and it reminds me of something Ian said on the day I moved into the Government Studies residence. He said the scales of justice symbolize the need for government to balance humanity and kindness with law and justice. Maybe if I find some of the Redirected students alive, it will balance the deaths I have been and will be responsible for.

Taking the recorders out of my bag, I explain, "I think Professor Chen and Official Jeffries know what happens to the Redirected candidates. If we encourage them to talk, we can record the conversation." That evidence might not sway Dr. Barnes's most ardent government supporters to end The Testing, but it will give us what we need to find Raffe's sister and everyone whom Dr. Barnes sent away. "Once we record what they know, we'll restrain them. The president and her Safety officials can be in charge of them after we have completed our mission."

Tomas's eyes darken. "If they are as connected to The Testing as the president believes, keeping them alive isn't an option. Not if we want The Testing to end."

"It has to be."

"Because one of them is Raffe's father?"

"No." Because watching Enzo in agony and seeing Kerrick die has taught me something valuable. While I'm capable of doing what is necessary, I'm not Dr. Barnes. "These officials have failed their country, but it's not up to you and me to determine their punishment. If the president and the leaders of the Debate Chamber want them to be killed for their participation in and perpetuation of The Testing, they will have to be the ones to do it." I have no doubt that the president will arrange for them to die, but their blood will not be on my hands.

"And what about the other three?" Tomas asks. "Do we detain them, too?"

"No." The apple feels like lead in my stomach. "For them we have no choice. Symon's hold on the rebels is too strong. Even if the Debate Chamber voted to remove Dr. Barnes and end The Testing, the attack Dr. Barnes and Symon have orchestrated would still happen. Who knows how many would die if that were allowed to take place? Zeen could be among them. If we want to end The Testing before Symon and Dr. Barnes have a chance to cause more death, we have no other choice. They have to be killed."

Our eyes meet. In Tomas's I see the resolve that matches my own. "Then let's figure out how to do it. I brought some things I think will help."

We empty our bags and lay our supplies on the floor. The apples, rolls, crackers, and cheese we put in the kitchen. Then we assess the rest. If Tomas is surprised by the weapons and explosives I've brought with me, he doesn't show it. However, while he is willing to handle the guns, he avoids looking at the knives and flinches when I touch their handles. I move them to the side so he will not have to be reminded of Zandri every time he sees them.

Some of the items Tomas brought with him I expected—clothes, food, water, and the radio I adjusted for him. But I'm surprised to see specimen containers filled with plants, a mortar and pestle, two small burners, and matches. When he sees me blink, Tomas smiles. "I wasn't sure what we would need, so I grabbed a bunch of plants from the lab before I walked out the door."

I pick up the containers and look inside. "They leave this stuff lying around your residence?" While I understand the need for Biological Engineering majors to have easy access to the genetic materials they are asked to work with, some of the plants, like the Purple Poppy or the Pokeweed Roots, have properties that should be kept under lock and key.

"Some of it." He shrugs. "My guide is in the advanced classes that study the best ways to negate the deadliest of the mutated plants. He prefers to work in a makeshift lab he created in one of his rooms instead of at the stadium. Our head of residence gave him special permission to take plants out of the greenhouse and work with them there. I went to his rooms to ask a question and had Kit drop by to distract him. While he walked her back to her rooms, I grabbed a few things out of his bag."

Tomas and I separate the samples based on properties. There are three plants that will kill when ingested, two that are used most often as sedatives, and several that will be useful if any of us are injured.

I place the deadliest of the samples in the corner of the room. Then I take a seat next to the rest of the pile to figure out how to get the answers we need and eliminate Dr. Barnes, Professor Holt, and Symon—all in the next twenty-four hours. Raffe said that he and Stacia would join as soon as they found a way off campus. If we need them to bring supplies, we have to let them know in time to retrieve the message.

"Zeen will have to eliminate Symon." My chest tightens as I realize that I still haven't heard from Zeen.

"Even if he does," Tomas says, "that leaves the four of us to question two on the president's list and eliminate two others, all in one night." Tomas looks at the array of materials next to us and frowns as he contemplates the difficulty of the task. "I guess we need to think of this like a mathematical proof. We understand the question. Now we have to list everything we know about the subjects, our skills, and the obstacles we face. Maybe then we'll find a way to solve it."

Easier said than done. There are too many variables: the

extra Safety official patrols; our unfamiliarity with areas we will have to visit; no estimate on how long it will take to achieve our goal when we reach each location. It's an impossible equation with our current numbers.

While Tomas goes to the kitchen to grab rolls and water for lunch, I hear a series of clicks. Zeen. I pick up the Transit Communicator, take a deep breath, and press the button.

"Zeen."

"Cia." Just hearing his voice brings emotions I've held at bay to the surface. But I cannot let him hear me sound weak or scared or he will come find me. As much as I want to see my older brother, I need him to stay where he is.

"How are the rebels reacting to the postponing of the president's proposal?"

"According to Symon, everything is going forward as scheduled. If the president really did postpone making her stand on the Debate Chamber floor, word hasn't reached us. The attack is still being planned for the end of this week."

Which means we have to complete our mission before then.

"Anticipation of the attack has emotions running high around here. That's why I haven't been able to contact you. This is the first chance I've had to warn you. You need to get off campus. Part of the attack is going to happen there. I don't want you caught in the crossfire," Zeen says as Tomas walks into the room.

"Already done," I say. "Something happened last night." I shake my head. This isn't the time to talk about Enzo. "Tomas and I were able to get off campus and are currently hiding while we wait for some of our friends."

"Good. That's good. If you stay where you are until after—"

"I'm not staying here. The president has asked me to help end The Testing and save the rebels and I'm going to try. But I can't do it without you."

"You shouldn't be involved in this, Cia."

"Are you kidding? I went through The Testing. I became involved in this the minute they chose me to come to Tosu City. There are things I've been asked to do that I hate, but I'll do them because the alternative is even worse. You can't stop me. But you can help me. Where is Symon now?"

"He's meeting with his team leaders. Ranetta wants to start deploying the attack groups of her rebel faction around the city tonight so they'll blend in. They don't want anyone to question their presence before Friday, when the attack begins."

Tomas takes the Communicator and asks, "Can you get close enough to Ranetta to talk to her?"

"Tomas? I would think if anyone could talk Cia out of this you could." When Tomas says nothing, I give his arm a squeeze. "Ranetta's pretty busy right now," Zeen continues. "I doubt she has time for someone like me."

"If you find a man named Dreu Owens, I bet you can convince him to get her to make time for someone from Five Lakes. He's Magistrate Owens's son, and we have reason to believe he's working with the rebellion. Find him and he might be able to help you stop the attack or get you close enough to permanently remove Symon."

"We need you to eliminate Symon, Zeen," I say before my brother can reply. "None of us will be able to get close enough to kill him. We can take out Dr. Barnes and the others on the list, but Symon controls the direction of too many of the rebels. You have to take charge of his removal. Otherwise who knows what will happen next."

Tomas and I look at each other as the silence on the other end stretches on. "Zeen?" I ask quietly. When he doesn't answer I say his name again. "Are you there?"

"I'm here. Dad used to talk about Dreu. He liked to follow Dad around to learn how to engineer new plants. Dad said I rivaled Dreu in the asking-questions department. If Dreu's here, I'll find a way to enlist his help. If not, don't worry. I'll kill Symon myself."

I close my eyes as feelings storm through me. Relief that Zeen will help. Pride that he is no longer speaking to me as if I am a child. And sorrow for making my brother vow to take a life.

I want to thank him but the words stick in my throat. How do you thank someone for promising to kill? I know that by doing so Zeen could die, and if he is successful, it will forever change his own life.

Swallowing hard, I tamp down the tears and focus. "We're waiting for the rest of our team to arrive. If everything works out, we'll begin our attack tonight."

"Then I'll try to be ready on my end. Signal me three times if you're starting your assault. With luck, I'll have found Dreu and will be in touch before then. And Cia . . . be careful."

"You too."

The Communicator crackles for a moment and then there is quiet. Worry festers deep in me when I think about the danger Zeen is in.

Since we still don't know how many of us will be working

to find our targets, I concentrate on one problem we are certain of. The extra Safety patrols that are traveling the Tosu City streets. As Tomas and I discuss this, I look at our supplies and have an idea. Since they have been instructed to keep an eye out for me, Tomas, and anyone we are with, the best way to go unnoticed is to make them think they have already found us.

Putting the three explosives containers I removed from the president's storage room in front of me, I explain my idea. The Safety officials will have been told about the explosion in my room. If they hear an explosion somewhere in the city, I'm betting they'll feel compelled to look for me nearby. We just have to make sure that the explosions occur in an area far away from our targets and that we are gone before they detonate.

For the next few minutes, Tomas and I go through the house looking for items we can use to make a timing device for the bombs we plan to build. A timer is trickier to create than the switch I used in my first bomb. That switch was manually operated. This device requires a remote so whoever places it has time to escape the blast. While I have never attached a timing mechanism to an explosive, I've helped my father create timers for irrigation systems. The principle behind them is the same and not all that complicated, but I'm not sure we have access to all the components we need.

Tomas and I find the electrical circuitry box in the kitchen closet and flip the main power switch to the Off position just in case. We widen a hole in the wall of the smallest bedroom and remove wires, circuitry, and switches. These will be valuable, but we still need a timer to trigger the detonation.

We go through the house again. When we come up empty, I unclasp the solar watch that I have hanging from the strap on my bag. I had hoped to find something else to use so that I would have a watch during our attacks. I will have to do without. So will Tomas. When he sees me opening the watch's back panel, he offers his identical watch. Removing the inner workings, I find it fairly easy to locate and detach the alarm wires. Without a soldering tool, it takes more time and some experimentation with the Bunsen burner Tomas brought to attach new wires to the leads. I hook up the wires to one of the coil relays we salvaged from the house's electrical system. When that is done, we construct a solar igniter similar to the one I built yesterday and complete the circuit with one of the solar batteries Tomas brought with him.

Once both timers are built, we decide not to attach them to the explosives just yet. We'll keep the timer separate until we need to arm the explosives.

Now that we potentially have something that will distract the Safety officials, we discuss the other issues we face. Our unfamiliarity with the areas in which our targets live is a problem. Stacia is similarly hindered. Raffe knows the city better than we do, so he will have to act as our guide. But as Tomas points out, no matter how effective our distraction is, there's no way all four of us can travel through the city unnoticed. We'll have to split into two teams. I will lead one. The other . . . I guess we will have to wait and see if both Raffe and Stacia make it here before we decide who will take leadership of the other. Tomas would be the natural choice, but I don't know how he will feel about separating from me. Regardless of who takes charge of the second team, we will have the pulse radios. Raffe will be able to help give directions if the second team gets turned around, and if something goes wrong, we should be able to let the other team know.

Knowing we will be divided into two teams, I take out my radio and record a message for Raffe to bring another flashlight if possible. While we wait for Stacia and Raffe to arrive, Tomas and I sort through the rest of our gear. Each of us takes two of the recorders that I lifted from the president's fifth-floor room. Then we each place a bottle of water, some food, and one of the timers and canisters into our bags. We also take another look at the list and information sheets the president provided. Based on the coordinates of each personal dwelling, we decide to split the targets into two groups. One team will go after Professor Holt and Professor Chen, who appear to live less than a quarter of a mile apart. The other team will target Official Jeffries and Dr. Barnes.

"I think that's as far as we can plan until the others arrive. If they don't make it, we will have to split up. If they do arrive, the most logical approach would be to have Raffe on the team assigned to his father, since he grew up in that area and knows it well. But Raffe might not be able to handle that. We won't know until we ask him," Tomas says as we sit on the floor with our hands clasped between us. All day we have found ways to touch each other. A brush of the arm. A kiss on the cheek. I know we are storing up memories in case one of us is not here tomorrow. I can see in the intensity of Tomas's gaze that he has accepted that possibility.

Tomas glances at one of the timers and sighs. "It's starting to get late and there are still a few things I want to do before the two of them get here." After brushing a quick kiss on my lips, he stands and grabs the mortar and pestle, the burner, and several of the plant samples and disappears into the kitchen. He comes back a moment later and takes the sample containers I placed to the side. Then he leaves the room again.

I rise and start to follow to ask him what he is working on. But then I stop. I trust Tomas to tell me what he is doing when he is ready. And I am glad for the solitude because I, too, have accepted that I may not live to see tomorrow, and so there is something I must do.

I take one of my charcoal pencils and several sheets of blank, gray recycled paper from the bottom of my bag. For a while I just stare at the pages. Then I begin to write. I don't know if these letters will make it to the intended recipients, but writing them helps organize my thoughts.

To my father I explain that I failed in heeding his warning. That while I cannot live my life without trust, I have learned better whom to give that gift to and that the things I do now I do with those who believe what I believe. They, like me, cannot know what I know and allow a broken process to continue. I apologize if the choices I've made make him unhappy or cause him and the rest of my family trouble, but explain that I cannot live my life pretending what I know is not real. He taught me that even the most corrupt patch of earth can be transformed into a place where living things thrive as long as someone is dedicated to that cause. This is my cause. I cannot make plants grow, but I can commit myself to removing the corruption in this soil. Maybe if I am lucky, something strong and good will grow in its place.

Tears stain the page as I sign my name and move on to the

letter for my mother. Hers is shorter but filled with love, as is the one for my brothers, including Zeen. Has he found Dreu Owens? Have they talked to Ranetta yet?

Forcing those thoughts to the side, I turn my attention to the final page and write. I have wiped away evidence of my tears and am sliding that paper into the side pocket of Tomas's bag when he returns from the kitchen with four water bottles, two in each hand. He puts down the ones in his right hand, takes my pencil, and draws a circle on the side of those two.

"This one contains a steeped mixture of the new strain of Valerian and lavender."

That combination should relax muscles and reduce pain. It could also cause some people to fall into a deep sleep. It should help if one of us is badly injured.

He puts one bottle in his bag, hands me the other, and then picks up the other two and marks each one with a large black X. "These have a combination of Rosary Pea, Pokeweed, and Oleander. This second bottle probably won't be needed, but I thought it might be good to have in case of an emergency."

I start to ask what kind of an emergency he envisions, but before the words can pass my lips, I understand. This bottle is not meant for the people on President Collindar's list. It, too, is meant for us. If we are caught by Dr. Barnes or the Safety officials, Tomas intends to kill himself, and from the way he looks at me I know he wants me to do the same.

I swallow hard and force myself to breathe as shock turns to horror. Whether we succeed or not, our lives could be taken. But while I accept that might happen, I cannot and will not make the choice to end my own life. To choose death is to say I am done fighting. That I give up not only on myself but on everything I love. I think of the letters I wrote and know I could never willingly abandon my family.

However, though I am determined to fight to the end, Tomas isn't me. I have seen the guilt and despair building inside him since The Testing. What happened at the stadium only darkened his sorrow. A seed of anger has kept him going, but Tomas's fuse is reaching its end. Once the fire is extinguished, his drive to fight will be gone, too. Especially if he thinks the fight has been in vain.

So, as much as I want to tell Tomas to leave the bottles behind or to promise not to use them, I don't. Instead, I take the bottle he offers and place it in the side pocket of my bag so it cannot be confused with the others. Taking a deep breath, I walk back to Tomas, stand on my tiptoes, and place my lips against his, infusing the kiss with all the love and understanding I can.

I barely register the click from the Transit Communicator as Tomas pulls me closer. It is only when the sound comes again that I understand.

"Zeen is calling." I feel embarrassment heat my cheeks as I step out of Tomas's embrace and reach for the Communicator. "Did you find Dreu?" I ask Zeen. "Is he there?"

"I asked a couple of people in my group. If Dreu's here, he's probably with Ranetta. A few of my friends are going to ask around for me since I told them Dreu and I are from the same colony. From what I can tell, he's been working on medical research and syphoning off resources for the rebels whenever possible. It sounds like he's not here very often."

Which means Zeen will be on his own. "Can you find a way to talk to Ranetta without him? Maybe if you say you know Dreu?"

"I'll try, but I'm not sure anyone is going to let me through to see her. Not now that things are so crazy. Groups of rebels are already starting to head into Tosu. If I'm going to get close to Symon, I need to do it soon. Otherwise he might leave the base. Once that happens, there's no telling where he'll go. But if I can get through to Ranetta before then, I'll let you know. Rumors are running rampant that some of the attack groups have been given different schedules based on whether they are in Symon's or Renatta's faction, so the tension is pretty high. When are you planning on starting your attack?"

Until the others arrive, we cannot know for sure. But with the rebels being deployed and the chance that the order to attack may be delivered before the scheduled time, there is no other option but to say, "We'll do it tonight. We plan on setting off a diversion to pull away the Safety patrols. Once you're done with Symon, you should come here," I say, and I read off the coordinates on the Transit Communicator. Zeen doesn't know Tosu City at all. Unless he manages to convince Ranetta that killing Symon is necessary, he will be viewed as a traitor in the camp. He will need somewhere to hide.

"If I finish and get off this base, I'm not going to hide. I'll be coming to help you."

Not if I can prevent it. Since he won't know where to find me, I consider this a promise he can't fulfill.

"I have to get going, but Cia . . ."

"Yes, Zeen?"

His words are barely a whisper when he says, "I'm not sure when we'll talk again, but I wanted to say—I love you. Be careful. Okay?"

Pressure builds in my chest and behind my eyes. "I love you, too, Zeen. And Zeen . . . don't do anything crazy."

"Who, me?" His bright laugh makes me smile. "I'll see you soon."

"I'm counting on it," I say. Despite the click from the Communicator, I continue to cradle it in my hands. As if holding it will somehow keep Zeen safe or bring him closer to me. Tomas tries to put his arms around my shoulders. I know he wants to offer me his support and comfort, but I pull away and walk to the other side of the room. While I love Tomas, I need to be alone with my thoughts of my brother.

I'm not sure how long I stand holding the Communicator, but the shadows on the floor have shifted when I hear the sound of low voices outside the boarded-up front door.

Someone is here.

"Tomas," I whisper. When he doesn't answer, I cross the floor and whisper his name again.

"What's wrong?" he asks as he appears in the doorway to the living room.

Putting my finger to my lips, I wait for the voices to come again. When they do, Tomas stiffens. Unfortunately, they are muted, making it impossible to know if they belong to Safety officials, our friends, or someone from the neighborhood who has grown curious about our presence. Slowly, I cross back to my bag, slide the Communicator inside, and reach for my gun. The voices are gone, but I notice the indicator light on my pulse radio is lit. I show the light to Tomas, who nods for me to press Play.

"We're outside. And we need to come in."

Raffe.

I put down the radio but keep the gun firmly in my hand as we go into the kitchen and open the back door. The sunlight is intense. I have to blink to focus my vision. When I do, I see Raffe and Stacia standing in front of me. Raffe is balancing their two bicycles, and after one look at Stacia it becomes clear why.

She has been shot.

Stacia cradles one arm to her chest. The hand she uses to protect her injured arm is streaked with blood. Her face is pale and she sways on her feet. I hand my gun to Tomas and lead her to the blanket on the floor. I ease off her jacket and use my pocketknife to cut away her shirt from just above the elbow so I can get a better look.

I see Raffe and Tomas standing in the doorway and ask, "What happened? Did a Safety official try to detain you?"

Raffe and Stacia look at each other as Raffe says, "Not exactly. Ian scouted the area and let us know the Safety patrols were concentrated near the main entrance so we could go to the north side and get around them. He gave me an idea of the best path to take and went back to our residence to keep the rebel students there distracted so they wouldn't notice that I'd left. Stacia and I were so busy avoiding the officials that we didn't realize two rebel students had followed us."

"It's my fault." Stacia winces. "They were fourth-year medical students. Both of them were known for hazing the first years. So I didn't think anything of it when they followed me out of the residence. I went into the History building so they'd think I went to class. When they walked away, I thought they'd lost interest in me. But they were waiting for us on the road outside the main campus exit."

While I am fairly certain Raffe has at least one weapon in his possession, I am amazed he was able to find a way to use it and get away after being taken by surprise. When I say so, Raffe shifts uncomfortably and says, "Actually, we didn't get away from them on our own. We had some help."

"Ian?" Tomas asks.

"Me," says a familiar voice from behind us.

Dread grips me as I turn toward the doorway in time to see an unmistakable figure stride into the room, wearing a wide smile.

Will.

CHAPTER 15

GREEN EYES MEET mine. For a moment I can't breathe as I remember the way those eyes glittered with calculation during The Testing when Will shot Tomas and turned his gun on me. I had thought he was my friend. I had thought he was on my side. I had been wrong.

I drop Stacia's arm. My fingers wrap around the wooden butt of my gun as I stand. No one says a word as I raise the gun, wrap my other hand around the handle for balance, and take aim.

Will doesn't flinch. He doesn't look to the others for help. His eyes stay fixed on me. Waiting for whatever I decide to do next. My brain tells me to shoot. I cannot allow Will to betray me again. I won't let Zeen be caught as a rebel traitor and killed. Will cannot be trusted. There is no choice but to eliminate him.

But I do not fire. Because for some reason Will saved Stacia and Raffe. Just as he saved Tomas and me on the plains when we were attacked. Why? During The Testing, Will decided to eliminate the competition in order to better his chances of being one of the twenty selected for the University. He could have allowed Roman to kill Tomas. He could have waited to see if I had the nerve to kill before stepping in to save us. He could have stood by and allowed us to die.

But he didn't. Ever since my memories returned, that fact has haunted me. Will wanted us dead. Yet he saved us despite his intent to kill. And now here he stands, calmly awaiting my decision after coming to the aid of two of my friends.

No, I am wrong. Though there's a lack of emotion on Will's face, he is not calm. The grip he has on the strap of his bag has turned his knuckles white. That and the rapid breaths he takes speak of the emotions swirling beneath the surface. But he doesn't speak. He doesn't plead for his life.

"You remember." The words are barely a whisper, but the way Will flinches tells me he has heard. Still, I say the words again in case I am wrong. This time my voice is firm. As is my need to understand this boy who has done good even as he has deceived. "You remember The Testing."

"No one remembers their Testing," Stacia snaps.

But Will doesn't look at her. His eyes hold mine while he says, "Not exactly."

"But you remember something," Tomas says, taking a step closer to Will.

Despite Tomas's obvious anger, Will doesn't move. His voice is steady when he says, "I remember enough to know that I've earned whatever punishment you and Cia think I deserve. Whatever you decide, I'll accept."

"What are you all talking about?" Stacia asks, trying to

climb to her feet. Raffe hurries to help her up, but she pushes him away. "Why would Cia and Tomas want to punish you, Will? You haven't done anything wrong."

"Yes." His voice is quiet but firm. "I have."

It is that calm acceptance of what he has done and the punishment he deserves that makes my finger ease on the trigger. If Will were angry or defiant or belligerent I would shoot. But I find myself remembering the boy I first met during The Testing. The one who heard me confess that I didn't finish one of my tests. Instead of ridiculing me or rolling his eyes as so many of the other candidates would have done, he thanked me for being willing to admit the truth. I saw Will's heart break when his brother didn't make it through the first Testing phase. I watched as he killed the boy who was about to kill Tomas in the fourth test, and I know that it's thanks to his insistence that I was freed from the locked metal box Damone wished me to die in during Induction.

Which is the real Will? The one who coldly killed or the one who helped me live? I don't know.

Slowly, I lower my gun. Tomas frowns as I ask him to get me a bottle of water from the kitchen so we can tend to Stacia's wound, but he does as I ask.

As Tomas leaves the room, Stacia shifts, winces, and says, "I don't understand. How do you remember your Testing? No one else does." Stacia looks at me. "Do you? Do both of you?" she adds as Tomas walks back through the doorway. Anger flashes from her eyes.

I choose my words with care. "During The Testing, I discovered a way to record some of what happened. I found the recording and started to remember."

"What about Tomas?"

"The memory-erasure procedure never worked on me." He sits down next to her and wets a cloth with water. "I've always remembered."

Tomas starts to wash Stacia's wound but she pulls away. Jerking her head toward Will, she asks, "What did he do?"

"I killed people during the fourth test," Will says. "Then I tried to kill both of them."

"Well, I guess that tells us you need to work on your aim." Stacia winces again but jerks her arm away when Tomas tries to tend to it. "How about me?" she asks, glaring in my direction. "Did I do anything that would make you want to shoot me? Or aren't I allowed to know what happened?"

"I don't know," I answer truthfully. "I only talked to you once during The Testing. You were with Vic and Tracelyn during the fourth test. You and Vic completed that test. Tracelyn never did."

"Do you think I killed her?" Stacia asks. The resentment has faded from her eyes, leaving only pain behind. Pain from the wound or from the thought of committing the murder of someone she knew? It's impossible to say.

"I don't know," I answer truthfully again.

"But you think I must have. Otherwise, why else would I be here, right?" Before I can reply, she turns to Tomas and asks for the wet cloth so she can clean her wound, saying that she is the most qualified owing to her field of study. Tomas hands her the cloth but stays nearby as she begins to dab the blood away.

The set of Stacia's jaw tells me she is done asking questions for now, so I turn back to Will and ask, "When did your Testing memories return?"

Will shrugs and sits on the ground next to the wall. "Right after Dr. Barnes told us we'd been accepted to the University. When I looked around and didn't see Gill in the room, I knew something was wrong."

I remember that Will had to be restrained and was taken away by officials when he realized his brother wasn't there. It took days before he returned.

While Will explains the flashes of memories he experienced, Stacia lets Tomas help finish cleaning up the bloody wound. I shift closer so I can see it. The hole made by the bullet isn't large. Perhaps a half inch in diameter. Maybe less. But the swelling and red rim around the injury are concerning. As is the blood that continues to trickle out. Since this is the only puncture in Stacia's arm, I have to conclude that the bullet is lodged inside.

Stacia comes to the same conclusion and decides to bandage up the arm instead of doing anything more to treat it. "I can't dig the bullet out myself. And even if I could I'm sure it would do more harm than good. I wish I had broken into the residence pharmacy and taken some of the good pain meds. All I have are some anti-inflammatories."

"I mixed some herbal remedies with water," Tomas says, taking the bottle marked with a circle out of his bag. "It'll take away the pain, but there's a chance it will also put you to sleep."

Stacia looks at the bottle and shakes her head. That simple movement makes her wince. In a strained voice she says, "I think I'm going to need a clear head for this. But if you don't mind, I'll hold on to it for later."

When Tomas hands her the bottle, she opens it and smells the contents. After a moment, she asks him to pour some of the liquid on one of the bandages she brought with her. I pull the ointment from my bag and hand it to Stacia for her to use on the wound as well. The easing of tension in her shoulders tells me that the combination might be enough to help get her through what is to come.

Before we discuss that, there is still something I have to know. "Why did you tell Enzo about the pulse radio in my room?"

"If I give the wrong answer are you going to threaten to shoot me like you did with Will?" She gives me the same smile I remember from The Testing dining hall. "Is this my test, Cia?"

"Would you pass?" I ask, conscious of the gun in my hand. "Not only was Enzo burned and almost killed, but it happened in my room. If it weren't for Ian, I would have been detained by officials. I might even be dead right now. You set that up. I think it's fair to ask why."

Stacia looks around the room. All eyes are on her. "When we went into the library, Enzo started asking a lot of questions about you. He said he was worried that you might be doing something that could get you in trouble with Professor Holt and he wanted to help. I figured it was the perfect opportunity. You hadn't come up with a test, and there wasn't any more time to waste. So I told Enzo you had found some recording that you thought was important and were trying to decide whether to turn it over to the president. He went after the recording and proved he wasn't on our side. I'm sorry he got hurt, but I did us a favor."

"All you proved was that Enzo wanted to see what was on

that recording," I say. "You have no idea what his motives were."

"Cia's right." Will speaks up from his spot in the corner. "Enzo could have been worried enough about Cia that he was willing to risk punishment in order to learn what trouble she might be facing."

"Or he could have been spying on her and was looking to collect a reward for turning information over to Dr. Barnes," Stacia shoots back.

And we may never know. As much as I want to believe Enzo will pull through, I saw how badly injured he was. It is impossible to imagine the pain he will endure and how he will survive it in order to come back from that.

"Worrying about what's been done isn't going to help us now," Raffe says. "Enzo will recover or he won't. We can't change that outcome. The only thing we can do is learn from the mistakes made and make sure we don't make the same ones in the future." When no one contradicts him, he adds, "The only way to prevent something like this from happening again is to agree that one person makes the final call on how we move forward from here. And the only reason we're having this discussion is because of Cia. She pushed for information about The Testing and found the truth behind Symon and the rebellion. The president asked for her help. Cia is our leader. From my position, whatever decision she makes on something should be final. Does everyone else agree?"

Will is the first to nod. Not that what he thinks truly matters, since he is not a part of this. Not really. Tomas studies Raffe and then gives his assent, which leaves only Stacia. I still do not know whether she believes in this cause or if she is only doing it for a reward she thinks she'll be given once it's over. Whatever her reason, it is clear she is not happy when she sighs and says, "Fine. Now can we talk about what we plan to do next? We don't have much time."

I push my worries about Stacia to the side. Now that the others have arrived, we are faced with two unanticipated problems. Will's presence and Stacia's injury. Tonight will be physically and emotionally challenging. I don't believe Stacia can handle it in her condition. However, I am certain she won't allow herself to be left behind. And from the way Tomas is acting, it's clear he is unwilling to discuss strategy with Will in the room. But we really don't have a choice.

Raffe doesn't seem to have the same concern since he asks, "So now what?"

Tomas and I look at each other. I can tell he doesn't want to talk, but as this group's leader the decision is mine.

Taking a deep breath, I tell them about my brother and what is happening now in the rebel camp. Raffe and Stacia merely nod when I mention Zeen. They listen as, pulling out the list, I explain the strategy Tomas and I have devised. Two teams. Four targets. All to be reached between dusk and dawn, starting tonight.

"But we might have to revise that plan now that Stacia is injured," I admit. "Maybe Ian . . ."

"No." Stacia shifts and winces but says, "I'm going. You can't force me to stay behind."

"She's right," Raffe says. "We need all of us to make this work. Even if we could get word to Ian, I don't think he'd leave campus. He's determined to talk to as many of the rebel students as he can and sway them to ignore Symon's orders. If Stacia thinks she can handle this, then she should try. If she starts having problems then we'll deal with it."

"Fair enough," Stacia agrees. "So which one of you is going to be lucky enough to team up with me?"

"I will," Tomas offers. "Out of all of us, I'd be the best one to help with the pain if it gets too bad."

That's not the real reason. The look Tomas gives me as I start to object tells me I'm right. Any one of us would be able to apply ointment or dab on some of the plant-doctored solution that Tomas has created. But while I am sure Tomas would prefer to face what this night will bring together, as we faced so much of The Testing, doing so would force us to trust the two members of the other team to do exactly as they say they will. Tomas does not fully trust Raffe. I do not trust Stacia. Knowing that, this pairing is the only one that makes sense.

Raffe asks, "Who's going after Symon?"

"Who's this Symon?" Will asks.

"He's someone who works with Dr. Barnes." Considering that enough explanation, I turn back to Raffe. "My brother is taking care of Symon."

Raffe studies me for a moment and nods. "Even without Symon, I'm not sure we can cover all the ground that needs to be covered in this time frame." He glances at the map I drew earlier with the locations of the targets. "If we want to draw the Safety officials away, the explosions will have to happen in the unrevitalized area on the other side of the city. Just avoiding the Safety officials is going to make getting there a challenge.

Especially since they must be looking for all of us by now. Then add in the time to scout locations where we're certain no one will be injured and set the explosions . . ."

"You need someone the Safety officials aren't looking for to set the explosions," Will says from the corner. "I volunteer." When I shake my head, Will says, "The Safety officials aren't searching for me. I can make it through the city faster than you can. We saw the outskirts of that area of the city during Induction, so I know where I'm going. And no one will think twice if they see me after the explosions go off. They'll be looking for the four of you, only you won't be on the city streets. When I'm done, I'll come back here and be ready to help if you need it."

I hate that he makes sense. If he were anyone else . . . "You're not a part of this," I say.

"Of course I am. They took my brother. And even if they hadn't, I'd still be part of this." His normally pale face is flushed with passion. "I know I gave you reason to doubt me. The Testing showed me things about myself. Things I'm capable of doing. But it's because of what I learned that I know I can handle this job."

I wait for Tomas, Raffe, or Stacia to say something, but they don't. Stacia's flat stare says it all. I am the leader. I decide. I feel the weight of this decision as it settles on my shoulders. Unless I ask for their opinions, they will leave it up to me. Me. The youngest of all of us. Yet, one thing I have learned since coming to Tosu City is that age does not guarantee better decisions or stronger leadership. The ability to put aside personal agendas and decide what is best for the whole does. That is what I now have to do.

Do I trust Will?

No.

Do I believe he can accomplish what he has volunteered to handle?

Yes. As long as he chooses to carry through with the plan. However, if he decides to run to the nearest University official in order to better his position after he graduates from the University, we will all pay the price.

I close my eyes, take a deep breath, and open them. "Tomas and I built the timers this morning." I get up and cross to where the timers and explosives sit. After picking up one of the timers and a canister, I walk over to Will. "You'll need to attach them when you get to the sites. One needs to be set to detonate at seven. The other should be placed a mile away and explode a half-hour later. That should convince the Safety officials to focus their search on that side of the city." Handing him the timer, I add, "We also have a third explosive that doesn't have a timer—"

"You can't possibly want him to do this. Think of everything he's done to us."

"I know what he's done, Tomas. But I also remember what I've done too," I say. "What we've both done. Dr. Barnes and The Testing are the reasons Will was put in a position to commit those acts. Will's here. He's capable. He deserves a chance to prove that he isn't the person Dr. Barnes's tests turned him into."

All of us deserve that chance.

"I'll show Will how to arm the timers." Deliberately, I turn my back on Tomas, signaling the discussion is closed. I can feel his anger and hurt. But if I am to be our leader, I cannot allow my feelings for Tomas to get in the way. So I demonstrate the timer to Will and explain how it is to be used with the canister.

Will explains the process back to me, asks several questions, and then checks the watch he wears on his wrist. "It's getting late, and I have a lot of ground to travel. I need to get going. If these things are as loud as I think they'll be, you'll hear whether or not I'm successful." As Will carefully packs the canisters in his bag, I walk to our stash of supplies and select a long, sharp knife and a loaded handgun.

"Here," I say.

I can feel Tomas's eyes on me as I hand Will the weapons. Will's hand closes over the butt of the gun and he tucks it in his jacket pocket. The ammunition goes into the side pocket of his bag, along with the knife and its smooth, deadly blade. I take Stacia's radio from her and pass it to Will. His hand closes over mine and stays there.

"Thank you." His expression is grim. Determined. "I won't fail you this time. I promise."

"Be safe," I say as he takes the pulse radio out of my hand. "We're counting on you."

"I know." Will turns away from me and walks to Raffe to ask his opinion about strategic locations to place the canisters.

Then, armed with Raffe's instructions and the weapons I have given him, he walks to the doorway, turns, and smiles. In that smile I see the boy who befriended me during the first test. That's the boy I am counting on.

"I'll let you know when I'm in position," he says. With a wink, he turns and heads out the door.

"How's that feel?" Tomas asks behind me.

When I look over, I see Stacia flexing her arm and nodding. "Better. I would never have thought of putting some crushed Valerian directly on the wound."

"That's why you doctor types need biological engineers to help you come up with the new drugs." Tomas smiles.

She smiles back. "Well, I hope Enzo's getting some of this right now." She looks at me. "I really did think I was doing the right thing by testing him. I never thought he'd break into your room and get hurt. Otherwise, I would have warned you first."

Her regret is for causing me trouble. Not for the injury to Enzo but for choosing a path without checking with me first. She believed I was taking too long to make a decision and did what she thought was necessary for us to succeed. I will have to remember that as we move forward. To keep Stacia from making decisions on her own, especially ones I do not agree with, I will have to make choices with more speed. If we come through this, I doubt I will ever be able to call Stacia my friend again. But just because I personally cannot feel comfortable with her doesn't mean she is incapable of doing what I need her to accomplish. If I have to be a stronger leader to make her do it, then that's what I will do.

Straightening my shoulders, I say, "We have two hours until Will sets off the first explosion. We need to be ready. We need to decide which team—"

"No, we don't," Raffe interrupts. "My house will be harder to find for someone who doesn't know the area. Besides, I need to be the one to deal with my father. Tomas and Stacia will take the other two targets. There are several landmarks that will help you know you're on the right track."

For the next ten minutes, Raffe gives Tomas and Stacia directions to their two targets. Professor Chen's house is near a small pond. Professor Holt lives only three blocks away in a large house surrounded by a tall wooden fence.

"Professor Holt never travels anywhere on foot. If her skimmer is parked in front of her house, you'll know she's home. If you can find the key to the skimmer, use it. Safety officials won't stop a University vehicle."

Tomas and Stacia ask many questions. I try to hand the Transit Communicator over to Tomas, but he shakes his head and says I need it to connect with my brother. Tomas says that if he and Stacia need help, they will send a message for Raffe. His knowledge of the city is more useful than the Communicator, which can't tell them what landmarks to look for.

It is six-forty by the time our bags are packed, plans have been coordinated, and Stacia and Tomas feel confident they can navigate the city streets quickly. I hold the Transit Communicator, hoping to hear from my brother. Instead, the message light on the pulse radio blinks to life. Will. The first charge is in place and ready to fire. Time for us to go.

Raffe and Stacia walk to the kitchen to get their bikes as I stare at the letters for my family that sit on the floor. When I look up, Tomas hasn't moved. He just looks at me. The silence stretches between us. In a few minutes we will separate. Once that happens, there's a chance we might not be together again.

"I love you." I cross over to him and look up into the face that is so dear to me, memorizing the curve of his jaw and the shape of his eyes. Standing beside him, I am struck all over again by how tall he is. How safe he makes me feel. I cling to that feeling as I reach out and take his hand. He stiffens but does not pull away. And when his fingers tighten around mine, I feel complete.

"I love you too," he says. The anger is gone. Only concern remains. "Stay safe."

"We'll see each other soon," I promise as we walk outside.

The sun is fading as we wheel our bikes out of the back door and around to the street. A child playing in a yard down the block sees us and runs up the stairs and inside. I look at the Communicator in my hand. Zeen still hasn't contacted me. Is he alive? Has he killed Symon? Have the rebels started a search for him or are they even now spreading out among the Tosu City streets, waiting for a sign to begin their attack? Worry gnaws my heart, but there is nothing I can do but hope he is safe and focus on what must be done.

I climb onto my bike. My gun is in my jacket pocket. Tomas takes my hand as the four of us stand on the road, waiting. I glance at the house next to us and in the fading light see the symbol etched on the stoop. Two lightning bolts. Two teams. The end of ignorance. The beginning of hope.

I glance at the watch on Raffe's wrist. Five minutes until seven.

I see a door to one of the houses open a crack. Part of me considers waving so they'll know we aren't threatening, but I understand that showing they have been spotted will only cause more anxiety. So I keep my eyes focused on the time.

Four minutes.

Three.

Two.

Somewhere to the west there is a rumble. The signal that the rebellion — the one Dr. Barnes never intended to truly exist — has begun.

CHAPTER 16

I LOOK DOWN at our joined hands and then up at Tomas as I try to memorize everything about this moment. We got through The Testing together. To succeed now we have to part.

"Are you ready?" Raffe whispers.

I swallow hard and after one more moment force myself to let go of Tomas's hand. "Keep your radio close. Leave a message if you're in trouble or if you've finished one of the tasks."

Tomas and Stacia nod and point their bikes to the north. I watch them ride down the block as I press the Call button on the Communicator to tell Zeen we are starting our part. When the two of them ride to the left and disappear from view, I turn my bike and head in the opposite direction, trying not to think about what might happen to Tomas.

Raffe leads the way. As the shadows lengthen, we zigzag around potholes, turn west, and keep riding. I catch sight of the white markings on a skimmer door in the distance. The vehicle belongs to a Safety official. But it never slows or turns in our direction. Whatever distraction Will has provided is enough to keep the skimmer pointed toward the west.

Raffe continues the fast pace. We spot another Safety skimmer in the distance and slow down. It, too, passes without incident. I wonder if Zeen is still at the rebel base and whether Tomas and Stacia have avoided the patrols as Raffe turns down the next street. This one is filled with large houses painted pale shades of blue or gray with white trim that shines bright even in the dimming light. Each structure sits on a plot of grass that is a healthy shade of green. The trees here are young but grow straight and true. Down the block kids race around a lawn, playing tag. Someone yells for them to stay close to the house.

A door opens to one of the blue houses. Raffe waves at the elderly woman who steps out the front door onto the porch and then looks at me as the lady waves back. "That's Mrs. Haglund. She's not wearing her glasses, so most likely she hasn't the slightest idea who I am. Even if she does, she's hard of hearing. I doubt she has a clue what's going on in Tosu or that Safety officials are looking for us. My parents' house is this way."

We turn down another block. The houses here are even larger than the ones we just passed and are more widely spaced, so that each one has an expanse of grass and trees on every side. Raffe stops as we reach the third house. He gets off his bike and starts wheeling it up a wide walkway that runs alongside the blue structure made distinctive by the large white pillars that frame the front door. He walks with his shoulders straight. His gait is unhurried. It's as if he belongs here. Which I suppose he does. I try to mimic his behavior as we lean our bikes up against the rear wall of the house.

"My father is typically in his office at this time of night."

"What about your mother?" I ask.

"Once we all graduated, my father decided that they no longer needed to use power after the designated hours the rest of the city follows. So she goes to a friend's house after dinner and doesn't come home until well after nine. They're the only two who live here. We should have time to do what needs to be done."

Raffe glances at his watch. Seven-twenty. Ten minutes until the next explosion is set to go off. I check the pulse radio. No messages. Are Tomas and Stacia standing at the back door of Professor Chen's house right now? Is Tomas turning the handle and stepping inside a kitchen as we do? Raffe closes the door behind me, reaches into his bag, and pulls out his gun. I engage the recorder and hand it to him. Nodding, he slides it into his pocket and then waits until I clutch my own gun before moving forward. I follow. Through the kitchen into a dark hallway that opens into a large living area.

Every step we take echoes in my head. I listen for sounds that Raffe's father is home, but aside from our breathing and my pounding heart, I hear nothing. Raffe leads me down another darkened hall. He doesn't turn on the flashlight as he moves confidently toward a closed door, beneath which a sliver of light glows. I hear papers rustling and ignore the way my muscles tense as I think through the strategy Raffe and I discussed. When we reach the door, Raffe touches my arm. I feel around the wall for the door he said was just outside his father's office.

There. I find the handle, turn it, and slip inside a small bathroom. I leave the door open so I am ready to act if necessary, and wait for Raffe to take the next step. My breathing comes fast as I hear a handle shift, a door creak open, and Raffe say, "Hi, Dad."

"Raffe." In the deep voice I hear surprise and relief. "Verna said . . . well, it doesn't matter now. I'll contact her and let her know that you're here and not off somewhere causing trouble with those colony students."

"What kind of trouble?" Raffe asks.

"It's not important. What's important is that you're here and that Verna and Jedidiah will see for themselves that you aren't involved in this mess. Of course, you should have known better than to leave campus when you're forbidden to do so. Your lack of judgment has caused people to question your loyalty. Do you know how that reflects on me?"

"I know where my loyalties lie."

"Be that as it may, Raffe, you can't just assume that my reputation will protect you from the consequences of your actions. I will not interfere with whatever punishment Dr. Barnes requires for this visit."

"I didn't expect you would. After all, you didn't help Emilie. Why would I think you'd help me?"

"Your sister had to take the examination on her own. There was nothing I could do to help her pass."

"You knew she would fail and you let her take the test anyway."

"The rules—"

"Dr. Barnes was prepared to break the rules to keep Emilie from taking the entrance exam because he knew what we all did. That Emilie not only didn't want to attend the University, she didn't belong there. I heard him make the offer. You turned him down. Where is Emilie now, Dad?"

The question hangs in the air. When Official Jeffries answers he sounds less confident. Warier. "You know where your sister is. She was assigned to a job in Five Lakes Colony."

I hear Raffe laugh. The sound is devoid of humor and makes my blood run cold. "Are you aware that two of the students you were worried about me leaving campus with are from Five Lakes? Until they were selected for The Testing, they'd never met anyone from Tosu City."

"They were mistaken."

"No, they weren't. Dr. Barnes offered to allow you to remove Emilie because he was worried you couldn't live knowing what the consequences would be if she failed. What are those consequences?"

I hear the sound of a chair scraping against the floor. A loud slam. Scuffling feet and the shatter of glass. I step into the hallway but I don't move toward the room—not yet. Raffe told me that he would call for help if he needed it and that I wasn't to come in otherwise. His father would never talk about the Redirection of Testing candidates and unsuccessful University applicants around me. The wall trembles as something heavy is slammed against it. Then everything goes still.

Through the open door I can see an overturned armchair and the corner of a desk. I hold my breath and listen. Nothing. I take one step closer when I hear Raffe ask in a low, angry voice, "What happened to Emilie? Where is she?"

"She's doing important work to help revitalize this country." Raffe's father's voice trembles with defiance, but under it I hear fear. I want to see what has caused the terror, but I don't want to interfere. Not when Raffe is so close.

"Where? And are The Testing candidates who failed there, too?"

"It doesn't matter where she is. What matters is that Dr. Barnes has allowed these students to contribute to our society in a meaningful way. They weren't strong enough to become leaders, but they are still able to assist our top scientists in understanding the worst corruptions that were inflicted upon our world and our race. It's because of her and the other students that we've been able to make such great strides in reversing some of the minor human mutations."

"Emilie isn't a scientist. She's not working in some secret lab, conducting experiments that will fix everything caused by the war."

"Of course she's not running the experiments."

My chest tightens as I understand what Raffe's father is saying.

"Then what is she . . ." Raffe's voice trails off. Has he come to the same terrible conclusion I have? If the failed Testing and University candidates are not in charge of the experiments, the only thing left for them to do is to take part in them. "You're running experiments on them?"

"Our best scientists are using the resources provided in order to fix the worst of the chemical and biological damage caused by the Seven Stages of War." Resources. The word makes me shiver, as does the conviction in Official Jeffries's voice—which grows stronger with every syllable. "Anyone who has seen the worst of the mutations understands why we've allocated some of our most promising resources to this project. Over the years, we've learned that subjects who can articulate the changes they experience are more useful than those who have no concept—"

The crack of a bullet makes me jump. I flatten against the wall as four more blasts echo in the house. Once the shots stop, I race toward the illuminated doorway. Gun raised, I prepare to fire. But I stop as I cross the threshold and see Raffe standing in the middle of the room, looking down at the figure sprawled on the woven gray carpet. Raffe doesn't move as I cross the room and kneel next to the man staring blankly up at the ceiling. I should feel horror at what Raffe has done. Up close I can see the resemblance. Same thick hair. Same square jawline and cheekbones. But there is nothing but a sense of sympathy as I check his pulse and confirm what I knew the minute I saw the bloody hole in the center of his forehead. Just as the president requested, Official Rychard Jeffries is dead.

"I didn't want to kill him," Raffe says in a dull voice, his eyes focused on the man whose blood he shares. "I wanted to think that my father wasn't as much a part of this as Dr. Barnes and the rest. But I was wrong. He is, and he didn't deserve to live."

The gun in Raffe's hand trembles. In the warm light, his face looks pale. Strained. The same expression I'm sure I wore when my knife punched into Damone's chest. Will told me once that the decision to kill is easy but living with it is hard. I understand those words now better than I did then, which is why I slowly rise and hold out my hand. "Why don't you give me the gun, Raffe?"

"I'm not going to shoot you, Cia." His attention does not shift from the ashen face lying at my feet. "I wouldn't hurt you."

It's not me I'm worried about.

"I know." I keep my voice soft and soothing, the way I used

to do when I handled one of the baby animals my father helped bring into the world. "Give me the gun, Raffe. Just for a few minutes. You should go to the kitchen and get some water. That will help."

Will it? I don't know. If nothing else it will get him out of this room. Raffe might hate his father now, but from what he has said, I know there was a time he felt love and admiration for the man. Soon those emotions will catch up with him, and when that happens, I'm not sure what Raffe will do.

I take another step forward and uncurl his fingers so the gun drops into my hand. When Raffe doesn't acknowledge my actions, I push aside my sympathy and sorrow. Yes, he needs to grieve. He needs to come to terms with what he has done. But this is not the time. A large clock on the wall tells me Will's second explosion should have detonated fifteen minutes ago. Whatever cover those explosions has given us will soon expire. The officials may understand that we are using them as a diversion, and widen their search. Raffe managed to get a large piece of the information we needed from his father. Had he not fired, we might have gotten more. I wish I could have guessed what Raffe would do when he heard the truth. If I had . . .

I push away the regrets. If we survive this, there will be time enough to sort through them. But now we must move on to the second part of our mission — Dr. Barnes. And since I only vaguely know the area he lives in, I cannot get there on my own. I feel uncaring for thinking of more than Raffe at this moment, but it can't be helped.

I take the recorder out of Raffe's jacket pocket, switch it to the Off position, and say, "We've done as much as we can here. We need to go."

My words are cold. Hard. Raffe's head turns toward mine. Shock and tears glisten in his eyes. For a moment I worry that I will not be able to get him to move. That I will have to leave him behind and continue on my own. His eyes close. His jaw clenches, and when he opens his eyes and nods, the tears are gone.

"You're right." He turns his back on his father's body and heads for the door. "Let's go."

Raffe doesn't look back, but I do. I put the guns I hold in the side pocket of my bag and briefly study the man on the floor. Rychard Jeffries helped shape, revitalize, and educate this country. What he explained to Raffe is terrible, but he must have done good things along the way to achieve the position he held. Raffe's passion and his dedication to his sister are proof that not everything Rychard Jeffries did was bad. For that alone, he deserves to be remembered.

I find Raffe washing his hands in the kitchen. He offers me a glass of water and I take a drink, then remove the radio from my bag.

The message light is on. Will's voice tells us that he has completed his part and is headed back toward the house. The rest is up to us. I cannot help the stab of disappointment I feel that the message wasn't from Tomas. Telling myself that restraining Professor Chen and getting information from her will be more complicated for Stacia and Tomas than what Raffe has just done, I record a response to Will, letting him know we have finished our first stop and are moving on to the second. I then repeat the message for Tomas's frequency, adding a request for his team to contact us with their status soon. I need to hear his voice.

After returning my radio to the bag, I find Raffe's gun and hand it back to him. "If you can't handle the next part, I need to know."

He opens his bag, pulls out the box of ammunition, and fills the empty slots. After snapping the chamber closed, he runs a hand along the barrel of the gun and shakes his head. "I have to finish what I started."

So do I.

The sun has set. The houses around us are quiet as we wheel our bicycles down to the street and climb on. The haze in the sky tonight makes it hard to see the moon. The lack of light is good for traveling unseen, but I have to work to make sure I don't lose sight of Raffe as we ride through the streets in the direction of the University. Dr. Barnes lives in a house close to campus. We will check there for him. Because it is night, there is a good chance we will find his family with him. Just the thought of what we might be forced to do if they are all at home is almost enough to make me stop pedaling. Only thinking about my brother, Daileen, and all those who have died in The Testing keeps me moving forward.

As we ride, I try to catch a glimpse of Raffe's face to gauge what he's thinking or feeling. After Zandri's death, Tomas was quiet. Withdrawn. At the time I thought it was just fatigue or disillusionment with the world around him that caused his depression. But now that I know what happened during my absence, I realize it was because Tomas was struggling with his conscience. Had I not been with him, I doubt he would have continued with the fourth test. Taking a life, especially one he knew and cared for, ate at his desire to save his own until the only purpose he had was helping get me safely to the end. Raffe's need to find his sister should keep him focused on us getting through the next several hours. After that, who can say what will happen. Perhaps if Emilie is still alive, Raffe will find purpose in bringing her home and helping her recover from whatever she has suffered.

Raffe turns to the left. I follow, although I notice that Raffe is farther ahead than he was before. Despite what has happened, the burst of speed makes clear that he has not lost his endurance. At first that thought encourages me. Then I realize that Raffe is not the one who has changed speed. I have.

I've been so concerned with Raffe's state of mind that I have not noticed the weight that seems to press on me with every turn of the pedals. At the end of the journey to Raffe's house was death. There had always been a possibility that I would come to Raffe's aid if he needed me, but it wasn't necessary. This journey is different. While blood stains my hands, I have never before set out to commit murder. Tonight, I am doing exactly that.

Raffe stops so suddenly, I have to turn my handlebars to avoid crashing into him. "Look," he says. I squint into the darkness, trying to see what he sees.

Skimmers.

At the other end of the block, traveling toward us without their running lights engaged. The lack of lights is both illegal and dangerous. Neither problem is likely of much concern to those who pilot the vehicles.

"This way," Raffe whispers, and he leads me off the paved

roadway and onto the grass. I cast glances behind me, trying to see if the skimmer pilots have noticed us, but the black of the night makes it hard to tell. Raffe must think there is a chance we have been detected because he doesn't slow as we ride in between two tall trees a hundred feet from the road. Riding on the rougher terrain has slowed his pace enough for me to keep up.

"This way."

Raffe darts behind the house to our right and stops. Putting a finger to his lips, he glances around the corner at the street to see if we are being pursued. I hold my breath. A minute passes. Two. Then I hear the hum of engines moving closer, but from the sound I can't tell if they are leaving the street or traveling along it. Finally I see a shadow darker than the rest slowly moving along the road toward the east. It's small. The same size as the skimmers we used during our Induction, although I am certain this one is faster and in better repair. A second skimmer appears. Raffe points out a third. The seeming lack of urgency suggests they are performing a basic patrol. Three patrols in one location seems excessive on a normal day, but I am not surprised to see them congregated here, since we are near so many of the dwellings where top officials reside. We were lucky not to have run into more trouble on Raffe's block.

Or were we?

I see the skimmers stop and watch as one by one they turn around and head back in the direction from which they came. If they were on basic patrol, they would keep going to secure the rest of the neighborhood. These Safety officials are guarding something. Since Dr. Barnes's house is only a hundred yards away, I can guess what that something is.

The lead skimmer passes our position as I hear the click.

And another. It's coming from the Transit Communicator in my bag. Zeen.

Raffe turns his head. A second skimmer comes into view. The click sounds three more times. When I don't pick up, a voice calls, "Cia, answer me." Zeen's frantic plea echoes in the quiet of the night. I reach into my bag to find the Communicator and shut it down. My fingers fumble with the fastener as Zeen yells, "I'm coming, but Symon is—"

I hit the Off switch.

Everything goes silent.

No. Not everything.

The hum of the skimmer engine turns to a roar. The running lights flare to life as the skimmer turns and heads across the grass, directly at us.

CHAPTER 17

TERROR FUELS MY feet. "Follow me," I whisper as loud as I dare, hoping my words can be heard over the roar of the skimmers' engines as they throttle up. These skimmers are bound to be fast and easy to maneuver. That's almost enough to make me think our fate is sealed. Our only chance is to ride around the far side of the house and double back toward the road before they see us. If they can't see us, they won't know which direction to follow.

I take a standing position to gain more momentum. The sound of Raffe's harsh, fast breathing tells me he's not far behind. We are almost to the edge of the house when my front wheel hits something. I jolt as the bike slows to a crawl. Panic flares as Raffe zips past and around the corner. I try to push the pedals again but they won't turn. Whatever I hit must be wedged in the gears.

Jumping off my bike, I lift it by the frame and run. Between the bulk of the bag and the weight of the bike, my movements are awkward. Engines roar somewhere behind me. I don't think they are close—yet—but I can't tell for sure and I don't dare take the time to look. My feet stumble. Raffe takes the bike from me and runs to a small group of bushes. He slides the bike under it and then grabs my hand and dashes toward the front of the house.

"Dr. Barnes lives two houses down on the north side of the street. I'll meet you there in ten minutes."

I don't have a chance to argue as he darts away. Without thinking, I run to the front of the next house and cross the street. The slap of my boots on the pavement makes me cringe. When I reach the grass on the other side, I brave a look behind me. The skimmers have not yet reached the end of the house we came around.

My heart pounds. I run as fast as I am able and drop to the ground near the wall of the house, and flatten myself against the dirt.

I keep my face lowered, hoping my dark hair will blend into the shadows. The sound of an engine comes closer. Slowly, I move my right hand. My fingers search for the side pocket of my bag and the gun I have stored there. I can feel the seam of the pocket, but I cannot slip my hand inside without shifting my entire body, giving myself away.

I hear the sound of the other skimmer. I press my cheek to the ground and squeeze my eyes shut as I wait for shouts, increased engine power, or anything that would indicate I have been spotted. My whole body quivers with the urge to run, but I force myself to stay put. The smell of rich dirt evokes memories of my father. My first memories are of the smell of earth that surrounded him when he'd come home after a day of working in his greenhouse. It's a smell I have always associated with hope. I cling to that as I wait.

Three gunshots slash through the night. Somewhere to the left. Perhaps a few houses away. Maybe more. Did a Safety official find Raffe? Has he survived? I want to look for him, but getting myself captured or killed will not help anyone. Instead, I bite my lip, force back tears of frustration, and hold my position.

The engine closest to me roars and disappears in the direction of the gunshots. I force myself to count back from fifty in case another patrol comes by. Fifty. Forty-nine. Forty-eight. Forty-seven. The seconds feel like hours. When I reach five, I lay my hands flat on the ground. Two. One.

Pushing to my knees, I blink at the darkness. There are no signs of skimmers or their running lights. Can I still hear their engines? No. My legs tremble as I climb to my feet. The pain that streaks up my leg makes my knees buckle. When I reach down to adjust the bandage, it is wet. My leg is bleeding. I consider my options. Go to the north and around the back of this structure toward Dr. Barnes's house or see if Raffe needs my help.

There is really only one choice. Raffe could be captured or dead. All I can do is continue to follow our original plan and hope for the best.

Slowly, I cross the grass to the back of the house. The breeze rustles the leaves on nearby trees. Somewhere in the distance I hear a dog bark. No engines. No sound of footsteps other than mine. I pass several windows as I walk but see no faces peering out.

When I reach the end of the structure, I glance around the

corner, toward the street. Nothing. I quickly cross the expansive lawn between this house and the next. The one that Raffe told me belongs to Dr. Jedidiah Barnes. The house is two stories tall. A flicker of light from a second-story window tells me someone is home.

As I walk to the back door, I glance through the rear first-story windows, but it's too dark to see within. The door is unlocked. I tighten the hold on my gun and start to push it open.

"Cia."

I turn the barrel toward the sound of my name and squint into the darkness for the source. When I can't make out the person running toward me, I raise my flashlight and hit the switch. After the events in the stadium, I think the risk of exposing my position is worth it.

When the beam illuminates Raffe's face, I let out a sigh of relief and switch off the light. "Are you okay?" I ask when he reaches my side. "I heard gunshots and thought you'd been killed."

"I used to play with some of the kids in this neighborhood," he whispers near my ear. "There are old water ducts at the end of the block. They're not easy to find if you don't know where to look. I fired a couple of shots to draw the Safety officials in my direction and then went into one of the ducts and crawled until I came out on the other side of the block, which is harder to do now than when I was smaller. Are you ready?"

Am I? Could I ever be ready for what I now must do? "I'm ready for this to be over," I answer.

"Then let's go."

Raffe pushes the door open and steps cautiously into darkness. I follow, closing the door behind me, then turn on my flashlight. We're in a large kitchen. My light shows dark wood cabinets, white and gray countertops, and a large wooden table. There are no dishes in sight. No glasses in the sink. My mother would approve. Raffe frowns.

"What's wrong?" I whisper.

"Probably nothing," he says. "When my father and I came to visit, Mrs. Barnes let me hang out in here. She always had flowers on the table and things her kids made on the countertop by the sink."

I shine my light again. The countertops and table are clear of decorations. Out of curiosity, I open one of the cabinet doors. In it are two plates, two bowls. The next one contains three mugs and two drinking glasses. I think of what my mother keeps in our kitchen. Because my father's job requires him to be close to the area he is currently working to revitalize, we move often, so Mom tries to keep our possessions to a minimum for ease of relocation. Despite that we have at least six or seven pots and pans, over a dozen plates, and a large number of cups. I have a hard time believing that what's contained in these cupboards is enough to service a family of five.

"Let's go." Raffe turns toward the door that leads to the rest of the house.

I keep the light pointed in front of us as we walk through a hallway that takes us to a large room. On one side is a wide staircase. A sofa, small table, and two blue chairs are arranged in the middle of the room. A shelf on the wall contains a number of books, but, as in the kitchen, there are no personal objects of any kind in the room. No paintings or baskets filled with knitting needles like I noticed in Raffe's house. The furniture and rug look comfortably worn, but still the house feels as though it's not really lived in.

Gun in hand, Raffe leads the way up the stairs. As I follow, I run my finger along the wood banister. It comes away clean. No dust. Despite the meager furnishings, someone still lives here.

We reach the top of the stairs and turn to the left. The light I saw from outside is coming from an open door fifteen feet away. The rest of the doors in the hall are closed. No lights shine from beneath them.

Raffe glances at me and nods. I turn off my flashlight, put it in my pocket, and nod back. This is it.

It is easy to keep our approach quiet. The carpet on this floor is thick. When we are steps away from the door, Raffe looks at me and mouths the word "Go." He races through the door. I step in after him with my finger poised on the trigger, prepared to fire. Only, no one is there. The chair behind a large desk stacked with papers is empty. The shelves in this room are stuffed with books worn from use. A large rocking chair sits near a window. Beside it is a small table stacked high with paper-filled folders.

Without discussion, Raffe and I walk out of the room and search the rest of the upstairs rooms. No one occupies them, but we do find answers of another sort. In the largest bedroom, we see a portrait of Dr. Barnes, his wife, and their children on the nightstand, but when we look in the closets we find clothes that belong only to him. There are no toys or clothes in the other bedrooms. Dr. Barnes still lives here, but his family does not.

Why?

We go back to the office to see if answers can be found there. Raffe stands at the desk. I walk to the rocking chair and sit on the floor next to a pile of papers. But before I can open the first file, I remember Zeen. Opening my bag, I take out the Transit Communicator, turn it back on, and click the Call button. When Zeen doesn't answer, I click the button three more times, hoping he will understand that I am now able to talk. That I have not heard the message that he took such a chance to relay to me.

The Communicator stays silent. Whatever Zeen is doing at this moment, he cannot hear me or cannot get to his Communicator. Biting my lip, I set the device to the side and search for the pulse radio. The message light is on, so I press Play and feel a tear slide down my cheek as Tomas's voice fills the room.

"The first step is complete. We are moving on to the second." His voice is strained. He promises to contact me once their next task is finished and then says, "I hope you are safe. Remember, I love you."

Warmth floods my body as I cling to one thought—Tomas is alive.

"He didn't say what happened with Professor Chen," Raffe says.

"No." I noticed that omission too. Perhaps Tomas is being careful, but his tone tells me something went wrong. Since there is nothing we can do about what has happened, I say, "They must have found her or he would have said they were unable to complete the first step. They might be with Professor Holt now. We have to decide what to do next. Where do you think Dr. Barnes and his family could be?"

"Dr. Barnes must have decided to move his family somewhere safe in case something went wrong with his plan. But I can't imagine he'd leave Tosu City."

I agree. Symon is in charge of directing the rebellion, but Dr. Barnes gives orders to Symon. He wouldn't leave. Not when the events he has orchestrated are about to be put in motion. "According to the president's information, he spends a lot of time at The Testing Center. I think our best chance of finding him would be there."

"Getting off campus was hard." Raffe frowns. "I'm guessing security is even tighter now."

"If we have to get past the Safety officials, we will," I say with more confidence than I feel. "But it would be better if we knew for certain if Dr. Barnes is there." I glance at the papers in piles around the room. "Maybe there's something here that will help. We might even be able to find evidence of what happened to your sister and the other students."

That kind of proof to supplement the death of some of the top Testing advocates might aid us in ending The Testing even if Dr. Barnes has gone into hiding. But we can't stay here for long. My gut tells me Dr. Barnes is still in the area. If we are going to find him, we need to continue our hunt. "Let's do a quick search," I say, opening the first folder in the stack next to me. "If we don't find anything after ten minutes, we should get going."

As Raffe flips through papers on the desk, I focus on the pages in my hand. At the top of the first page is a name. Ayana Kirk. Beneath it are listed grades for twelve years of studies as well as notes that say the student especially excelled in physics and music. There are several recommendation letters from teachers. In a different hand, I see notes in the margin questioning whether the student's musical proclivities make her too sensitive to withstand further education or whether she might be better served by a mid-level education job instead of reaching for a higher position. These questions must have been sent to those who wrote the recommendations because more letters follow, addressing the concerns, as well as a note that an invitation to take the University exam was sent. I flip the page and my heart sinks as I see the words "Redirected and assigned to resource program under Professor Cartwright." Beneath that is Dr. Barnes's signature and a date. This student failed her examination last year. The signature is in the same hand as the notations in the margins throughout the file.

I skim through the next file. Another failed student. Another Redirection. This one also from last year. As I quickly scan the pages, I notice that all the files stacked here are from the past ten years. No students previous to that time are included. All were Redirected. The older the application file is, the fewer notations in the margins. Not a single question is written for those who applied a decade past. As I do the math, I notice something else. Unless files are missing, over three times as many students were Redirected ten years ago than last year.

"What did you find?" Raffe asks.

"I'm not sure," I say. Or maybe I am and I don't want to admit that what I'm seeing is real. Dr. Barnes is the force behind The Testing. He's the one who created tests that kill and who turned failed University applicants into resources to be experimented on. And yet, if these files are authentic, he's been working to convince applicants he believes are doomed to fail to choose another path before they make a choice they cannot take back. Just as he did with Raffe's sister. Why?

"Maybe officials who traveled to the colonies began to notice that none of the Redirected students were ever seen there," Raffe suggests when I explain what I've found. "Limiting the number of unsuccessful applicants means fewer questions he'll have to answer for officials and families here in Tosu."

That makes sense. Especially since President Collindar took office just six years ago. I glance at the clock on my watch. Our ten minutes are up. We need to get moving.

"Did you find anything?" I ask.

"A couple of reports suggesting The Testing be limited to a hundred candidates. During the past several years a larger percentage than is acceptable to Dr. Barnes has been eliminated during the first examination. Nothing that helps figure out where Dr. Barnes is now." Raffe frowns. "Although there's also a calendar that shows the scheduled meetings for this year's selection of Testing candidates, along with the preliminary names."

Raffe holds out the papers and I cross the room and take them. The first page is a list of potential candidates. My soul aches as I read name after name, along with the colonies they belong to. Finally I come to Five Lakes Colony and the names Daileen Dasho, Lyane Maddows, and Christoph Nusman. All students I know. I have played sports with them and studied beside them. All three will celebrate their selection for The Testing, not knowing that the price of failure is more than they should ever be forced to pay. Pushing aside the emotions that threaten to overwhelm me, I flip to the calendar. There was a meeting of the committee earlier today at The Testing Center. I doubt Dr. Barnes would have missed it. The meeting must have ended hours ago. Dr. Barnes could have left after it was over, but this is the only clue we have as to his whereabouts. We have no choice but to follow it.

When I tell Raffe we are headed to campus, he says, "Before we leave, there's something you need to see. There's a file here with your name on it."

He places the file in my hand and watches as I open it. The paper is the same gray color as the one given to me by President Collindar. Only this time, instead of finding Dr. Barnes's name and information inside, I find my own.

Malencia Vale.
Age at Testing: 16
Colony: Five Lakes
Group: Wide range of aptitude
Defining attribute: Mechanical Ability
First round Testing: Pass
Notes: Strong emotional reaction to candidate self-termination. Will watch to see if this affects future Testing.
Second round Testing: Pass
Notes: Again, strong emotional reaction to candidate failure. Yet still completed this test.
Third round Testing: Pass
Notes: Unusual need to aid teammates when allowing those teammates to fail would bring candidate closer to achieving her goal. Her personal beliefs are in conflict with the committee's criteria for passage to the University. However,

strong demonstration of candidate's ability to trust her in-stincts and persuade others makes her unique. I believe she is my best chance and have taken steps to go around my col-leagues in an effort to aid and test her further in round four.

Best chance? I read the line again. Best chance of what? Was Dr. Barnes the reason Symon gave me food, water, and the vial that helped me in my interview? From what I see here, it ap-pears he must be. But why? I don't understand.

Fourth round of Testing: Failure recommended by staff. Candidate is not questioning enough of others and not com-mitted enough to her agenda to do whatever is necessary for the country's future development. Does not have a strong enough personality to make difficult choices.

Failure. I shake my head and read the words again. Not a strong enough personality. If the committee sought to elimi-nate me as a candidate, why was I accepted?

Interview: Candidate surprised committee with emotional restraint and strongly worded responses. Some have been swayed to allow her passage. Most have not.
Committee recommendation: Failure
Final result: Pass

Despite everything I did, the committee believed I had failed. Those words on the page make my knees go weak. It shouldn't matter what The Testing officials believed. But seeing proof that I was not good enough or strong enough to them is like a slap in the face. My best wasn't worthy of their acceptance.

"None of this makes sense," I say, looking up from the folder. "Why did I pass The Testing if the committee recommended I fail?"

Raffe shakes his head. "It looks like Dr. Barnes intervened. Maybe that's the reason Professor Holt has been upset about your presence at the University from the first day you arrived in her residence. She would have known you had been marked for failure and yet somehow survived. What do you think it means?"

"I don't know." And there is only one way to find out. I pick up my bag and shove the folder inside. "We have to find Dr. Barnes. Let's go."

Raffe glances around the room. "I don't know if it's important, but it just occurred to me what's been bothering me since we got here. The lamp in this room was on. Dr. Barnes would never have left a light on all day by mistake."

"Why . . ." I don't ask the rest of the question because I guess the answer. Dr. Barnes left the light on because he wants people to think he is here. The Safety patrols that roam this street, even though all other officials are looking on the other side of the city for whoever set the explosives.

This is a trap.

CHAPTER 18

RAFFE AND I look around the room for a sign that I am right and find it beneath the desk. A black box with wires and a blinking light. An explosive. Is it on a timer or is it waiting to be tripped by something else? It's impossible to say. Only one thing is clear. "We have to get out of here."

Raffe must agree, because he grabs his things and is right behind me as I hurry into the hall. We are halfway down the stairs when a door somewhere below us closes.

I turn off my flashlight and consider our options. Going upstairs will get us out of sight, but this is the only staircase down. If we hide in one of the second-story rooms, we risk being stuck in our hiding place. So I hurry down the stairs as quickly as I can. The front door is only about twenty steps to the right, but when I calculate the time it will take to get there, unlock the door, and get out, I discard that option. Especially since I hear the sound of footsteps from somewhere in the back of the house.

Grabbing Raffe's hand, I race down the last six stairs, race to my left, and duck behind the sofa. Raffe joins me just as the lights in this area flare to life.

"You two, stay here," a familiar voice says quietly.

Symon. If he's here, what happened to Zeen?

Raffe stiffens beside me. He too has recognized the voice.

The carpet dulls the sound of footsteps as Symon climbs the stairs, but what I do hear makes me think more than one person made the ascent. A few minutes later, Symon calls down, "He's not here yet. We'll wait. Turn off the lights. One of you go to each end of the block and hold that position. The minute you see him, signal me."

The lights blink out. Footsteps disappear down the hallway, toward the back of the house. A door slams upstairs. The minute Raffe hears that, he peers around the side of the sofa. He waits for a moment and then whispers, "Stay there," as he slips out from behind the couch. Several seconds later he returns, taps me on the shoulder, and motions for me to follow him.

Slowly we cross the dark room, careful to steer clear of the furnishings and avoid making noise. I want to go up the stairs, demand to know where my brother is, and put a bullet in Symon's head. But if Symon sets off Dr. Barnes's trap, I don't want to be caught in it too. I brush my fingers along the wall to guide me and am relieved when the hall opens into the kitchen.

When I head for the door, Raffe grabs my hand and whispers, "We have to split up. If you move fast, the two people he sent to guard the ends of the street won't yet be in position. You'll get out of the area without being seen and be able to get back to campus. Go to The Testing Center. I'll deal with Symon. You have to find Dr. Barnes."

"You saw what's in his office. You can't go up there."

"Symon's working with him. He has to know about the bomb. There's no choice. We have to eliminate him."

"Then I'll stay." If Symon knows anything about Zeen, I might be able to find that out before I pull the trigger.

Raffe shakes his head. "The minute a gun is fired, the guards will come running. Knowing this neighborhood is the only thing that's going to help me get away." He walks me toward the door and takes my hand. "This is our only shot at getting them both. You know I'm right."

I don't want to agree, but I do. Raffe has a better chance alone. I have to trust him to do this. Just as he is trusting me.

"I'll see you soon," I whisper.

Raffe leans forward. His lips press against my cheek. His fingers tighten around mine as he whispers, "You will. Be careful when you get to campus. The rebel students could cause you more problems than the Safety officials. And just in case something goes wrong here, I need you to do something for me. Find my sister and tell her I'm sorry. I never thought I'd trust someone the way I trusted Emilie, let alone someone from the colonies. But I believe in you. You'll do what's right."

Then he's gone. He slips into the shadows of the hallway. Out of sight.

Outside, the breeze is cool on my face. I close the door quietly behind me and slowly look from side to side. When I see and hear nothing, I consider which way to go. Since the guards are posted to the west and east, I run north and realize why Symon did not worry about someone approaching from this direction. Fifty yards from the house is a large wall that stands at least eight feet high and spans the length of this block. The barrier is made of smooth stone. There is nowhere to get a good handhold, and I can't reach the top without a boost.

Squinting into the darkness, I spot a tree about twenty feet away and head for it. The willow tops the wall by five or six feet. The tree is fairly young. Probably about four years old. I pull on one of the lower-hanging branches. It's thin. Supple. Not ideal for climbing, but this is the only one I see that is close set enough to the stone wall to be of help.

Still, the tree stands about eight feet away, which means I will have to climb as high as possible for this to work. I shift my bag so it doesn't get caught on the branches, put one foot on the trunk, and pull myself up. The lowest-hanging limb bends under my weight but doesn't break.

I reach as close to the top as I dare, position my feet on two V's near the trunk where the branches are sturdiest, and take a deep breath. The sound of gunshots makes me flinch. Raffe. I force myself not to look behind me. Instead I grab the thin center of the tree as the branch under my left foot breaks and smashes to the ground.

I hear shouts. More shots. The limbs sag as I quickly step from one fork to another. At the third fork, I push off hard and extend my arms as I jump toward the wall. My chest makes contact with the top of the stone barrier. I bite my lip to prevent myself from crying out as I start to slide down. The stone grates against my fingers but I refuse to let go. My arms tremble. Sweat breaks out on the back of my neck. I almost lose my grip as an explosion roars behind me. I finally find a good holding spot with my boots and use my leg muscles to propel me up and over. Before I drop to the other side, I catch a glimpse of smoke and licks of fire coming from Dr. Barnes's house. I allow myself five seconds of hope as I scan the area for Raffe before I let go of my grip, drop to the other side, and run.

I race across the grass, run between two houses, and reach the street on the other side. Beams from flashlights cut through the darkness as people awakened by the sounds come out of their homes.

Everyone looks scared. I'm certain I do. Between the spectacle of the fire and the fear, no one gives me a second look as I walk quickly down the street. Away from the flames. Away from Raffe. If he survived the explosion, he might at this very moment need my help. But I do not turn, because he would never forgive me for risking our mission. As I walk, I can only wonder who will be next and if anything we do is worth the price paid.

When I can no longer hear the shout of voices, I duck under a bush and pull out the Transit Communicator. I select the coordinates for the Government Studies residence that I saved in the device during Induction. I am a half mile from campus. If I start walking now, I should be there in less than ten minutes. I look at the moon and try to judge the time that has passed since Tomas, Stacia, Raffe, and I left the house. Two hours? Three? It seems impossible that so much has happened in so little time. Raffe is probably dead. Zeen still does not answer my calls. Tomas and Stacia were okay when Tomas left his message, but who knows where they are now.

I push to my feet. My legs tremble as I shift my bag back onto my shoulder and start walking. Slowly at first, then faster until I am running as fast as I can. The sooner I find Dr. Barnes, the sooner everything will be over. The Testing. The experiments on Raffe's sister and the other failed students. The deaths I've been asked to execute. All of it. It has to end.

My lungs burn. My pulse pounds. Both make me feel alive. It isn't until I see familiar landmarks that tell me I am only a block from the University gates that I slow. I click the Call button on the Communicator one last time, not caring if Zeen speaks and someone else overhears. I need to hear his voice. But the device stays silent. I feel a part of my heart go still as I slide it back into my bag and exchange it for the pulse radio. The indicator light is dark. Recording a whispered message, I tell Tomas, Stacia, and Will that I am currently headed to where we began this journey. Then I press Send. Instead of putting the radio back in my bag, I slide it into my jacket pocket to keep the thought of Tomas close, and I start moving through the shadows.

The archway of the University entrance comes into view. Seeing it again, I remember how I felt the first time I rode beneath it. Tomas, Malachi, and Zandri were beside me as we spotted the wrought-iron sign that reads THE UNIVERSITY OF THE UNITED COMMONWEALTH. Despite my father's warnings, I felt excitement and hope. I do not cross under the archway now. If anyone suspects I'm on my way here, this is where they will wait. Instead, I head toward the TU Administration building on the edge of campus.

I'm careful to keep my tread light so no one nearby hears me as I walk through the darkness, listening for sounds of officials or rebels lurking nearby and thinking of the day I left Five Lakes Colony. Before The Testing. When I trusted others but was not always sure I trusted myself.

Heading toward where this all started, I think I finally understand why The Testing was created. In a time when each decision could mean the difference between a country rebuilt and one that becomes too broken to repair, the founders of The Testing were not willing to trust anyone's best intentions. They needed leaders who were not just smart or kind or nice, but who were capable of making the tough choices that most people would not want to make. Of putting necessity above all else and acting on it without hesitation.

Stacia is right. President Dalton faltered. His wasn't the worst mistake, but historians say that by the Fourth Stage of War it was clear that peace talks had no chance of prevailing. Despite so many deaths and so much destruction, the leaders of the main alliances still believed their desire for conquest could be fulfilled. They had invested too much to step back. Doing so would have been akin to admitting they were wrong. The only measure that could have stopped the Fourth Stage from progressing would have been to eliminate the leaders who were marching the world toward destruction. Had that happened, perhaps those who took their place could have seen the futility of the devastation around them and taken steps to end the war.

But that didn't happen. The leaders pushed forward with their war and the world collapsed. The United Commonwealth rose from the ashes of that world, and The Testing was created to ensure that leaders would not fail like that again. But while The Testing seeks to push candidates to show what they are capable of, it fails to recognize that different circumstances bring about different results. The Testing committee believed

I should be cast as one who failed because I couldn't do what was necessary. How I passed is still a mystery, but the journey I make now shows how wrong they were.

The sound of boots slapping against pavement hits me, and I slip behind a bush. The footsteps are somewhere to my left. I squint into the darkness and spot two people racing south. Officials? Rebels? There's no way to know. When they disappear, I wait for several minutes before walking in the opposite direction. I see the edge of the fence in the distance and hurry to reach it. When I do, I'm glad for the lack of windows in the back of the TU Administration building and I slip around the fence onto campus.

Gunshots sound in the distance. A siren starts to wail as more gunfire erupts. I flatten myself behind a bush and wait. A scream rises above the din. Other voices shout and more shots are fired. All of it sounds as if it is taking place on the other side of campus. When another round of gunfire rings out from somewhere far to my left, I clasp the gun and stand.

Careful to keep to the shadows, I cross behind the building and head toward the stadium, trying not to think of what happened there only yesterday. But I do think of Tomas. Is he safe? The radio light stays dark.

Just past the stadium I see it. Five stories tall and almost hidden in the darkness because of its black steel and black glass exterior. The fence that surrounds the area around it also blends into the night, but I know it is there along with the small bronze sign that announces the purpose of the work that takes place inside.

The Testing Center.

The last time I was inside that building, Dr. Barnes announced that the twenty of us seated in the room with him had been accepted to the University. Tomas and I were together. Without my memories of The Testing I had just passed through, I was happy.

I spot a figure standing in the shadows near the front of the building and go still. Without getting closer I can't determine whether the man is one of the rebel students or a Safety official. But all the activity to the south has not pulled his attention, so I know he will not be drawn away easily. I will have to find a way around him or another way inside.

A back door or windows on the main floor would allow me to enter without being seen. I don't recall the presence of either, but I circle around to the back of the building to check. The black fence that surrounds the building grounds is only chest high and easy to scale. Once on the other side, I confirm what I hoped was not true. The guarded entrance is the only way inside.

As silently as possible, I cross the area behind The Testing Center. The upper-story windows are darkened, making it impossible to know if Dr. Barnes is inside. Have I ever seen light coming from the windows here? I don't think so. The only time I remember being outside this building during The Testing was in the daytime, when we were waiting for the results of the first test and they allowed us to go outside. Zandri, Malachi, Tomas, and I sat near a small pond. As I approach that spot now, I remember how Zandri's hair caught the sunlight and the way she made Malachi laugh. Last year the fountain in the middle of the pond was broken. To pass the time, Tomas and I worked together to repair it. The fountain is currently turned off, and I wonder if there's a way to use it to create a diversion.

The gunfire has stopped, but the siren still sounds as I find the power box nestled discreetly in a pile of rocks. As I did months ago, I remove the cover with the screwdriver attachment of my pocketknife, and this time use my flashlight to view the contents. Everything looks as it did when Tomas and I fixed the fountain last summer, and I think I should be able to make the motor whine and grind enough to attract the guard's notice.

It takes several tries to make the adjustments to the motor, wrap long pieces of grass around the impeller blade, and block the water-return pump in a way that will cause the now-hindered motor to be even more overworked. The combination should tax the machinery to produce rumbling and a high-pitched whine. Or the motor might overheat and stop working altogether. There's only one way to find out which.

After taking a deep breath, I get ready to run and hit the power switch. The water gurgles in the fountain as I dash toward the building. The sound of the grinding motor begins as I edge my way along the back of the building toward the north side. The motor lets out a screech loud enough to be heard over the siren. It only lasts for a few seconds before the damage I did causes the motor to give out with a loud bang.

Was the noise enough?

Yes! I hear footsteps and duck around the corner of the building as whoever was in the front now looks for the source of the sound. Hoping to get inside before he returns, I race to the entrance, but I start to panic as I see the small keypad next to the door. I remember Michal using a code with six numbers to gain us entry, but I didn't see what they were. Even if I had, I doubt they have remained the same. I turn away from the pad and focus my attention on the lock above the door handle, hoping I can jimmy it before the guard returns.

The sound of running feet and the voice yelling for me to stop tell me I'm too late. I do the only thing I can. I turn, aim at the Safety official as he raises his weapon, and fire.

I meant to hit the man's leg. Instead, my bullet punches into his stomach. His weapon goes off as he hits the ground, and I press against the door behind me and feel it give way. The lock wasn't engaged. The man behind me groans in pain. I want to help him, but I tamp down that instinct and step through the doorway. Between the unlocked door and the man I shot lying on the ground outside, someone will soon discover I am here. I have to find Dr. Barnes, fast.

Clicking my flashlight, I shine it around the building's entrance. Everything in the lobby is as I remember it. White walls. Scuffed gray floor. Gray wooden chairs in the corner. The Testing storage room and personal preparation rooms are on this floor. I will not find Dr. Barnes in those. If he is in this building, he will be on one of the upper floors. I run down the long white and gray hallway to the bank of elevators we rode during The Testing to reach the upper four floors.

But I don't want to be trapped inside an elevator if someone discovers that I am here. So I walk past them, down the hall, looking for stairs.

I find them at the end of the corridor and begin to climb. The building is large. The task of finding someone in this place is daunting. When I reach the second floor, I step out into the hallway and shine my light down the corridor. I could search floor by floor, and I will if I have to. But for now I follow my instincts, turn back to the stairs, and climb to the third floor. It was on this floor that Dr. Barnes spoke to us about each phase of The Testing and gave us each set of instructions. This level was also the location of our interviews. It was during mine that I learned Tomas was responsible for Zandri's death, although Dr. Barnes refused to tell me how. When I step out of the stairwell into a dimly lit hallway, I am certain that Dr. Barnes is near.

Sliding the flashlight into my bag, I pull out my gun and walk toward the lecture hall. Blood pounds in my ears as I approach the large double doors that lead to the room where I began and ended my Testing. When I take hold of one of the door handles, I feel the same anxiety and fear I did when I entered this room for the first time months ago. Inside, the stage is dark. In the shadows I see the same podium Dr. Barnes spoke behind standing at the center. The tiered seats are empty, but if I close my eyes I can see the faces of those who died. If Dr. Barnes has his way, this room will soon be filled with more candidates ready to be tested. Knowing that steadies the gun in my hand as I turn and walk to the very end of the lecture hall toward the room where I was interviewed. I see a thin slice of light under the door.

I put my hand on the knob. In my mind I list the names of the candidates who walked through the doors of this building. Those names give me courage as I slowly turn the knob, push open the door, and step inside.

Seated at a black table near the back windowless wall with a pen in his hand is Dr. Barnes. I wrap both hands around the butt of the gun, plant my feet firmly on the floor, and prepare to fire as Dr. Barnes looks up from the table and smiles.

"Good evening, Cia," he says. "We've been expecting you."

Before I can wonder who "we" is, I hear a click and feel the cold metal of a gun barrel as it is pressed against my head. And I know I have failed.

CHAPTER 19

A HAND REACHES out and wrests the gun from my hand. Another person grabs the bag off my shoulder and laughs. I know that laugh. Turning, I see a sneer spread across Griffin's face as he drops my bag to the ground.

"You might want to be careful with that." Dr. Barnes rises from behind the table and crosses toward me. "Ms. Vale may have one or two more tricks up her sleeve." He reaches out and takes my gun from a third-year Government Studies student I have never spoken to. "Thank you for your assistance. Now, if you don't mind waiting outside, Ms. Vale and I have matters to discuss. You'll both be rewarded once our conversation is complete."

Annoyance flickers across Griffin's face as he stalks toward the door. The other boy follows. When the door clicks shut, Dr. Barnes picks my bag off the floor, walks back to his chair, and places the bag on the table. "Please, have a seat. I know you haven't gotten a lot of rest in recent weeks. You've been quite busy, Cia. So busy, in fact, I was concerned something might happen to you before you had a chance to meet me tonight. That would have been a shame, since there's much to discuss."

He motions for me to sit in the black chair that is situated across from him at the table. The smile Dr. Barnes wears is familiar. It is filled with warmth and concern and is designed to elicit trust. His expression turns puzzled when I do not take a seat. "You did come here to talk to me, didn't you, Cia?"

"I came here to kill you."

"Of course you did." His smile widens as he sets my gun down on the table in front of him. "And I intend to let you. Of course," he adds, "you will still have to deal with the individuals outside if you succeed. I apologize for that, but I couldn't take the chance of you killing me before we had this conversation."

"You're going to let me kill you?" Confusion, nerves, and fear make me laugh, although nothing has ever seemed less funny.

Dr. Barnes leans back in his chair. "You don't believe me, Cia?"

"No."

Now he laughs. "I suppose I don't blame you, although do you really think you'd be standing here right now if I didn't intend for you to complete your agenda? You've come a long way since first stepping into this building, but there's still much for you to learn."

I think of the lock that was disengaged downstairs, the lack of dishes and clothes at Dr. Barnes's house, the papers and files in plain sight in his study, the explosion that burned his house, and the ease with which I crossed campus despite all the fighting going on. Even the guard outside who had the chance to fire at me before I shot him. While the plan that I embarked on was well thought out, I could not have made it this far without some kind of help. Help Dr. Barnes is now claiming he provided. Why?

"You're right," I say, shifting my gaze to the gun. While this room is small, the gun is too far away to reach before Dr. Barnes does. I'm not sure if Dr. Barnes's nod of approval is for my decision not to take that risk or for my understanding of the help I have received. And it doesn't matter, because he's correct. We have to talk. I need answers that only he can provide. Once I have those, I will find a way to get the gun, because I do not believe for a moment that Dr. Barnes intends to die.

Crossing to the black high-backed chair, I take a seat. "I do have more to learn, Dr. Barnes. But somehow I doubt you and Professor Holt will allow me to return to class after everything that has happened."

"Professor Holt would certainly stand in your way. She's been suspicious of your abilities since you first arrived for The Testing. She was especially unhappy when you were passed through to the University despite her objections. She never understood how you received enough votes." He gives me a pleased smile. "However, due to tonight's activities, Verna is no longer a consideration. Neither is MayLin Chen. So they won't be around to complain if you decide to continue your education. Then again, after everything you've been through, you may wish to leave Tosu City and return to Five Lakes. If so, I'm certain your family will be happy to see you."

Hearing Dr. Barnes mention my family makes it hard to

breathe, but I keep my emotions off my face. I will not give him the satisfaction of knowing that his verbal jab connected. Keeping my tone flat, I say, "You went to a lot of trouble to arrange this meeting. I doubt it was because you want to talk to me about whether or not I'd like to go back to my colony."

"You don't believe I'd allow you to return home?" He leans forward and rests his hands next to the gun.

"No." I cannot take my eyes away from his fingers as they brush the butt. "I don't believe you."

"I have no reason to lie," he says, wrapping his hand around the wooden handle. "Of course, I don't expect you to take my word on that."

Gun in hand, he rises and crosses the room to a small bench I failed to notice before. On the bench is a tray. Atop that tray is a glass filled with clear liquid. Dr. Barnes takes the glass with his free hand, walks over to the table, and places the glass in front of me. "That's why I provided us with a drink you might remember from the last time we were in this room."

As Dr. Barnes walks back to the other side of the table, I pick up the glass and study its contents. There is nothing to distinguish it from water. Not the look or the smell. It appears innocuous. But it could be the same liquid as the one I was required to consume during my interview, and I know looks are deceiving. Even after taking a serum that was designed to counteract the effects of the interview drug, I still felt a sense of euphoria once I drank it and the desire to tell those who questioned me everything they wanted to know. Thankfully, the serum allowed me to think before I answered and to control my responses. I do not have the benefit of that serum now.

"I'm not going to drink this." I set the glass down on the table.

"And I'm not going to insist that you do. The drink is for me," he says. "I'm just offering you the opportunity in case you doubt my claim about what's in the glass."

I'm confused. Is what he has to tell me so important that he would willingly consume the truth drug he once forced me to take? The one that, with Symon's help, I beat. "How do I know you haven't taken the serum that negates it?" I ask.

"You don't." Dr. Barnes leans back in his chair and nods. "You are always one to trust your instincts. What do you think?"

I don't know what to think. This is another test—perhaps the last one I will ever face—and I'm not sure of the correct answer. None of what has happened tonight makes sense. Not the unlocked door, Dr. Barnes's booby-trapped house, or his claim that he wants me to kill him. For these things to be true, Dr. Barnes must have always known what I've been doing. Nothing I've done has been in secret. But there have been no cameras. I disabled the tracking device in my bracelet. He couldn't have planted something in my clothes because I have not always worn the same . . .

My eyes fall on the University bag that sits on the far edge of the table. I've rarely been without it since it was given to me after The Testing. The bag is constructed with strong material to prevent it from ripping. The bottom, especially, is thick to ensure the bag can hold all the books we have to carry around campus. At least that's what I assumed. A bag. Like every other bag. Without memory of The Testing, I had no reason to question it when it was given to me. And once I did remember, I never gave it a second thought.

I put the glass back on the table and lean back in my seat. "Was The Testing bag designed to monitor our movements, too?"

"I'm impressed, my dear. You're correct about this bag containing a device that allows me to better understand your daily activities, but the satchel you carried during The Testing did not. My staff believed the recorders in the bracelets were sufficient to obtain the information we needed. You proved them wrong then as you have here at the University. Just as I hoped you would."

"You hoped?"

Dr. Barnes reaches across the table, picks up the glass, and toasts me with it. He swallows some of the liquid and frowns as he sets the half-empty glass back on the table. "I forgot how unpleasant that taste is. It was something we always meant to fix but never got around to. Not a surprise, I suppose, since no one who drinks it remembers the bitter flavor once The Testing is over. Ah, well, perhaps now you will allow me to explain in my own way."

He places his hands on the table and begins to speak. "When the United Commonwealth was formed, it was decided that a different selection method would be necessary to ensure our country did not fall victim to the mistakes of the leaders in our past. For a while that selection was easy, since the boundaries of our country did not extend beyond the city. It was a simple matter for officials to observe those who naturally assumed leadership roles in the work they'd been assigned. However, after the first colonies were established and our population grew, there were problems. Leaders struggled to be decisive when faced with difficult decisions like power distribution. Fights broke out in parts of the city where power allocation was at its lowest. To stave off frustration and violence, two new colonies were established and tens of thousands of people sent out of the city to revitalize areas far to the east. Due to rushed decisions, those areas were poorly scouted. Only a handful of those who left the city survived."

We studied the failed colonies in school. Those who survived talked of poisonous windstorms, vicious mutated animal attacks, and contamination in the ground that caused anything that was planted to die within days. My father always wondered how the scientists who reviewed those areas missed such deadly contamination, and believed mistakes were made. He was right. Thousands of people died because of those errors.

"Those who returned shared their story. They questioned the current leadership. The civil war that loomed would have torn apart the city and the country. To prevent that, a compromise was reached between the current leaders and those who opposed them, ensuring that new leadership would not commit the same mistakes. The University, under my grandfather's guidance, was charged with selecting students with the qualities necessary to lead and with preparing them for the positions they would hold. A year after that change was made, The Testing was established."

Gun in hand, Dr. Barnes stands and walks the length of the room. "It's hard to determine what makes a good leader and to test for those qualities. For the next ten years, The Testing was comprised of written and hands-on challenges meant to determine whether a candidate had the knowledge required to help lead the revitalization mission. Those who attended the University were the brightest and most promising minds our country had to offer. And yet, many of them faltered when it was their turn to lead. After all, no matter how intelligent and skilled a person is, it is impossible to know how a person will behave in a certain situation until they are faced with it. So my grandfather created two versions of The Testing as an experiment. One for colony students and the other for those from Tosu City."

When Dr. Barnes turns away from me, I realize this could be my chance. Slowly, I slide to the edge of the chair. There is a knife in the side pocket of my bag. If I can reach it . . .

"The colony candidates' Testing became harder. More stressful in order to see which students could succeed in spite of the pressure and which would break under the strain. Perhaps it shouldn't come as a surprise that the largest advancements in genetic manipulation, medicine, and in cleansing our water have been made by those who came from the colonies and passed through The Testing. Successful candidates like your father and President Wendig. Over the years, The Testing has proven to be an effective tool, which is why President Collindar is now insisting that all applicants for the University, including the ones from Tosu City, be required to take part in it."

Icy shock streaks up my spine. "That's not true. President Collindar wants to end The Testing."

I know Dr. Barnes is lying. Until recently, the president didn't understand what candidates were forced to go through. Her desire to learn more about The Testing was one of the reasons she had me assigned to be her intern.

"No, my dear." He sees my proximity to the bag and extends the gun in front of him. His eyes hold mine, waiting for me to make a choice.

Slowly, I sit back. With a smile, he lowers the gun and continues. "While you would like to believe differently, ending The Testing is the last thing President Collindar wants. After a hundred years, other countries in the world are reaching out. Some in friendship. Others . . . well, let's just say that our leaders will need to stay strong in order for our country to survive what comes next. Despite my growing concerns about the elimination of so many bright minds through The Testing, President Collindar believes that those losses are minor compared to the number of casualties we'll incur if our leadership should falter."

My mind races back to my conversations with President Collindar about The Testing. In each, she talked of ending Dr. Barnes's control of the process. Never once did she actually say she intended to eliminate The Testing itself. But that proves nothing. I look at the half-empty glass sitting in front of Dr. Barnes. Is he telling the truth now? There's no way to know.

I tamp down the uncertainty rising inside me and ask, "What about the Redirected students? Does President Collindar know that you and your scientists are experimenting on them?"

"Ah, you have been busy learning all of our secrets." But his frown and the flicker of confusion that crosses his face make me wonder if he truly knows everything that I have done. "Yes, the president receives monthly reports from Professor Cartwright and Dr. Bates that outline the success of their resourcing program. She's fully aware of their progress in the study of human mutations caused by the wars, although she believes Professor Cartwright is being too cautious in his use of the subjects. Results are important. Especially if the reports we are getting from beyond our country's borders are accurate."

I want to ask about the reports he has hinted at, but as important as those are, it's the faces of those who did not pass the first rounds of The Testing that haunt me and make me ask, "Where are they? Where are the experiments being conducted?"

"In Decatur Colony."

"There is no Decatur Colony." I would have heard. Everyone in the Commonwealth would have. Five Lakes was the last colony established, and that was more than twenty-five years ago.

"The colony isn't like the others. It was established as a base for research close enough to the boundaries of the fourth test that unsuccessful experimentation can be released into a closely monitored environment." It is the way he looks at me. Expectant. As if he is waiting for an answer. Unsuccessful experimentation . . .

Horror squeezes my chest. I see the eyes that met mine when I raised my gun on the unrevitalized plains and fired.

Angry.

Bitter.

Human.

I remember the screams as my bullet made impact and took a life. If Dr. Barnes is to be believed, it might have been the life of a former Testing candidate who was Redirected. Turned into a resource and then discarded.

Before I can recover my voice, Dr. Barnes goes on. "President

Collindar and I disagree on a number of things, which is why you, Cia, are here. I chose you to be our own personal test. A candidate from a colony we have not selected a student from in years. One who is unlike the type of leader President Collindar and the rest of the Testing committee insists will be necessary for our country to survive the future. The president was positive a student with your background would crack under the pressure, that you'd be incapable of doing what is necessary to keep your country safe."

A piece falls into place. "Symon helped me during the fourth phase of Testing because you told him to."

He nods.

"Why?"

"I needed you to think clearly about your interview answers so that I could make a case for you being accepted to the University. Many on the committee had already expressed concern that you were too emotional and displayed qualities they felt were inappropriate in our leaders. I needed you to be in control during those final moments of The Testing so no one would ask too many questions when you were passed through to the University, which is what needed to happen. Because that was the only way you could be here at this, your final and most important test. President Collindar has agreed to abide by the results. If you pass this one last exam, The Testing program will end. If you fail, it will move forward as it currently stands and students will continue to die."

"What is the test?" I ask. Vaguely, I am aware of the sound of footsteps and raised voices outside the door. But that doesn't matter. Nothing matters except this moment. My throat is dry and my heart pounds as I stare into Dr. Barnes's eyes, looking for the truth. "What do I have to do?"

"Why, that should be obvious." He walks around the table to where I sit and turns the butt of the gun toward me. "It is up to you to make sure that I die."

I stare at the handle of the weapon in his hands. In my mind, I take it. I aim. I fire. The Testing is ended. All of this is over. But all I can do is stare at the gun, trying to decide what new test lies behind Dr. Barnes's words.

"I don't understand," I say.

"Of course you do." He smiles. "I want to end The Testing. For that to happen, sacrifices need to be made. It seems only fitting that I am the one to make this one, since I have been a part of this process for so long. And truly this is the only way for The Testing to come to an end. The Testing has helped our country get through the darkest time in our history. People have come to trust the system and the leaders it produces. They believe in it."

"Because they don't understand what The Testing entails," I insist.

"You aren't that naive, Cia," he chides. "They might not admit it, even to themselves, but more people than you think understand what The Testing involves. Most choose to pretend they're ignorant of the facts because the system works. The idea of changing it scares them more than giving it their tacit approval. But you, my dear, are here to test whether the system really does function as well as we believe. In previous years, despite your grades and your performance in the fourth test, you would never have passed The Testing. Without the drug provided by Symon, you would have answered the interview questions truthfully. Your natural inclination to trust and your lack of killer instinct would have been apparent. Those qualities that have rallied friends to your side would have caused you to fail, because those characteristics are viewed as weaknesses by the selection committee. Today, you will prove that The Testing and the reasoning behind it are flawed. The president doesn't believe students like you have what it takes to do what is required when your country demands it. By killing me, you prove that I am right in my convictions and she is wrong. Kill me, and this all comes to an end." He places the gun in my lap, takes a step back, and folds his hands in front of him. "I am sorry, Ms. Vale, but after all that you have done, I have to ask that you take this one last test. You now have all the facts at your disposal. What will your answer be?"

CHAPTER 20

I WRAP MY fingers around the gun and stand. Slowly, I extend the weapon in front of me. I walked into this building resolved to kill, but I could never have imagined that Dr. Barnes would stand quietly in front of me asking me to take his life.

He created the tests, selected the candidates, and forced them into situations in which giving the correct answer was not enough. The president has asked for his death. Killing him will mean an end to The Testing.

His eyes fill with sympathy. The expression on his face is one of understanding and acceptance. I steel myself against the doubt that swirls inside me. Dr. Barnes calls this a test. If so, it's one I don't completely understand and one I cannot fail. I have to shoot. For Zandri, Malachi, and all those who did not pass. For Daileen and the others who could be a part of The Testing in the future. For me.

I jump at the sound of voices raised in anger. Running footsteps. Someone is coming. Friend? Foe? It doesn't matter. All that matters are the gun in my hand and the man waiting for my answer.

My hand trembles as I search within myself for the truth. Something crashes into the door, making it shake.

Dr. Barnes's eyes meet mine. "Your time is almost up, Cia."

I do not take my eyes off the man who stands before me. Is he the monster I have always believed, or someone who is now making the ultimate sacrifice as a means of righting wrongs and finding redemption? The answer shouldn't matter. But it does.

Everything depends on this moment.

I need to fire.

I need to kill.

But I can't. No matter how much I want to succeed, I know that Dr. Barnes was wrong to choose me. Because I can't look into the eyes of an unarmed man and fire. No matter what answer I give to this test, I know that ultimately it will cause me to fail.

Out of the corner of my eye, I see the door to my right open. Lowering my weapon, I turn and see Symon standing in the entryway with his gun raised. Behind him are two more men. Both armed. And their weapons are all pointed at me.

"Put your gun down on the table, Cia. After your surviving this long, it would be a shame for it all to end here." Symon takes a step toward me. His shirt is torn. Blood and char streak his pants. He must have still been inside Dr. Barnes's house when it exploded. The hand that holds the gun poised to fire at me does not tremble. Symon's eyes are flat and cold. He will not think twice about ending my life. I know I have no choice. My fingers tremble as I set the gun on the table next to me. Nodding, he calls over his shoulder. "Guard the elevator and the stairs. The president might have sent people here, too. Once we have a plan in place, we'll be leaving."

The two men hurry down the hall as Symon turns his attention to Dr. Barnes. "When you missed our meeting at your house, Jedidiah, I was worried. The person who attacked me and the bomb that went off there concerned me even more. The students here on campus have been leading an unauthorized assault on the officials Professor Holt assigned to keep the campus locked down."

That's what the fighting I heard outside was. Ian must have convinced the rebel students to turn against Symon.

Dr. Barnes frowns. "I thought you said you had the students under control."

"I did, but things have started to unravel. Ranetta is refusing to deploy her teams around the city. Instead, she has convinced most of them, including many in my faction, to stay in camp. I don't think we can wait for the rebels to hit first. If they're going to be eliminated—"

"The rebels aren't going to be eliminated," Dr. Barnes says.

Symon goes still. "I don't understand."

Dr. Barnes smiles and puts his hand in his pocket. When he pulls it out, he is holding a small gun. "The president and I have come to an understanding. Too many people know about The Testing, the rebellion, and the Redirection project."

"The rebels—"

"Not just the rebels, my friend." Dr. Barnes's face is filled with sorrow as he steps toward Symon. I am forgotten while they study each other. I slowly reach for my gun as Dr. Barnes says, "The time has come for all three to come to an end. The country is better for them, but they have served their purpose. I wish you had died in the explosion I created. After Ms. Vale's heroics, I thought it appropriate. And then I wouldn't have to do this."

Symon understands the words a moment too late. I jump at the crack of gunfire. Symon reels back. Blood blooms on his shoulder, just inches from his heart, as he screams and fires back. Dr. Barnes shouts and another gunshot explodes as I turn to flee.

A familiar figure fills the doorway, blocking my path. Sweat glistens off Griffin's head and he raises a large black gun. This time I don't think. I pull the trigger. Surprise crosses Griffin's face and he grabs the door. I fire again. Red spatters his face. As he falls, I run.

I race down the hall. Three shots ring out from the room behind me. Someone inside is still alive. At the end of the hall, I see the outline of a man raising a gun. I run to the left, toward the double doors, as he fires. I slip back into the lecture hall, close the door, and lock it. The lock will not keep them out for long, but it buys me a few seconds to figure out what I need to do next.

The room is black as night. The door handle rattles. I run my hand along the chairs beside me to keep my balance as I navigate the stairs as fast as I dare. There is shouting on the other side of the door. Two voices. Symon's is the loudest as he yells for the other to stand back. I reach the bottom of the stairs and hurry across the aisle between the stage and the front row of chairs as five gunshots slam into the door.

I duck down behind the chairs as the door crashes open.

Lights flicker to life above me. I hold my breath and crouch as low as I can while still remaining on my feet so I am ready to flee. To my right is the stage where Dr. Barnes once stood. The podium is there. Far to the left I see a narrow door. Too far away for me to reach now, but maybe I can find a way.

Someone is on the stairs. Another is near the back of the hall, moving down the aisle. From the hall outside the room, I hear more footsteps. The other man Symon brought with him? Two against one is bad odds. But three against one? I tighten my hold on the gun. I will only get one chance to fire. Whoever is with Symon will see me the minute I rise. He will fire too. I will die. But so will Symon. I will not allow myself to die without a fight.

The person coming down the stairs is moving slower that the one in the back. His footsteps sound heavier. Like a man who is injured. He will be my target.

A voice shouts from the hallway. Whoever is out there will be here in moments. Then I will face three opponents. I think of those I love and have the whisper of Tomas's name in my heart as I swallow down my fear and stand. I was right. Symon stands three quarters of the way down the side aisle. His eyes widen in surprise as he sees me. Blood coats the hand holding the gun that takes aim.

The footsteps in the hall stop. Three figures appear in the door as I squeeze the trigger. Sound explodes around me. Symon drops to the ground and rolls down the last two stairs to the front aisle as searing pain pierces my right arm. I turn toward the man who shot me and fire again, but miss as he darts to the left. And I'm not sure if I would have hit him anyway.

The burning ache in my arm is making it hard to keep a grip on the gun.

Symon's man turns and takes aim as a voice calls my name. Tomas.

Another shot cracks the air. Symon's man stumbles backward into one of the chairs. Blood seeps from the wound in his chest as he sinks to the ground.

My arm is on fire. The world spins in and out of focus, but none of that matters as Tomas races down the stairs toward me. His clothes are covered in dirt and a ragged cut runs down one side of his face, but he is here. Whole. Alive.

Over Tomas's shoulder I see two other people running down the stairs. One is Will. The other, Zeen. I look behind them for Stacia but don't see her. Did Tomas have to leave her behind because of her injury? Or is she looking to make sure Dr. Barnes is dead?

I am about to ask when my brother says, "I want my Transit Communicator back."

Despite the pain I feel, laughter erupts out of me. Zeen flashes the smile that I grew up idolizing as he rushes toward me. I start to reply when I see movement to my left—the barrel of Symon's gun as it is placed in position. I push Tomas to the side and raise my weapon, but I know I will be too late. That after all I have been through, I will die as Symon pulls the trigger.

Gunfire fills the room. A scream rips from my throat, but the bullet never finds me because Zeen gets there first. My brother jerks as the bullet punches into him and groans when he hits the ground next to Symon. I do not hesitate as I squeeze the trigger of my weapon. A wound blooms in Symon's chest.

A second—from Will's gun—appears in his left temple, and Symon drops to the ground.

Zeen. I can barely whisper his name as I kneel next to him, ignore the pain in my arm, and roll him over to see the injury he has sustained. I choke back a sob as I see the hole in his chest. Instinctively, I reach for my bag to find something to help, but my bag isn't here and even if it were, I know there is no healing this wound. Zeen's lungs have been damaged. Maybe his heart. It won't be long before both stop working.

Despite what I know to be true, I scream for Will and Tomas to find someone to help us. I don't care if I am arrested and punished. Zeen needs to live. There has been enough loss. Enough death. Too high a price has been paid. I can't lose him. Not now. Not when we are finally together again.

Will yells that he'll go to the Medical residence to find help and disappears out the door. When Tomas finally moves, I think that he too is going to look for aid. That he believes there is a chance Zeen could live. Instead, he kneels opposite me, next to Zeen, and takes Zeen's other hand in his. I see tears streak down Tomas's face. I want to cry, but there are no tears to wash away a loss this huge. Dr. Flint used to say that the severest wounds often cannot be felt by the victim because the nerves are too damaged to transmit pain. Seeing Zeen in my arms, struggling to breathe, has cut too deep for tears.

He coughs and I smooth back his hair and whisper encouraging words like he used to do when I was little and scared or sick. I tell him that I love him. That I am so glad I am with him now. That everything will be okay. But it won't. Because Zeen's breathing is becoming shallower. His heartbeat is slowing, and his eyes are filled with anguish.

"Do you still have your bag?" I ask Tomas. "Can you give him something for the pain?"

Tomas looks down at Zeen and nods. He stands and walks to where he dropped his bag. He pulls out two bottles. One marked with a circle. The other with an X. I see the question in his eyes as he holds them out to me.

Zeen coughs. His hand tightens around mine. His face has drained of color. His chest barely rises as he takes his next breath. I reach out and take the bottle with the circle on it and help him drink. Maybe it is selfish of me, but I want these last moments with him to last as long as they can. It will be hard enough to go on after Zeen is gone. I cannot be the one to bring about the final moment of his life.

"Cia," Zeen whispers. "Remember what I said when you graduated. And tell Mom and Dad I saved you. They'll be proud."

They find us sitting with our hands joined. Tomas, Zeen, and me. Zeen's heart has stopped. He is no longer in pain.

I try to console myself with that as Safety officials do not shoot but instead ask us to stand. When I try, I find I cannot. I am too dizzy. Too tired. Too overwhelmed. They let Tomas help me into one of the chairs as a medical team works on my arm. Tomas sits beside me as they clean and bandage our injuries. When I ask about Stacia, anguish crosses Tomas's face and I know before he says it that she is dead. Tomas tells me he'll explain everything later, but that she died at Professor Chen's house. When he falls silent, I don't press for answers because I have had enough of death.

My arm throbs, but the pain lessens when the medical team applies an ointment and begins to wrap the wound with a bandage. They have done all they can here and will need to treat me further to prevent infection or a terrible scar. As if anything they can do will prevent the scars I will wear from this night forever.

A team of officials in purple appear. I think they must be coming to arrest me, but instead they walk to where Zeen lies. I scream when they try to carry Zeen's body out. That's when President Collindar arrives. She tells them to leave Zeen with us and orders her staff to remove Symon and to keep everyone else out. When the medical officials are finished, she asks them to leave us alone. She allows Tomas to stay, which is good. He would have refused to go.

Once she is alone with Tomas and me she says, "There is much we need to discuss, but most of it can be done in the days and weeks ahead. My officials found Dr. Barnes down the hall. He and Symon are both dead. But that is not true of everyone on the list I gave you."

Dr. Barnes is dead.

I close my eyes and try to feel relief that someone succeeded in killing him when I could not. After all, he is the reason my brother and so many others lost their lives. But there is no joy in his death. Only sadness and a sense of confusion, since I will never know whether his final words were the truth — that he believed The Testing should end and was willing to give up his life to make sure that it did.

I open my eyes and choose my words carefully as I reply to the president's unspoken question. "Since Symon had a hand in creating the list, I decided it was best to learn what I could about the people on it. Of the twelve, only five were involved in the University and Testing process in a way that eliminating them would affect your agenda. Those are the ones we opted to remove."

"I'm impressed." President Collindar smiles. "It is not always easy to lead with caution, especially with so much at stake. After giving you the list, I began to wonder if Symon included some opponents of The Testing. Had they been killed, you would have eliminated those who could have been influential dissenters."

Are her words the truth, or did she herself have reason to want those people removed, as Dr. Barnes's explanation suggested?

The president's stolid expression provides no insight. "For your sake and the sake of your friends," she says, "we will make a public announcement that the deaths of several prominent officials and members of the University came at the hands of one Symon Dean—the leader of a group created to destabilize the Commonwealth and our revitalization mission. He will also be blamed for the explosions that occurred here on campus and on the other side of town, as well as for the deaths of the students and officials who have been fighting tonight. I have already talked to the leader of the students who believed they were doing what was necessary to help end The Testing. He and his fellow students will be given amnesty for their actions, as will all those who followed Symon."

"And is that when you'll announce that The Testing will end?" I ask.

President Collindar straightens her shoulders. As she looks at me, I recall the words Dr. Barnes spoke tonight. Does she know that I was not the one who killed Dr. Barnes? Have my actions been sufficient to prove that I am strong enough to be a leader even though it was not my hand that accomplished that task? If Symon killed him before coming after me, then there is no one to tell her differently. But if someone else was behind the act, and Dr. Barnes was being honest, I'm not sure what she will do.

"Yes." She smiles again. "I will also announce that the University selection process known as The Testing will end. Once the University and its programs are legally shifted under the Debate Chamber's jurisdiction, I will direct the Chamber to choose a new head of the school and institute some necessary changes."

"What kinds of changes?"

"It will be a while before that can be determined, but I can promise you that none of the candidates for our University will have to go through the trials you did."

Her smile is reassuring but her words are not. My brother and my friends did not sacrifice their lives for half promises.

"What about the students who failed to pass The Testing?" I ask. "The ones in Decatur Colony. What will happen to them?"

For several heartbeats there is silence as President Collindar studies me. Gauging how much I know. How much she should say. "I've only recently learned that there is a research group known as Decatur Colony. Perhaps you will be interested in taking a trip there with me to see what work is being done."

I think of Raffe's final request that I find his sister Emilie, and I nod. "I would."

"Good." She smiles. "I assure you that changes will be made. There are a number of challenges ahead, and whether someone attends the University or not, I intend to see that the brightest minds from the colonies and Tosu City are put to the best use possible. Because of that, it is my plan to allow students who are unhappy with the University to request to return home to their families. I'm certain those who do will find a way to contribute to our revitalization mission from there."

Tomas's hand tightens on mine, and I know he is thinking the same thing I am. We can go home.

"Do you have any more questions, Cia?"

I have dozens. But I'm sure I will never hear the answers to the most important ones. I look at President Collindar's sincere expression and think of the tension I felt between her and Dr. Barnes the day I was assigned to my internship. I think of the worry she expressed at the number of candidates and students who came to the University and failed to graduate. She spoke of the desire to remove Dr. Barnes in order to end the practices that he perpetuated, and charged me with helping her create that change. I want to believe her. To deny that anything Dr. Barnes said about her was real. After all, he was the one who watched my Testing roommate's body be cut free while explaining that her suicide proved The Testing's methods worked. Could that man, who was responsible for so many deaths, have really wanted The Testing to change? Was he right about President Collindar? Is it true that she not only knows the fate of those who have been Redirected, as her own words indicate, but approves of what has been done to them? Does she believe The Testing should be made even more difficult and be inflicted upon more than just colony-born students? Despite what she says now, will The Testing that Tomas and I were forced to participate in really end?

Dr. Barnes said that my greatest asset is my ability to trust my instincts. I have to trust them now. Do I believe Dr. Barnes?

I don't want to, but I do. And now that he is dead, there is only one way to know if I am right.

"Do you have any other questions for now, Cia?" President Collindar asks again.

"Yes, I do," I say. "Would you mind if I get my University bag from the interview room?"

She rises. "Of course not, although you understand that any tools you might have borrowed to complete your task will have to be returned to the storage facility in my office."

It takes me two tries to get out of my chair. The room shifts but I stay on my feet. Tomas offers an arm to help me balance as I navigate the stairs, but I refuse. This is something I must do on my own.

President Collindar follows us out. I feel her eyes on us as, side by side, Tomas and I walk to the end of the now brightly illuminated lecture hall. A purple-clad official wipes blood off the floor near the entrance to the interview room. Griffin's body has been moved. As I step through the doorway, I see a body lying on the floor with a small gun near one hand. Blood pools near the head, matting the gray hair that had given the man an air of authority and wisdom. His face is turned away from me, and though I know who it is from the clothing and the gun, I move several steps closer.

There is a bullet wound in Dr. Barnes's shoulder that was not there when I last saw him. But that wasn't what killed him. The three bullet wounds clustered near his heart are the obvious cause of his death. I wonder if those three holes will give me away, because never could I shoot with that kind of skill.

"As soon as we leave, they will collect the body. I gave you this task, but I wasn't sure you would be able to see it through.

When your friend told me that you had, I was pleased to know that the faith I placed in you and your abilities was not mistaken."

"My friend?" I look at Tomas, who shrugs. He is not the one who claimed I killed Dr. Barnes. Then who?

"Yes," she says. "The dark-haired boy with the green eyes."

Will.

"I saw him after I heard Dr. Barnes had been killed and asked him what he knew. He was worried you'd feel guilty after everything that happened and that you wouldn't accept the credit for what you had done. He thinks you're a hero."

"I'm not." After everything that has happened, it is the only thing I am certain of.

President Collindar smiles. "I had a feeling you'd say that. The decisions that leaders have to make are never easy. Including this one. You took a life, but just think how many more were saved."

Not Zeen's. Lives were saved. Yes. But not by me. By Will.

I look again at the bloody hole in Dr. Barnes's shoulder and the three precise gunshot wounds in his chest. Symon must have caused the first as he ran to find me. Symon was injured when he fired. I am not sure he could have fired with the accuracy it would have taken to create the fatal wounds. But someone who was a known marksman, like Will, could have. His main skill lies with a crossbow, as he demonstrated in the fourth test, but I remember how he took down Roman and know his skill with a gun doesn't lag far behind. Symon might have inflicted the three wounds that killed Dr. Barnes, but my gut tells me no. This was Will's work.

Will wasn't here when Dr. Barnes explained his bargain

with President Collindar. He couldn't have known that crediting me with the kill was the only way to end The Testing we both despised. Yet, that is what he did. The Will I knew during the fourth test would have taken the credit for his actions. He would have wanted whatever reward he thought would come with bringing down the president's foe. Instead, this time, he passed to me whatever accolades he felt would be delivered. Because Will isn't just the boy who shot and betrayed. Just as I am not just the naive girl from Five Lakes. Now I have to decide for certain whether Dr. Barnes was the man I believed him to be and whether President Collindar is the person she says she is.

Walking to the table, I look at the glass Dr. Barnes drank from, and the liquid that remains at the bottom. I put the glass to my lips and take a small sip.

The flavor makes me grimace as Dr. Barnes did. Metallic. Bitter. The taste that I remember from months ago in this same room. When Dr. Barnes watched and waited and hoped that I would be confident and coherent enough to pass through to the University. He hoped I would prove that The Testing was flawed and that by my hand and through his sacrifice it all would be ended.

"Are you ready, Cia?" President Collindar asks.

Everything Dr. Barnes told me was the truth.

"Cia, are you ready?" she asks again.

I look at the president and then around the room, my mind filled with questions. Only some of which I can answer. For the rest I will have to do what is necessary to obtain the truth.

"Come on, Cia," Tomas says, taking my bag from the table. "Let's go home."

CHAPTER 21

HOME.

On the outskirts of Five Lakes I sit under an oak tree that my brother Zeen helped create. My father and I have visited this site every day since I have come home. Today, I am here alone. In my hands is the Transit Communicator that Zeen once owned. The mate to this Communicator is buried next to him. Tears that I could not shed the night he died fall freely now that I am surrounded by reminders of him. The night of my graduation, we stood under an oak like this. On that night Zeen spoke to me the words that in the moments before he died he asked me to remember. Back then the two of us stood in the shadows together, both disappointed about our futures. Me, because I thought I hadn't been chosen for The Testing. He, because he felt trapped by the boundaries of Five Lakes and the lack of recognition for what he had achieved. In that moment he told me, "Things don't always work out the way we hope. You just have to pick yourself up and find a new direction to go in."

Nothing about what has happened this past year has turned out the way I had dreamed of. Yet remembering Zeen's words has given me comfort, and knowing he died to save my life has made me more determined to see that his sacrifice is never forgotten.

Above me, leaves rustle on the tree. Sunlight, bright and filled with hope, shines on the four grave markers beside me. Each etched with a symbol and a name so that the sacrifices of those who died will live in the memory of everyone from Five Lakes. Zeen Vale beneath two crossed lightning bolts. An arrow under the name Malachi Rourke. A stylized flower and the name Zandri Hicks. And Michal Gallen with the symbol of an anchor. He wasn't from Five Lakes, but I insisted he be included. Honored for the help he gave and the sacrifice he made. Without him, change would not have come. And there has been change.

Three weeks have passed since that night in The Testing Center. I spent much of that time in the University Medical building getting treatment, talking to Enzo, who is still in the early stages of the healing process, sitting with Tomas, and watching Raffe through a window as he fought for his life. The medical team is amazed that Raffe has survived this long and that each day his vital signs get stronger. Caught in the blast that was meant to kill Symon, Raffe is determined to live. And now he has an even larger reason to fight for his life.

The president stood by her word. Three days after that night in The Testing Center, I accompanied her and her team to Decatur Colony. Since Tomas is not part of the president's staff, he was not allowed to join us. I'm glad, because I am uncertain how he would have handled what we found there. I'm not sure what I expected, but it wasn't a community twice the size of Five Lakes Colony with medical facilities more advanced than any I'd seen in Tosu City located on the outskirts of the colony. But unlike those wards, these contained patients in various stages of chemically induced mutations. Not as many as I would have thought, considering the number of Redirected students sent here every year. Four in each of the five stages being studied. Two male. Two female. Those in the worst stages arched their backs and extended their claws as researchers stood behind glass walls, taking notes. When I asked, I learned why there are so few. The others deemed beyond help were turned out onto The Testing grounds to mingle with the mutations that were created by war instead of by this lab.

The scars on my arm tingled as I stared into their eyes and wondered if these patients knew the mutated humans I shot during the fourth test. I wish I knew their names, but the newly appointed head of Decatur Colony's research team, Dreu Owens, does not know the identities of those I killed or whether they were research subjects or natural mutations like the ones scientists are hoping eventually to treat and cure. Dreu told me that after being assigned to Decatur Colony, he wanted to leave when he realized most residents and test subjects were former Testing candidates and Redirected University students. But he didn't because, now that he understands the work being done, he can't leave behind those who suffered. Not if there is a chance of curing them. And from the partially cured human and animal mutations Dreu showed us, I believe there really may be a chance.

But not if those in charge continue the practices that have been employed up till now. Because while many former candidates and students are content to be working in labs and helping to discover a cure, there are others who are bitter and angry. Who believe that the methods being used are wrong and who live in fear that they might be chosen as the next subject for experimentation. Dreu has already announced that he will limit research to subjects who have already suffered mutations and that those who are unhappy in their current work will be able to request a transfer to another project.

Over the president's objections, I insisted on taking two Decatur Colony residents with me — Raffe's sister Emilie and Will's twin brother, Gil. Both had been assigned to work in the labs and seem to be undamaged. It appears they had escaped scientific testing. After seeing what they could have been faced with, I am glad they are untouched. Both have been reunited with their brothers. The smile I saw on Will's face was the same one I remember him wearing the first time we met. He and Gil exchanged jokes and finished each other's sentences as if they'd never been apart. Seeing their happiness made me hold back the questions I will someday ask. About Dr. Barnes. The bullet holes. The credit Will gave me. But even without hearing the answers, I can see the truth when Will's smile fades and he thinks no one is watching. He is living with the memories of what he has done. Something his brother and Emilie do not have to do.

All memory of the time spent in Decatur Colony has been

removed from them. The president and her advisors believe limiting the memory of those who return from the colony and the public's information about the research done there is essential to retaining peace. Another secret kept for the good of our country. When I consider the president's logic, I cannot disagree. And yet, part of me wonders if we can ever truly learn from what we have done if we continue to suppress or erase the past.

And yet, there is hope that we have learned something. Last week, I watched from the Debate Chamber gallery as President Collindar kept her bargain with Dr. Barnes. Standing at the podium, looking out on a filled Chamber and observation area, the president announced the disbanding of the University selection process known as The Testing. Current University students will continue their education under the temporary direction of Professor Douglas Lee — head of Early Studies and professor of history. Meanwhile, the president and her office will work closely with the Education Department to create a new selection system for the University, one that will be the same for both Tosu City and colony students.

The city is buzzing about the traitor who killed Dr. Barnes, Professor Holt, Official Jefferies, and Professor Chen. I know now that only three of them should be dead. In the days following the attack and Dr. Barnes's death, I learned that Professor Chen was pushing for a reevaluation of The Testing's purpose and the method of selecting new students. Tomas and Stacia learned of Professor Chen's true intent when they went to her house. Once she was restrained, Tomas wanted to leave but Stacia refused. A bullet at close range from Stacia's gun killed Professor Chen. Stacia was determined to follow the president's instructions. The United Commonwealth president was Stacia's leader. Not me. Stacia died moments later. Tomas says it was self-defense. I have not pressed him. Perhaps because I can see the real answer in the shadows that fill his eyes. Maybe someday he will tell me why he killed Stacia, but I doubt it. In his mind, what happened is over. It is time to move on.

My name has not been mentioned in conjunction with Dr. Barnes's death or the elimination of the others. Nor have the names of Tomas, Ian, Raffe, Stacia, and Will, though our friends from our former study group helped us create a marker decorated with the symbol Raffe created to honor Stacia. We placed it next to the one Professor Holt hung for Rawson. A fitting tribute, I hope, for a girl who wanted more than anything to be important. She and I might not have agreed on much in the end, but for better or worse, she was still my friend. I miss her.

Thanks to the president's official version of events, I can go on with my life without anyone knowing about the task the president gave me and the choices I made. Tomas is grateful. I suppose I am, too, although I have already told the truth to my family around the same kitchen table where I learned how to divide and multiply. I notice my brothers no longer tease me as easily as they used to. My mother tries to pretend nothing is different, but I have seen her watching me. I know she wants me to be the same girl who left home, and I try my best to act like her, but we both know I am not. My father is the only one who truly understands. Perhaps because he too has been Tested.

I stand and look to the west. Far in the distance I see the current boundaries of Five Lakes Colony and the unrevitalized area beyond. There is much good I can do here. I love being home, even though once again I am sleeping in front of the fireplace to avoid hearing my brothers' snores. Magistrate Owens has already asked me for ideas about enhancing our communications with Tosu City and the other colonies as well as my thoughts on better ways to create and manage our colony's power.

Tomas is happy because he has been offered a place on my father's team. If he proves himself, he will be able to create a team of his own. Being home has lifted Tomas's spirits. He's more like the boy I knew before leaving for Tosu City. Surrounded by family, he's begun to heal, though he too will never forget. Despite our not having graduated from the University, everyone here considers Tomas and me leaders. The opportunity we've been offered to help our colonies is exactly what we dreamed of when we hoped to be selected for The Testing. Tomas is eager to start working with my father, and to build our lives here.

I long to stay. To be happy.

But as much as I want to be with Tomas and my family, each day that passes convinces me that I cannot. Five Lakes is as wonderful as I remember. I will visit as often as I can and will always find peace here. I wish I could go back to who I was, but I'm different. This is my home, but it is no longer where I belong.

Holding the Transit Communicator tight to my chest, I slowly walk to town, where Tomas waits for me. I'm going to tell him that I have to go back. But he will know my choice the minute he sees the bracelet that circles my wrist. This is not the path I dreamed of while growing up, but it is the one have to walk. Because the only way to be sure The Testing we had to survive never happens again is not to trust our leaders. It is to be one of them.

I walk up the hill and into the square. Tomas stands near the fountain that sprays sparkling, clean water into the air. When he sees me, a smile filled with love spreads across his face. In his hands are daisies he must have picked on his way here. As I walk toward him, I smile back with all the love in my heart. Tomorrow I will return to Tosu City. I will move into a new room at the University and will complete my studies and my internship. I will tell Brick, Naomy, and Vic the truth behind what has happened. And when Enzo and Raffe recover, I will ask them all to help me keep watch over the president and our other leaders to ensure that nothing like The Testing ever happens again.

If I have to travel the path I have chosen alone, I will. But as Tomas's mouth meets mine, I hope deep in my heart that he will understand the choice I have made and will once again make the journey to Tosu City with me. Because despite what I have learned and what I have done, I am still the girl from Five Lakes who wants to lead and help my country. And there is so much still for me to do.